CONVERGENCE

by

Jerry Sander

THE WAY IT
WORKS
PRESS

Created in the United States of America
Worldwide Rights

The following document has been authenticated as genuine and unaltered and is published and distributed in its entirety by the Restored United States of America in Exile (RUSA-IE) in the Year 2046. (Archived, RUSA-IE Library, Port Huron, MI 5/46).

"Author" (Sander) should be construed as the receiver of this document, not an affiliate of the RUSA-IE, which is solely responsible for its edited content.

Its distribution is not an endorsement of the points of views, opinions, political direction, or attitudes contained within. Publishing this unaltered and as-written is a statement of confidence in the inherent intelligence of our reader-citizens.

The only additions we have made can be found in the Glossary at the end of the document, which the reader is encouraged to refer to in order to assist with understandings of arcane technology and phrases no longer in current use.

The victory of any protracted revolutionary struggle requires knowledge of where we've been in the past, recent and otherwise. This includes an understanding of what has failed, a humble appreciation of the heroism of those who've come and gone before us, and remembrance of the treachery of our enemies.

To Zokaya, in love and appreciation.

The battle is not over. Trust your eyes, your gut, and your brain.
Distribute, discuss, and report breaches through trusted channels.

I Pledge Assistance to The Convergence
of the Technological Present,
The Triumvirate,
Which brings Peace to All,
Jobs for All Who Want Them,
and Security from Religious Attack,
None Excluded.

—The Pledge of Convergence

Table of Contents

Arrival

They still called it California even though the United States was long gone.

It was the Year 13. Why wasn't air-travel better? I'd left Liberia early the night before and spent ten hours traveling just to get to the connecting flight at Heathrow. I was hungry and tired.

The plane cruised lower and lower, and my ears popped with the change in pressure. I rubbed the sleep out of my eyes and looked out the window. California rose beneath us, variations of copper and green, higher elevations coming into focus first, then the valleys and fields, the sun now streaming through our cabin.

The Center for Advanced World Studies wasn't even my first choice. I wanted to study with Wen's group, in China, but their hiring had trickled to a halt in the years since they'd bought Apple for 4.28 trillion. There was no application process to work there, no strings my teachers could pull. If Wen's group wanted you, they'd find you.

The Chinese were ascendant now—every child in Liberian elementary school was taught that, along with conversational Chinese. Every passing year proved it. Their infrastructure projects in Monrovia, the success of Chinese solar power all through Africa, South America, and Asia, and their legendary charity work across the globe meant they were the Big Dogs now.

A sudden swing right made me open my eyes. My stomach rumbled. The food on both planes over had been terrible. I needed something that tasted like home. I remembered my mother's chicken peanut soup. I pictured her sprinkling in the cayenne, and I could smell the coriander

I was the only Liberian going to California.

Just two weeks ago Mr. Sayeh, my high school teacher, stood in front of our class, his grey shirt stained with his usual armpit sweat, explaining why the most ambitious of us had to leave Liberia.

"Wen seized Apple for a fire-sale price. Rival search-engine giant, WhoozHooz was blind-sided by this, so they quickly set up the Centers for Advanced World Studies, in California, Greenland, and Australia to compete. The Religious Wars, the New York City subway bombings, the arrests...The United States was worn down and merged. The Triumvirate is where all the action is now. It is either CAWS or Wen, in China. Nothing in Africa. California is The CAWS Mothership."

I looked out at the land drawing closer, and I wondered about who my roommate was going to be. I suddenly remembered the going-away ceremony they'd held for me back home. Food, pictures, speakers, my

1

mother clapping, wiping tears from eyes when they introduced me. I remembered her laughing when the Education Secretary said, "If you don't have a seat at the table, then you are probably dinner."

The businessman next to me started making grunting sounds. Suddenly, he was leaning over into my seat-space, shoving his HIVE-TV wrist-device in front of me.

"Look at this," he said.

The screen was an off-shade of blue. I immediately recognized it; the Army of the Righteous. That was their trademark color. It made blood look vivid. Were they still around?

"It never changes," the businessman said. "Over and over and over."

The soldiers held the family members by their hair to make sure they were sitting upright for the camera. There was bad Southeast Asian music.

I knew there'd be screaming, crying, begging, and then horrible sounds, so I looked at the businessman's leg instead of the screen. I was right. There was wailing and desperate attempts to bargain for their lives. I didn't need to see this. He didn't either.

It also wasn't clear whether this was straight film footage, or one of the Synthesized Creative Reality Apps (SCRAPS) that had become big in Year 9. The professional in me accepted it as a challenge. I glanced back at the screen.

Death. Blood. The shadows seeming to fall in the right places.

"Child murderers," the businessman blurted.

This was my arrival into California. Hideous stuff on HIVE-TV, as worn on the wrist of a businessman next to me. I looked one last time.

The positions the bodies fell in looked real.

It was upsetting on any level, more so if it were real. There had obviously been post-production work. Humans didn't ordinarily sound like that. An enhanced SCRAP, most likely. But, then again, I'd never been in such a situation, so I couldn't judge. No one I'd ever known had either.

"Animals," the businessman said.

"It's fake," I said. "Not real."

The plane touched down with early morning ease.

"Worse than animals. Y'know, where those murderers are now? Dust."

He didn't seem interested in my assessment of the media.

"Dust to dust," I said. That was a phrase my father used to say when I was little, when we watched the news. I thought of Saturday morning motorcycle rides on the back of Dad's Royal Enfield, him smelling of Bay Rum, the two of us leaning into the curves. He always said we should hop on the bike, "because we can," and we'd share a smile. Then he stopped being in contact with all of us. He disappeared. I preferred to think he was on an important, secret mission of some sort. "Is that from The Religious Wars?" I asked.

He nodded. "And they say they're still out there. Hiding. Religious Ones. Waiting for a moment to pounce. They never accepted losing," the businessman said, unbuckling his seatbelt and standing as the plane finished pulling up to the arrival gate. "You here for school?"

"Yes."

"Keep your eyes open," he said, retrieving his luggage from above and walking forward "Not everyone is nice. Even in California. I don't know if they tell you that where you came from."

I thought back to the last thing Mr. Sayeh told me in school: "Believe nothing of what you read, nothing of what you hear, and half of what you see."

The pilot came on over the speakers. "Ladies and gentlemen, welcome to Bill Gates International Airport, Los Angeles, California. The temperature is 76 degrees, the local time 7:06 a.m., Pacific Standard Time."

#

The transport van had to pick up other kids from a variety of other airlines. We stopped to make pickups at Korean Air, Lufthansa, Norwegian Airlines, British Airways, and Qatar Airways. It was a swirl of colors, the sounds of doors slamming and luggage being slid into the back by men in uniforms expecting tips. I sized up the kids as they each loaded their belongings. Only about half of them gave tips. I wasn't intimidated, though a lot of them wore glasses. They all looked smart, but I didn't feel bested yet.

On our way to CAWS, the driver, who introduced himself as Miguel, told of a cheese and crackers reception at the conference center. "You must be some very important people, huh? For still being young people, right? I pick up people all the time, they don't get cheese and crackers. It's an honor, right? What did you guys do to get that? You invent stuff?" he asked, swinging his head back to check us out.

I felt sorry for him. What would it be like to have a life of just ferrying people back and forth to the airport? On top of this, no one was answering him. "We're important in a very small circle of people," I said. "We like cheese and crackers. We are cheese and cracker people."

He laughed. "That's a good one! 'Cheese and cracker people.' I still think you invent things. You know The Next Big Things, right? You know what's what, right? What's coming down the pike? Because you're not old." He nodded. "I get it. Smart. That's smart, bringing you guys."

I had just turned eighteen. Microsoft, Instagram, Facebook, and Snapchat – all things we'd studied about in school – were no more, having merged into FruitEdge, a lamely-named company attempting to capitalize on some sort of Apple-ish/fruit imagery. It was failing rapidly. Most of the things I learned even in tenth grade were now obsolete.

We pulled into CAWS and saw what must have been an acre of smooth, green lawn in front of the entrance. "That's artificial," Miguel informed us as he unloaded our luggage. "Better for the environment, they say." I gave him a twenty-dollar tip, not really knowing if that was too much or too little. "Stay yourselves," he said in an odd farewell, waving before driving off.

I expected him to tell us to invent cool things.

I joined the small group walking through the lobby and following the signs for the Woodcrest Room, where the cheese and crackers waited for us. The first person I truly focused on was Rudra, a handsome young man with long black hair, who looked like he was from India. He was, like the rest of us, putting on his goofy CAWS name-tag, and he came up an intriguing lapis blue color on my Predictive Friend Advisor. The PFA, which could now screen and compare name, character, and personal attributes through a centralized registry, comparing it to mine, worked within .18 seconds. It was getting faster and faster, and the one going into kids now was said to be .07.

The retinal color-coding—a brief wash of color that swooped across your field of vision and then disappeared—was easily understood as an expression of how likely it was that two strangers would be compatible. It was proximity-activated and uncannily accurate. The warmer the color, the better the match. We were all extremely used to the colors coming and going. How much attention you paid to them was up to you. The PFA was a packet of internal apps carefully constructed to be limited. The HIVE couldn't record or maintain archives about PFA responses due to restrictions the developers baked in them. It was no spycam. This ended up being more important than we knew. In fact, this ended up being key. The PFA could only offer you advice and, as they said at the time: "It just works."

No sooner was I basking in Rudra's lapis blue glow and feeling like perhaps another international visitor from a different continent was here with me to provide some company than I saw Elizabeth, standing over by the food, reaching for a plate. She was talking from the first moment I saw her and, as soon as she turned in profile, she came up brown/green on my

PFA. Not good. That, combined with an intimidating British accent, kept me away.

She lectured a smiling shorter girl, who seemed to be in awe of her, standing there adoringly, practically wanting an autograph. The two of them were filling their plates with grapes, cheese, crackers, and slices of apples before sauntering off to a small, comfortable reception area with low tables and cushioned chairs. They sat, and Elizabeth kept talking. Rudra walked over and sat down with them, listening.

"The HIVE replaced old 48G coverage when we were still little wankers. Before Year Zero. Same time as The Filament. Integrated, so no more *coverage*, just wake up, instant-on and Bob's-your-uncle HIVE-Weather, traffic, terror warnings… Doesn't matter if you're in a cave, underwater or in the loo. 'The HIVE never sleeps…so you can,' luv, remember? The billboards?"

I'd already heard about Elizabeth. Rumors in the geek world that there was some big-mouthed British mega-hacker who'd gone over as part of a plea deal of some sort to advise her government—and possibly The Triumvirate?—about next steps to be taken to protect themselves from someone like her. But no one knew her name. Only her hacker name: The Prime Minister. Something told me, as I watched her talk, and talk, that she took that seriously.

"You'd think that the powers-that-be could distribute our actual schedules ahead of time so we're not walking around in circles smashing into walls, bumping into one another when we start tomorrow, maybe? I mean, come on!" (She pronounced it "*shed*-you-als.") "But, oh, right, we're in California, Land of Avocados and Self-Esteem, everyone slurping down vegan protein shakes, balancing their chakras. Pardon me, I just want to get to the projects, advanced systems design and implementation," she said, flipping back her dark hair. She wore glasses that looked like they were from The Geek Shop. They probably were.

When she said *chakras*, Rudra stared at her sharply.

"I'm not mocking, luv," she offered. "Not the Indian-Indians. Hindus, yoga-people, what-have-you. It's just the ones from Palo Alto, you know? I mean, most of the world is in the Year 13, not great-grammy's love-beads in your hair, hello?"

"It's alright," Rudra said. "My chakras don't need anything from California."

"Big fan of chakras," Elizabeth said. "Wouldn't leave home without 'em. But...just organize this Academy. That's all that I'm saying. Don't dither."

I'd never in my life known anyone who used the word *dither*.

I approached her. "Are you The Prime Minister?" I asked.

She turned, looked up at me, and actually was silent for a second. I wonder if her PFA told her the same thing mine did. "Who is asking?" she wanted to know. "People pay money for that sort of info." Then she looked back at her admiring girl and laughed.

"I'm Zokaya Kpelle," I said, sitting down in a fancy green cushioned chair across from her.

"Zokaya...Zokaya. What is that, Tanzanian?" she asked.

"Liberian."

"I knew someone from Ghana once," she said.

"Yes. Different country," I said with some crispness. "Are you The Prime Minister?"

"We live different lives at different times, don't we, luv? Next thing you know we're all here, ready to learn how to surf!" She went back to giggling with her girlfriend.

"The Prime Minister did some fancy work in her day," I said. "Above and beyond. Taking down the international banking systems? For an hour and a half?"

She stopped laughing. Her face suddenly focused, and she looked ten years older. "Do I know you?" she asked. "I don't believe I've heard much coming out of Liberia."

"No, you don't know me. I've been in interactive-looped HIVE healthcare learning systems," I offered. "You'd have to have been looking. Can I ask you something?"

"Sure."

"Are you here as a condition for your release? Some sort of insider-plea-deal thing?"

"I'm here for the same reasons you are," she answered. "Fame."

It didn't feel right. It might've been right for her. But we weren't all there to be little Elizabeths. I knew, right then, that she'd be my major competitor. And that the difference between us is that she wanted to be a celebrity. Mr. Sayeh warned us about celebrities the first time our class talked about tech developers; they were people who were "well-known for their well-knownness."

I just wanted to be the one noticed by Wen. I wanted to know what Wen was up to, not CAWS' next project. Wen thought big. Everyone knew this. I belonged there, not here. I never settled for second-best. I'd been identified early on as exceptional in the field of HIVE encoding and bio-evolutionary sequencing because I was.

Some of my work was speculative, but with the right resources, it wouldn't remain that way for long. I was midway through developing a two-way HIVE/individual health-loop that would allow for remote medical care, sleep, and personalized hormone control. I could finish this in a year. If I did this at CAWS, it would make sense that I could jump ship to Wen's crew by my second year. Wen had to have people looking to poach the best from CAWS. CAWS and WhoozHooz just seemed to aim so low. Daily- living things that made life-schedules more pleasant. I wanted to make technologies that were transformative. I didn't want, in Year 13, to be working on developing a better can opener. Not when ultimate healthcare as an ever-evolving mutually-transacted HIVE-loop was within our sights.

I was contemplating the reality of just having met someone I didn't like, the first one since getting off the plane, when a blonde woman sauntered into the room. I wasn't sure if she was one of us, a teacher, or something else entirely. There was a stealthy quality to her movement, as if she were trying out this body in this way before committing to the room, and to our company.

She wore an old rucksack slung over one shoulder, had short hair and was extremely pale. She found a chair alone around a different table. She wasn't tentative, though, once she decided she was in the right room. I felt an aura of an unknown presence that surprised me. My PFA sprung into a golden-warm reading. Her face looked completely calm. Kristina looked like she didn't need to speak. She popped some lip balm out of her rucksack and applied it. I don't know how I understood it from such small gestures, but I had the distinct feeling of being in the presence of great power.

I had a surge of missing home. Something about her face made me feel both a longing and a sense of aloneness. There was a whole level of sound back home, the way that words and laughter and sing-song expression went together, that was missing here.

I walked over and sat across from her. To my relief, she smiled. "Zokaya," I said, not really knowing if I should shake hands or what.

"Kristina," she said, tilting her head to the right, and scanning me.

I sort of half-waved, and we both laughed, because she half-waved back.

"Liberia," I said, as if she'd asked me anything.

"Sweden," she volunteered back.

I hoped her PFA was telling her good things about me. My next thought was that they must hardly have any sunlight in Sweden because she was one of the fairest-skin people I had ever met. We sat there as the quiet ones, for a moment, before Elizabeth's voice crackled through the room, loud enough for all to hear. We turned.

Elizabeth continued on: "What, pray tell, is the purpose of Pacific Standard Time, anyway? Why not just use Mountain Time? A need for California to be special again? Some more? I'm asking! For real."

"You know perfectly well the rationale for Pacific Time," Rudra offered. "It is familiar enough a time zone to not raise hackles but different enough to cultivate regional identity."

"Isn't it so sad that they need *that* in order to feel good about one's self?" Elizabeth pondered out loud.

An announcement came on, telling us to pick a partner and go for a walk on the designated Health Trail. You could also, optionally, run it. The announcement said it was now a requirement that this be done at least once a day, and it was fine with me. Rudra approached me and raised his eyebrows, which was the invitation to walk, and I gave him a nod.

The Health Trail was warm and sultry in the late afternoon. I was happy Rudra had asked me. Maybe he would be my first friend here. We both had different roommates, and neither of us had met them yet. He walked like he was ready to own this place. He stood tall and looked like an adult.

I kept feeling like anyone watching us would think a member of the staff here was giving me a tour. As with Elizabeth, I felt like I might've met my match. Whereas my ambition was to be the one who would work with Wen. Rudra's, I imagined, was to somehow be involved in running the whole world.

But then there was the side of him that could laugh. We laughed about the trip as we walked and compared miles traveled to get to CAWS. I came 6,963 miles, he came 8,688 miles, winning by a long shot, entitling him to two more airline meals.

The trees had a hushed sound as the breeze came through. I asked him, "Does this place remind you of home at all?"

"Can't say it does. There's a sense of place that's very particular, but I'm guessing it'll take a year to get my bearings." He answered the way an adult would. "Liberia for you, right?"

"Yes."

"I don't know a thing about Liberia," he said.

"What do you want to know?" I asked.

"What's it like?"

"Beautiful. Lush. Warm. Peaceful. Then not beautiful. War. Then beautiful again. Then not beautiful," I answered. "Ebola, then a cure, tribal hatreds, more Ebola, economic growth, lots of Religious Ones."

"Sounds like India," he said. "Different diseases."

"Good people, though. My people. They don't waste everything like they do over here," I said. "At home, restaurants don't throw out unbought food. Even at the airport, I saw them throwing out enough to feed two villages."

"In India we waste more than people know. People like to think of the fairy-tale India," Rudra offered. "We have mountains of discarded computer junk. People think if they land in India and talk to someone with a beard, they will be healed of whatever ails them. It's a good place to grow a beard."

It felt good to walk after the plane. The crunch of the small stones on the trail under our feet felt restorative.

"How old were you when you got implanted? I was five in Year Zero," I said. "The same timing over there?"

"Yes," Rudra said. "My mother refused to call it Year Zero all year long. She kept saying '2026.' She kept thinking it was going to be like a monster movie operation, instead of just a microscopic Filament in the back of the neck. She calmed down after they showed her the size."

"They did all the newborns from Year Zero on, here, within the first eighteen days, retrofitted the rest of us, up to age twenty-one. It's a birth-entitlement now. Updated every two months. Same thing there?" I asked.

"Yes."

We crunched on ahead in some silence again.

"Where's the worst food you ever ate?" I asked.

"Easy," Rudra said. "Hands down: England. Elizabeth's pride and joy. The native specialties: inedible. Unknown with a gluey sauce. Worst food you've eaten?"

"Haggis. Sheep heart, liver, and lungs. One of The Religious Ones ate that back home, shared a taste. From Scotland."

"Maybe we're talking about the same things," Rudra said. "I couldn't for the life of me figure out what it really was. I just couldn't stop eating fast enough."

I heard a bird singing out a message to its partner high up in the trees.

"Do you ever think The Religious Ones got a raw deal?" I asked. "I mean, they're just…different, right?"

"They behaved like savages. They started the whole war. It was on every continent."

"Middle East first?"

"No, coordinated. Everywhere at once. In North America, before it was The Triumvirate. That was the hot spot. If it fell, everything could fall," Rudra said with authority.

"I would say it didn't fall."

"Hardly. The Religious Ones paid the price for trying to bring it on The End of Times. It was the end of their times, not ours. And I am grateful."

"You don't feel sorry for how they were treated? The revenge attacks?" I asked. My mother told me this happened in Liberia, France, Iraq, Poland, Russia, and England. And, of course, North America.

Rudra looked at me. "You do understand they fought against everything we are trying to accomplish here, right? They stood against human order and progress."

We walked in silence. The jet lag had almost completely left me the more we moved and breathed. The lapis blue PFA had been right about Rudra, it felt good hanging around him.

With the sun sinking lower in the sky, everything was still radiant and warm. The Californian people I'd met so far, in passing, seemed smart, easy, and relaxed. Except for the businessman on the plane. It was us international talents who weren't so easy or relaxed. Particularly Elizabeth.

"How many girls do you think there are at CAWS," I asked, almost immediately regretting how young I sounded.

"They've raised the acceptance rate for females to fifty percent of the total student population. But a lot go independent instead. So, there could be thirty-six. How come?"

"No reason," I lied.

I had a girlfriend for about five months in Liberia—Akeelah—but she backed away immediately when she found out I'd be going West. It seemed cruel, but I would have done the same thing in her position. Most who go West only come back to visit, not to live. Not since Year Zero, anyway.

Seeing Kristina earlier punched up feelings of what was missing in my life. It made me feel both lonely and excited at the same time. I tried imagining what dozens of other girls might look like.

"You liked Kristina, huh?" Rudra asked.

I was embarrassed. *Liked* made me sound like a schoolboy. How did he even know?

"No. Just that she looked retro. Stood out."

"Well, that's how things start, right" Rudra asked, smiling.

"How about you?" I asked. "Anyone back home?"

He seemed caught off guard. "No. Not really. Perhaps. I don't know. It's hard to tell. I'm focused on padding my resume and going looking at the intersection of HIVE-linked-productivity loops and monetization right now." There was some awkwardness to the silence.

"You're going to figure out a way to make a lot of money from all this?"

"Without a doubt, yes. A lot."

We both saw a black and white rabbit in front of us, nibbling on plants, nowhere to go that would be better, nothing to do to be happier.

Then we heard feet fast approaching us from behind. The rabbit skittered off. "On your left," a voice shouted as we felt and saw the woman jogger zip past. Brown/green PFA. It was Elizabeth. "Don't stop me to talk, I'm making time!" she said, presuming that the idea would've crossed either of our minds.

"What do you make of her?" I asked Rudra.

"Smug. Bossy, and smart," he said. "First impression. Should do well here. Could be an obstacle."

"Obstacle?" I asked.

"To me," he said. "I get that she thinks she's in charge. I don't like it."

She was waiting for us up around the next corner, holding two of her fingers to the pulse point of her neck and checking her progress.

"One-ninety-six," Elizabeth said. "Not bad. Could come up."

We ignored her and kept walking. She caught up and started walking next to us.

"The two of you saving the world?" Elizabeth asked.

We ignored her.

"I didn't mean to startle you. I'm on a strict physical regimen. I'd been becoming of those tech-toads who sit behind screens all day guzzling carbonated sugar-water and I was almost five stones too fat. Three-and-a-half down."

She walked with us a little and seemed, briefly, to want to fit in with our quiet. "I wanted to tell you Affinity Groups have been assigned. I think ours is top-of-the-pops. The two of you, me, Kristina, and someone else on their way tonight. Affinity Groups keep tabs on each other, challenges and inspires each other's growth. That's from their guidelines." She sounded like a SCRAP for this place.

"How many people attend CAWS?" Rudra asked.

Elizabeth was quick to say, "I think it's about eighty. But we're the ones they're counting on for big things."

"How do you know that?" I asked. "About who they are counting on?"

"Because I'm in your group," she said, putting her hand back on her neck-pulse and starting to run again. "And I just hacked a WenBook."

We both stood dead in our tracks. This was not possible. We'd all seen the SCRAPS, as kids, that showed how WenBooks were impervious to attack and were only for educational purposes. This were the two things that set them apart from all other machines.

Rudra tilted his head and said, "That's not possible. It's military-grade. And there are billions of them in circulation, all secure."

"I'm not saying it was easy," she said, starting to run away. "Mirrors upon mirrors. Had to think way outside the box. Not much of a way in. But I've been working it for years."

"There is, in fact, NO WAY IN," Rudra sputtered, eyes glaring. "How did you do it?"

"Oh, c'mon, that would take all the fun out. Sharing it with you two, wouldn't it?" she said, running off and disappearing.

I felt my stomach churning and fingers tingling. Elizabeth had just told us something that should be immediately reported.

Was this a test?

Hacked

"What should we do?" I asked Rudra. The Main Building was in sight again as we rounded the last bend. There were only two things I could think of: that we were supposed to turn this information over to our Advisors, in all likelihood, and that I was now in possession of information that could be invaluable to Wen and Wen's group, should I decide to leverage them. If I could learn how she did it and get that information back to his group, I'd be in with Wen without a doubt.

"I don't know," Rudra said. "I'm thinking."

We walked back into the lounge area of the Main building. There was now lemonade out for us where the cheese and crackers had been. I saw Kristina sitting in the corner reading. My PFA, again, was golden warm. She was reading, of all things, a paperback book. It had to be from about 2025. I walked over to say hi, and saw the title: "The Force."

"What's that?" I asked. "The book? Something supernatural?"

"No. A police novel. A lot of clichés. But—"

"You like cop novels?" I asked, laughing.

"When I can find them," she said, smiling. "Yes. Antique bookstores are your best bet. Only three left in Sweden, the best I can tell. You know we have a meeting in the Auditorium in a minute, right?"

I'd forgotten. I was still wondering if Elizabeth had been bluffing back on the trail about the hacking. Hackers were notorious liars. "What's the point? Of the meeting?"

"To meet The Advisors. The ones who tailor projects and certifications," Kristina said. She, too, sounded so mature to me. Why was I the only one who sounded my age?

"Have you met them?" I asked.

Elizabeth, walking in, brushing out her hair after having obviously taken one very fast shower, interrupted us. "I have," she said. "Orlinsky and

Cote. Orlinsky's the one I've met already. Bit of a strange bird. Cote seems to be the major-domo, though."

"Cote…French?" I asked.

"No, Canadian," Elizabeth reported.

Rudra wandered over. "Did you tell her?" he asked, pointing his head to Kristina, and clearly meaning the hack.

"No. Not yet." I said. "We've got an assembly in a minute. How many people do you want to tell, anyway?"

"Anybody here ever been to Canada?" Elizabeth asked.

There was silence. It was a little awkward. Since Year 1 direct conversations between people my age (face-to-face ones) were rare, and it felt like we were running out of things to say.

"That's where they have moose?" I asked. "Right?"

Three rich sounding *pings* filled the air, meaning—we all figured—we were to walk into the Auditorium for Orientation. As an Affinity Group (the smartest one, according to Elizabeth) we were still missing our expected fifth member. We walked in together, looking around to see bunches of kids we hadn't yet met. I started sweating, as if we had to go up to make a presentation or something. I hadn't been around a group of so many super-achievers ever, and I wasn't sure how to behave. I was worried about being so foreign to them and worried about what they'd make of me.

The auditorium was cooled to perfection, and it felt like something very efficient was about to happen. Some sharp-sounding, busy-people-doing-things music came blaring out of invisible surround-speakers and we knew to sit down. It was quite an international mix of people, and I counted about fifteen people of color – though I remained one of only three from the entire continent of Africa. And the three of us were very aware of each other, as we'd heard about each other in the whole "best and brightest" competitions in high school. None of us, apparently, had made it to Wen's group. Not yet.

The lights dimmed on us and rose on the stage. Two men walked in through the side auditorium doors. The one taking the lead was tall and elegant with short-cropped gray hair and a prominent nose. Together, with large eyes, he looked like a hawk in an expensive linen shirt. The much-younger man next to him looked like he could've been an actor in a movie from my parents' time, or a singer in a band from Year 5. Brown-haired, handsome, and quietly intense. Medium PFA readings for both.

"Good afternoon," the older one said. "I am Mr. Cote, one of your two Advisors. This is Mr. Orlinsky, on my left," and he paused as Mr. Orlinsky gave a half-wave to a smattering of applause. Cote continued, "Our job is to keep you on track as you identify and implement projects that will occupy a significant chunk of your young-adult lives. These projects should be ones that positively influence the world we live in and shape the one we want to live in. To this end, our first requirement is to keep you, and the systems we work on, safe.

"We enjoy an unprecedented mutual level of cooperation with all the major players who've contributed to the development of The HIVE, as well as cooperation with others." This was, no doubt, a swipe at Wen; he was the *others*. "You will be working on advancing programming projects within your Affinity Groups, yes, but what this boils down to is that there are no secret projects at CAWS. That applies to you just as much as to CAWS' programs in Greenland and Australia. What YOU are working on is what WE are working on. It is essential that your Advisors know, and approve, of what you are doing. The media loves a good rogue programmer story, but that's not what we do here. The HIVE didn't get as far as it has by everyone doing their own thing."

There were a few chuckles at this.

"The time you spend on your advanced programming will be supplemented by mandatory LAMP curricula. I am responsible for everything about tech. Questions about your LAMP course—Literature Art

Music Phys/Ed—go to Mr. Orlinsky." Turning towards Orlinsky, he asked him, "Do you have anything you'd like to say to them?"

Orlinsky shook his head. "No," he said. "I think it's been said." I wondered if Orlinsky was used to being steam-rolled like this. It seemed so.

Cote wrapped up by saying, "By now, you've received your Affinity Group contact assignment. I'll be meeting with each of your groups throughout the year. Get some rest tonight and be ready to hit the ground running tomorrow. Let's have a good year. Good night."

As we rose to leave, he walked down the five carpeted steps leading to the ground from the stage, jabbed a finger at Rudra and Elizabeth and said, pointedly, "Stay." His hand then swung to point at me and Kristina as well. "Your whole group. I want to meet with you now. Follow me."

This was more than a little scary. I'd just been getting ready to whisper something to Rudra about how strange Cote looked when he approached us. We followed him and Orlinsky off to a small conference room on the side. We walked in, and Orlinsky closed the door.

"Sit," Cote said. And we did, around the small, empty conference table. "We have a problem. It is not a small one. I will talk to your group, and your group only, about it, and I will have your support on this without this information getting around. If I find that it has, you'll all be out of CAWS and sent packing by tomorrow afternoon. Is that understood?"

I looked around at the others. Rudra was nodding, and Kristina just looked to be studying Cote's face. Elizabeth seemed to be working hard to contain any emotion at all, looking studiously blank.

"I asked you if that was understood?" Cote asked, in a louder voice. "I don't hear you."

"Yes," we murmured, more or less together. Rudra was still the only one actively nodding.

"A WenBook has been hacked. That was always an infinitesimal possibility, but extremely unlikely," Cote said. "They're far beyond

16

military-grade encryption, more than six times minimum cryptosecure emerald status, for those of you who need a refresher on WenBook specs. They auto-report when even an attempt is made, but in this instance, it reported a location of the middle of the Indian Ocean. And a depth of 2,500 feet. So, whoever did this was good."

Rudra and I made a determined effort to not look in Elizabeth's direction.

"What was the point of the hack?" Kristina asked, in what was the first time, really, she'd spoken in front of our group.

"Just that the hacker could do it. My code is bigger than your code. The usual," Cote said.

Elizabeth cleared her throat and spoke up. "I might be able to shed some light, here," she said. "I am the one who hacked it."

Cote took a half-moment and looked her up and down. "How do you expect me to believe that?"

"Because it is true. I did it," Elizabeth said, standing her ground.

"That's easy to say now. Why didn't you tell me this beforehand? You claim this right after I told you it's happened?" Cote asked, glaring at her. "I told you all there are no secrets here. We work on the assumption you've tell us everything we need to know. And that means everything. Anything else is deceptive and grounds for being expelled from CAWS. This place is bigger than you, Elizabeth."

"I can show you how I did it," she said. Then she looked around and said, "In private."

"That still doesn't prove you did it. It only proves you COULD do it.," Cote said, his face getting more flushed and tighter. "There is one thing that you definitely did, though; and that is earn a disciplinary letter in your file. We can forward them to future employers for ten years after graduation. Here's the challenge, Elizabeth: if you say you did it, let's see you reverse it. Just fix it If you can't, then it wasn't you. Fair enough?"

"Whole different ball of wax," Elizabeth said, her voice rising in protest.

"There are no rogue operations at CAWS," Cote said. "If you come to my attention again, Elizabeth, it had better be for some reason that makes me extremely happy or I'll be in instant communication with English authorities and what happens next will make your head spin."

No one said anything.

"Do the rest of you understand this?"

The silence continued, until Rudra finally broke it. "Why are we so concerned about Wen's problem? Won't he have his best people on this right away?"

"Because we don't know what else cracks when someone cracks Wen's coding. He's off in Wen-world over there on the other side of the globe with top-secret everything…waterfalls, lotus flowers, and tons of secret ingredients we're not privy to. We don't know what's linked to what. He doesn't do things like us. Has he put anything at risk? I don't know, and that is the problem. Not knowing in the ecosystem of HIVE-encoded-biolooping is unforgiveable. Your job is to repair the WenBook hack by morning and suggest coding amendments to protect it."

None of us heard the door that must've opened behind us as the fifth member of our Affinity Group entered and sat down in a back row.

Cote wasn't done yet. "This is a once-in-a-lifetime opportunity for us to see how Wen does things. To see the guts of the coding and architecture. Taste the secret sauce. And learn how to improve upon it."

"Do you mean steal?" a highly-accented male voice coming from behind us asked, loudly. We all turned to look. He stood.

"This is Aharon Chayot," Cote said, gesturing with his arm, but looking at the young man coolly. "From The Protectorate. He's your fifth."

Aharon was tall, skinny to the point of almost gaunt, and his eyes seemed to be focused far beyond this room. I didn't know what had happened to him before he arrived, but it must've been big. He set down the messenger bag that had been slung over his shoulder and sat in an empty chair near us. He looked tired and hungry, of course, we all did when we arrived, but this was much more. He simply looked haunted. My PFA flickered between two washes of color: white and light tan. I didn't know how to process this. It was a weird, ambiguous color.

Cote continued, directing this to Aharon. "There's no such thing as stealing in HIVE development," he said. "The history is one of borrowing from all existing ideas. You can use legal semantics and pay out big settlements if you need to, but it's all just progress." He looked at all of us in an uncomfortable silence. "Get in to Wen's world and get out. Learn as much as we can and fix it by morning."

"We're going to give Wen the fix as a gift?" I asked Cote, speaking out at the same time as I was raising my hand.

"Precisely," Cote said. "Just colleagues helping colleagues."

"After stealing their secrets," Aharon said without emotion.

I wanted in on this. However, or whenever, the communications or discoveries went to Wen, I wanted to be there. That meant me being the one to fix it, I figured.

Cote glared at Aharon. "Is there anything you want to tell us about how they're doing things in The Protectorate these days?" he asked Aharon. "Anything relevant?"

We were all quiet. The Protectorate was what the Internationally occupied Middle East had been called since the last few days of Year 10. Aharon was the only of us who came from a simmering war zone. I felt protective of him and was rooting for him to not say anything.

"Relevant? I don't know if we've ever been relevant. Not to California. It's more of the same. Fewer explosions in the street. A few snipers who don't know it's supposed to be over, oh, five years ago, shooting at anything that moves until someone comes and shoots them dead."

"I thought there was extended calm," Kristina said.

Aharon stifled a laugh. "They confiscated chemical weapons and whatever else they found. Declared peace in Year 10. All governments had to resign or face IOME military response. Seven countries and twenty-eight guerrilla factions became one Protectorate. Better luck this time, right?"

I could feel deeply the sadness he carried with him. "Where in The Protectorate were you from?" I asked.

"Israel," he said.

"Right. Ok," Cote said. "Back to the present. Wen has a broken system right now and will surely make an announcement in a few hours. He doesn't want people waking up to it being hacked. He knows we know. He's going to act swiftly to secure it. Could you please get to work before that happens?"

"What if we can't fix it?" Rudra asked.

"Then we'll know no one can. Don't let it go to your heads. Greenland and Australia CAWS are working on it, too. Get in touch with me as soon as you crack this," Cote said as they left. "I'm going to sleep. Make me happy when I wake up. Welcome to CAWS." And then both he and Orlinsky left.

We got to work. Elizabeth looked like there was a lot she wanted to say but was deciding to keep her mouth shut and her lips pursed. She wandered off to where she said she'd be comfortable. She needed the right chair, always, she said. She found one in the corner by the window of the common area down the hall, near where the girls' dorms started. Almost predictably, the rest of us gathered to work there, near her. There were pillows, a few desks, a sofa, and a lot of serious looking lamps.

There was a knock on the door, and a smiling girl from Student Services wheeled in a cart with food on it, saying, "Mr. Cote says to help yourself and there will be coffee available round the clock."

Then she handed Aharon a special plate.

"What is it?" I asked.

He looked, sniffed, and offered the slightest bit of a smile. "I think it is supposed to be hummus and tabbouleh."

After about five minutes of silence, Kristina asked Elizabeth, loudly, "Why did you do it? The hack?"

"Because anyone who was able to would," Elizabeth quickly responded. "I've been working up to it. It's a master challenge. Just horses for courses, that's all."

"Then you know the way to fix it?" Rudra asked.

Elizabeth didn't say yes or no. She started to explain to us advanced hack pathways used in the past and why these don't work with WenBooks. I followed it carefully. I memorized every move she showed me to write down later, but it was clear she wasn't divulging exactly how she'd executed it. She may have wanted us to invent the fix, do the work for her. Maybe Cote was right and she was bluffing.

We went back to our chairs and desks, and it felt like she was the teacher and we were the students, and we were supposed to report to her. I resented it. If I found the fix, it'd be for myself and Wen.

The more I worked the more I saw that all avenues we were pursuing, even through multiple backdoors, looped back to the rigidity of the system programming. In fact, the system seemed to get more rigid with our every attempt, as if it were learning about us more than we were learning about it.

"I'm not getting anywhere," Rudra said after a quiet hour working.

"Me neither," said Kristina.

I had just kept poking at it, and it kept shutting me out and turning me away. I tried mirroring, simulated creation sequences to literally re-invent it, I've tried altering reproduction systems in the outside code. And there was no way in. "It won't allow a fix," I told the group.

Elizabeth seemed to be growing concerned. It was 2:30 a.m. She was muttering a lot to herself. "Can't be. Can't have learned that. Probability is nil. Approaching nil…"

After another half-hour of us knocking our heads up against the Wall of WenBook, I saw that Rudra was resting his eyes, his head down on his hands, on the desk. Then I heard him snoring. Aharon had moved to a densely padded chair in the corner, had turned out the lights, and was sleeping with his head back. I wanted to be home—home, home, not here—in bed.

But I was wide awake enough to hear Elizabeth's first snort. It was a more-important-than-usual snort. She was crunched up into the window-sill now, sitting uncomfortably, typing about a hundred words a minute on some old laptop.

"What's going on?" I asked.

Rudra awoke. Aharon was less certain he was awake.

Elizabeth looked at the screen intently, looked away, and then looked back. "Ummmmmm…people?" She cleared her throat loudly now. Aharon popped up with a startle. "There's something I have to tell you. Wake up." The room seemed to come alive at the same time, and Elizabeth kept looking back at the screen saying, "Uh-oh. Uh-oh, uh-oh, UH-OHHHHHHH…"

"What?" we practically shouted.

"*Hell on Earth*," Elizabeth said. "It's here in twelve minutes"

We looked at each other. I thought I was dreaming, that maybe all of us were.

Hell on Earth was a nightmare, an urban legend, a Boogie Man. It was the much-rumored-about unicorn of a gaming program that no one had ever seen. It was said to be able to alter the brains of whomever attempted to play it in rapid, violent, and permanent fashion. Addictive ultra-violence. It was what old people talked about when they were scared of change and trying to frighten people into never moving forward. But it was fake. Fake News. It just didn't exist. There was even a ban on attempting to copyright the name, or any variation of it, ever since Year Zero.

"Nine minutes," Elizabeth said, looking visibly agitated. "I think it might be real. Stop looking at my WenBook and turn on yours. See what you see."

We did. The same screen she'd been looking at was on all of our WenBooks. The screen suddenly zapped into some horizontal visual noise. A message appeared: "You have temporarily lost HIVE connectivity." I was shocked. I had never seen that in my life. There were some solid moments of static and visual confusion. It was upsetting and disorienting. Then a brief Wen Enterprises logo screen appeared, complete with lotus flower. Then that went black. More static. Then a black welcome screen appeared, with fonts that were stark, though not large.

"*Hell on Earth* arrives in six minutes." Somehow, even seeing these words on a WenBook looked obscene. We'd gotten so used to only seeing educational content on them that this, alone, was shocking.

I watched as the words changed to: "Don't Even Try to Prepare for *Hell on Earth*. You Can't."

"Shouldn't we HIVE-Snap Cote?" Rudra asked as we all looked up. "Orlinsky?"

"Too late," Elizabeth said, looking ashen. "HIVE-Snap them if you want, but there's nothing they can do."

"I'm on it," Rudra said.

"Was this from your hack?" I asked, angrily. "Did you open this gate?" She was silent. "I don't know what this is."

"Why should we follow this, then? This isn't our mission," I said.

"Because it might – as a byproduct of the hack – have breadcrumbs in it that lead to the fix," Elizabeth said. "If we can subdue it."

"Welcome to *Hell on Earth*," said the screen. There was a big rectangular box in the middle of the screen to click, and the words: "BRING IT."

Instructions

Rudra was the first one to go in, after running to get total-body VR suits for us from the dorm's tech supply room. I watched him slip into his, with all the pulse points, heart, hands, neck, stomach, and several areas of the face attached." He was suddenly motionless and silent. Then a simple "Whoa."

"What?" I asked. He didn't answer. We all stared at him.

"What is going on?" Elizabeth demanded.

"I didn't click on it," Rudra said. "You don't even have to click on it to have it start. You better come on in and see for yourself. "

It felt very military, all of us suiting up at once. It might've been standard-issue body-suiting for California, but it was nicer than anything I'd seen back home. Just sturdier feeling. The one back home felt like you were walking into a plastic garbage bag.

I went on in. It just started.

"Entering Hell," said the screen when I put on the visor. I was utterly unprepared for the look of the game.

I was looking into the eyes of a young boy. Enormous eyes. Filled with sadness. Or was it shock? I could see every pore on his skin, every eyelash. The colors—his dusky skin, his blue sweater, the top of the red shirt sticking out over his collar.

Then everything started to rumble, a deep, resonant, unstoppable vibration all through my body. From my toes to the hair on my head I felt the rumble of hundreds of tanks approaching as they came into view. Five across, an endless row, advancing with no pause, across the field of dirt, broken glass, twisted metal, and concrete. The boy stood in front of the tanks. No weapons. Behind him, and next to him, were six other young people; two of them girls. The tanks now seemed within fifty feet of the people. The civilians lifted signs high above their head. "No War!" and "We Are One!"

The tanks smashed into the boy, knocking him onto his back with force, tank treads rolling onto his legs, running over him without pause. Amidst screams, rapid-fire automatic weapons rang out and the others dropped, bodies crushed in place. Each line of tanks ran over their dying bodies. I didn't know what I was watching. I'd been expecting the beginning of a game. The sounds of bones crunching rang through my head beneath the relentless motorized throb of the machine.

Another minute went by like this before everything froze and the words: "Choose Sides Quickly" appeared, with a 5-second countdown on the screen. 5-4-3-2-1. It was a multi-player game, and you had to choose a tribe: Savage Hill Survivors, The Denizens, Erase All Witnesses, The Natives, or Autopsy on Request. Suddenly, thousands of other people could be seen, running, and scrambling to choose sides. I chose The Denizens became the name seemed less psychotic.

I was teamed up with a guy named Denny. We were given guns and assigned a mission: we had to break into a small elementary school, steal computers, and spray paint our tribes' tag all over. Simple enough. But then the police arrived.

"Shoot them?" a prompt suggested.

"What do you think?" asked Denny, lifting his gun.

I joined him, choosing the fatter of the two policemen to shoot first. It ended up with both of us killing them with forty-eight shots to the heads and bodies. I was ahead of him, 48-34, in shots, but he caught up once he noticed. Denny peppered the cop's body, and was laughing as it danced on the floor with each bullet impact.

I had been staring at that, evidently. I still couldn't shake the feeling that on some level this wasn't cool or funny or even fun) when I lost sight of Denny. The next thing I knew he was behind me with a knife to my throat.

"What?" was the last word I said before he pushed me onto my knees, and then kicked me into the path of an oncoming cop car. I felt the car slam into me, a brutal *thud* as everything went dark, and I was, apparently, done. I had died. The last thing I saw was the fender of the car.

The screen went pitch black, then came up with an image of a translucent body. "YOU HAVE DIED" came up next.

Denny had killed me.

While I'd ignored some brief command that might have floated around as a VR suggestion while the cop was dying, Denny had opted to betray me for some fast gain on points for the level system, advancing quickly towards Level Two.

I was angry. No one kills me. In fact, no one touches me unless I want them to. I wanted to play this game again and get it right.

"RETURN TO HELL?" the screen asked.

This time I looked for the prompt to betray whomever I was teamed with, fast.

The request came quickly: "Do you want to try Level One again?" I motioned with hand, fast, and the game started. The same boy, the same blue sweater, red shirt, sandy colored skin, the same huge rumble of tanks, the same crushing of him, shooting of the others, only this time, I noticed the tanks rolling over arms and legs that were still quivering under the unforgiving pressure of the tank.

I joined Erase All Witnesses this time. I chose a knife at the outset, instead of food, as basic equipment. We had to set a church on fire while children were downstairs in classrooms, still learning whatever they learn in churches. My partner was Rick. I leapt at him the first moment I saw the prompt, grabbing him from behind as he was lighting some newspapers to throw onto a pool of gasoline. He struggled, but I slit his throat before he could understand what was happening. My hands felt wet and sticky, and my heart raced. I lit the fire just as he had started it, and ran out, encountering no one and trusting no one.

My heart rate was rising. When I ran out of the burning building, I heard my name being called. How did anyone know my name? I never volunteered it.

But it was being called in real life. "Zokaya! Zokaya! Come out of it. It'll auto-pause. Come out."

I took off the hood and saw Elizabeth and the others staring at me. I realized I was sweating and still breathing hard.

"Where were you?" Rudra asked. "What were you doing?"

"Same thing as you, I would imagine," I said.

"Then why did it take you so long to get out of it?" Elizabeth asked.

"I don't want to talk about it," I said, wondering if any of them had been killed, too, or if I were the only one.

"Well, I'll talk about it," Elizabeth said. "Here's what I say: That's it?" she asked. "Burning a few churches, well-designed fire and music from pre-Zero? Some tempting naughty bits waved in your face? Been there, done that. LAME! I expected a lot worse. Wasted opportunity if you think about it. Not worth losing sleep over."

"It seems that quite a few people disagree with your one-star rating," Kristina said, consulting a non-WenBook laptop. "There are 8.2 billion people in the world, and thirty-two percent of us are under twenty-one. That means Wen distributed over 256 million WenBooks. And it seems that over five million of us just finished playing Level One already and have chosen to go on to Level Two, as of this moment. And it's just been released an hour ago."

"Where are you getting that from?" Elizabeth demanded.

"Sources," Kristina said. "You're not the only one here with secrets."

"Umm...we have visitors," Rudra said, interrupting, and gesturing behind us, pointing towards Cote and Orlinsky. Cote was, for some reason, staring at me hard, and he looked as if he thought I'd been lying to him about something. Orlinsky was trying to look neutral but looked concerned.

I suddenly felt embarrassed and dirty, seeing them. I wasn't sure why. But I still wanted them to leave so I could finish Level One.

"Where are we? What do you have for me?" Cote asked.

"*Hell on Earth,*" Elizabeth said. "We're all playing it."

Cote snorted. "That's the Loch Ness Monster," he said. "Older than me. It doesn't exist."

"Yes, but I just told you we're playing it right now," Elizabeth said curtly. "My guess is if you turn on HIVE-News, you'll see others are, too."

"So, you're not working on the hack?" Cote continued.

"It appeared," Kristina said. "It just appeared on the WenBooks as we were working on a way in, OK? It doesn't even care if you click it. It just auto-plays."

"So, it's not just on your WenBooks?" Orlinsky asked, finally speaking.

"There is no way it is just on our WenBooks," said Rudra.

Orlinsky turned on HIVE-News on the large wall-monitor. It was 3:00 in the morning, L.A. time. The authoritative male anchorman was mid-sentence: "…serious breach of what we all thought was an un-hackable system. Reports are coming in from Africa, Asia, and Europe, as well as The Triumvirate, all saying the same thing: *Hell on Earth* is here."

"I guess it's real, huh?" said Aharon.

Cote looked stony. Part of his left cheek started twitching.

"Authorities strongly recommend putting down the WenBook and ignoring any invitations to play a game," the newsman continued. "There are too many unknowns, and if you play, you may be triggering an even larger spyware/malware epidemic. The best advice is to simply walk away from your WenBook. A statement from Mr. Wen is expected at 7 a.m. New York time."

"What do you want us to do?" Elizabeth asked Cote. "Do you want us to be up on what millions of people will be experiencing shortly, or do something else?"

"Play the game," Cote said. "Get through it as fast as you can. Let me know everything worth knowing." He and Orlinsky left.

"How are you?" Kristina asked me in a concerned voice.

I hadn't even seen her walk up. It took me a moment to focus on her, and then I tried to figure out what she wanted me to say. "I don't want to talk about it," I found myself saying. She walked away. I shouted over to her, "How are you?" Kristina didn't answer and left the room. I guess she wasn't playing. Or already had finished Level One.

I wanted to go back to playing.

"What time is it?" I heard someone ask.

"Who cares?" said Rudra (I think). I put on the VR-hood, and all the sensors and the game immediately picked up with the sounds of the church fire crackling and screaming in the background. I tucked my knife away and pulled out a short sword. The weight felt just right in my hand. To test it I ran around the corner of some rubble and stabbed one of the Denizens through the back. He dropped and the blade pulled out with some difficulty. It must have snagged on part of his lungs. I was shocked at how good, and how deep, the haptics were on this suit. It felt detailed down to the neural level.

A large one of the Autopsy on Demand guys came running at me from out of nowhere, blade in hand. I deflected his lunge and killed him on the way down. He fell by my feet.

I knew what to do without being told. I scrambled to the top of a hill of rubble and spotted The Natives huddling by a campfire, planning something. I found an overturned storage container to hide behind while the five of them took positions in different directions. When the guy near me was far enough away from the others, I leapt out in front of him. Before he could say,

"What?" I stabbed him in the throat. He fell, and this time, it was harder getting my blade out of him. It must've been snagged on vocal cords.

I whirled around to run, and there were three guys suddenly on me. They were Savage Hill Survivors. This was going to be the end of me. My sword was knocked out of my hand, and I threw myself at the guy who did it, both of my hands wrapping around his throat. I squeezed and squeezed even though I knew the others would get me by stabbing me in the back. I watched the last breath leave him, his color turning to red, then purple, his tongue flicking out as his mouth gasped, pleading, then growing slack, tongue hanging loosely.

And before anything else could happen, the screen said, "Welcome to Level Two." Apparently, killing one of each of the other tribes got you the advancement. And it was an entirely different scenario. I was alone on a beach. No one was trying to stab me in the back.

Without knowing why, I whipped the VR hood off, and everything stopped. My breathing was fast. I bent over with my hands on my knees. I didn't want to see anybody. I didn't want to have to talk to anybody. Not anyone real, anyway.

I wanted to walk away, but I knew if I did, I would run away. I would leave this place, the real place, this real place. I would head south. In my mind, my poor, confused mind, that would lead me back home. When, in truth, there was no returning home.

So, I put the hood back on.

I was still standing on the beach. Next to me were my people. Together, we were Erase All Witnesses. There were men, and there were women. There were some teenagers but no children.

I could smell our sweat. The sound of pulsing distorted electronic music was growing louder, along with what sounded like industrial machines slamming against something, over and over again. I had never known a moment like this, not even in games I'd played as a high schooler.

I was seeing, with such clarity, and feeling, and feeling all through my muscles, what I knew would be happening next: us doing something together, without a leader, without saying anything, like birds changing direction all of a sudden, or bees, hunting to ensure that our will prevailed?

Yes, the killing stuff was old news, but the knowing about doing everything together, combined with the lustful, energized feeling of knowing it would be something filthy and wrong and deadly, with none of us bearing responsibility for, that felt new. And delicious. It was much easier to do what we were about to do because we were a unified mob. We really would Erase All Witnesses.

A set of instructions appeared, advising me on how to fly. "Arms out for speed," said a soothing female voice. "Slower by separating your palms more."

I went aloft, leaving the landscape, gently cruising, swooping in loops that felt deliciously sexy. I don't know why the loops felt sexy. It was power. Power to fly.

Then I saw the mass of people far below. The townspeople. The ones who'd been fleeing us.

"DIVIDE BY SEGMENTING FROM ABOVE," the female voice said as the words appeared, superimposed over the townspeople.

I tried, hovering, and moving several fingers of my right hand up and down allowed me to segment them into two suddenly-separate groups. I watched as they were physically shunted to one side or another, several feet, by an unseen force. I could hear the screaming. It seemed out of proportion to what was happening, though. To me, it was just a line drawn, with two little cup-shaped groups resulting.

My ability to fly, and hover, wasn't affected. I was just in the sky, drawing the lines any way I liked to. I experimented, bringing the line down and to the right, creating a cup-shape as I came up again on the right side, and I watched the segmentation happen again. The group in the *cup* now had a special status.

More instructions appeared, as a series of choices to make.

"CHOOSE A LABEL," the instructions read, as the soothing voice spoke the words. The choices were: DISEASED, RAPISTS, or THREAT TO WAY OF LIFE. I chose the last one by grabbing the choice-box with my fist. The choices disappeared, and the entire group became highlighted with the color blue as I grasped at the box.

"DISPOSE OF THREAT," the voice soothed, as the words appeared. "CHOOSE METHOD: FIRE, GUNFIRE, or CHEMICAL."

I was startled, and it seemed like gunfire was the most humane. That's why I grabbed it.

"DIG OWN GRAVES?" the voice asked, as the check-boxes appeared. I grabbed "YES" without thinking. I regret it now.

I was able to zoom in on the picture by spreading the scene below me open with my fingers. Shovels appeared and were distributed to the masses, by three ERASE ALL WITNESS members. People reluctantly received them and, after a few moments of verbal exchanges that I couldn't hear, burst out into tears. I watched a young girl clinging to her mother as the mother howled, looking up (right at me?), refusing to move in any direction. She was poked by a rifle, and when she wouldn't respond, her daughter was shot in the head, and then her.

I couldn't get the mother's look out of my mind. She didn't look like a CGI character. She looked like she was truly in pain. To my whole body and mind, in this moment, this felt real. I had just done this.

Everyone else began digging. The crying was sobbing and gulping for air in between tears now. Why could I hear this when I couldn't hear the exchange of dialogue before this? Technical glitches in this game? Why were the people obediently digging their graves when there were hundreds of them and only three big guys with guns?

I hovered over the sight but came down lower. I was jolted by the sounds of shooting. They were mowing them down now, and they were falling into their newly-dug graves. At least the crying got softer.

I turned myself left and left again and accelerated my flight away from the site. I tried to fly outside of the whole game, so that I could see the structure from a different angle. It wouldn't let me out.

In fact, it bounced me back over the bodies. The three shooters had walked away now, and it was a quiet field. But around them, off to the sides, were the others, the ones who hadn't been THREATS TO WAY OF LIFE. They were screaming, loudly. It was a mixture of fright and warning. They had seen what just happened. Their hysteria was growing louder and louder and a few people were looking up, at me and pointing.

Words appeared, and I heard the soothing whisper: "MUTE OTHERS?"

I waved my hand over them, clenching in my fist, grasping, and highlighting them. They turned blue. I grasped again and all the noise stopped.

Sweet silence.

I turned and flew away. This time I was allowed to.

For the shortest of moments, I saw the image of a sexy, short-haired young woman, undressing, in her bedroom, her back towards me. A blouse being lifted off, her tight jeans being pulled down, next. White panties. Her head turned partially towards me, half a smile almost visible. Then the flash of words, too fast to take in, then gone. I would learn later what they said.

I was still flying. I was swooping low now. The beach was almost in sight. But first the word "MANAGE STRAGGLER" appeared, as the voice whispered it in my ear. I noticed, far below me, an old man, limping. "DRONE-SHOT OR CHEMICAL?" I grabbed at DRONE-SHOT because I wanted this over fast. An arc shot from the box I had selected and the man disappeared in a cloud of dirt. "

I was back over the beach now. I let my hands rise over my head, and I gently set back down to the warm sand. It felt good.

"WELCOME TO LEVEL THREE," said the beautiful, beautiful voice. I wondered if this was the voice of the woman I'd just seen.

I took off the VR suit and sat, exhausted and full of feelings I could not identify. Too much, too fast. I didn't think I even knew what I had done.

But I did.

Clear, Simple, and Wrong

Only Rudra was in the room with me. It took a while for my eyes and head to adjust to not playing the game. He was seated in a chair with his back to me, looking out the window. I didn't know what time of night it was.

"Where is everyone?" I asked.

"Don't know. Asleep, I guess."

And that was it. That's all he said, and I didn't feel like talking either.

I was staring at a wall, half-asleep. I kept seeing that woman's face. The woman they shot. The one who wouldn't dig her grave. I kept hearing the sounds of shovels assaulting the earth, digging up gravel and dirt, the pause and then the gunshots. Even though my stomach felt queasy (hunger or nausea?) I wanted to resume playing the game. That is what I was going to do, and that is what I started to do when Elizabeth walked in and threw on the lights. Kristina walked in, behind her, rubbing her eyes.

"Were you—?" I started.

"Sleeping? Yes. Can't recommend it enough. Good stuff," Elizabeth said.

"Did you—?"

"Finish Level One? Yes, we all did. What a lot of muck. Distressing at best, been-there-done-that more than I'd expected. The programming values, though are high-grade," Elizabeth conceded. "Luxurious visual density, seamless contextual interface recognition and transition, deep sensory integration."

I wondered if she'd seen, and done, anything like I had. What had the others seen?

"I finished Level Two," I blurted out.

"Why?" Kristina asked. "Didn't you want to get some sleep?"

"No," I volunteered. "I wanted to play it. Didn't Cote say to do that?"

"You are the only one to take that seriously, Zokaya. Even Elizabeth slept."

I looked over at her. She nodded.

"This is Wen's cock-up," Elizabeth said. "Poor coding. The hack will get fixed in time."

"By Greenland? Or Australia?" Rudra asked.

"How much should I care? Cote didn't believe me in the first place!" Elizabeth said. "Leave it broken for a few days and see what happens. That's my vote. And now," she announced loudly, in her best BBC-English, "It's Wen-time. Seven a.m. New York time. His Majestic Excellency with Subpar Coding Abilities will speak momentarily." Aharon woke up from the couch he'd been sprawled on, startled by her voice. "Probably from within a waterfall, or riding on a unicorn."

Elizabeth was right. The scene was of media people milling around in front of a moss-covered cave. The sun was going down on what had been a sunny day. It was 6:30 p.m. in China.

Standing in front of a beautiful element of nature was trademark Wen. It wasn't always a cave. The last two times had been in front of gentle waterfalls. Insane rumors about him abounded; that he could hypnotize spiders and get them to perform tricks, or bend light with his hands. Wen was never, ever seen behind a podium or from the inside of an office.

Wen walked forward, exiting from the cave, flanked by three associates. He was a slender man wearing a regular white business shirt and gray pants. He managed to make that look cool somehow. He brushed some of his healthy-looking, long black hair towards the right side of his face and spoke directly, and warmly, in Chinese-accented English, a Chinese translation quietly rolling in the background. I could understand him in Chinese, though.

"Good evening," he began. "Good morning to my friends in the West. Earlier today misfortune hit us in the form of hacking of our beautiful creation. We labored for years to create WenBooks. Rich or poor; all have the same WenBook. They are state of the art. This is unacceptable.

"We will find how this happened and who is responsible. We will restore all the benefits for all of the people. We have the best people working on this. WenBooks will come back stronger than they have ever been. They will be one-hundred percent safe to use.

"Please be patient while waiting. Do not proceed with any screen instructions on a WenBook until you hear from me that it is safe to do so. We are hoping this will be within hours, two days at most.

"Thank you."

We turned it off.

Aharon asked whether they really had the best people working on it and Elizabeth said, "Yes; us. The five of us."

"Is our mission to work on the hack or follow-through on this game?" I asked.

"Assume they are one and the same until proven otherwise," Elizabeth said. "That's the working hypothesis."

"Then why are they sending us into a school today instead of just working on this?"

"What? What kind of school?" I asked.

"The local public school," Rudra said. "You didn't get the memo?"

"No. How come?"

"To observe the impressionable little brats," Elizabeth said. "To see whether the wankers still continue to behave like little wankers before, and after *Hell on Earth*," Elizabeth lectured. "Cote must be taking heat from parents or the school system. They want us to show face, do a meet and greet, tell them that their little Suzys and Johnnies are o.k. So catch another hour and a half of sleep, ladies and gents. Or stay up and reverse the hack. You know how I'm voting," she said, disappearing down the hallway, and into her room.

I curled up into the seat I was in and was asleep in less than a minute.

The next thing I knew we were woken by Elizabeth, who found a way to blast "Rule, Britannia" for an early morning alarm over the HIVE screen.

"Bugger off, Elizabeth," Rudra shouted. From his blanket-covered spot on the floor. "Can't you just wake us up in a normally aggravating way?"

"Hear, hear," I added.

Kristina padded into her room, carrying her shoes in her hands but otherwise dressed and ready for the day.

"Where's Aharon?" I asked.

"He's going to catch up to us outside," Elizabeth said. "Hard to believe, but he's out jogging."

"Do we get to eat or anything?" Rudra asked.

"No. Not here. You can buy some school breakfast with the 8th graders," Elizabeth said.

"Come on," Kristina said, closing up her rucksack and swinging it onto her. She was wearing a beautiful dark blue blouse. She was a swirl of sunny, casual beauty in this day and I felt something in me open. "We're supposed to meet Cote and Orlinsky outside. We're all walking there."

Aharon was waiting right outside. I fell in next to him and watched Rudra and Kristina walk ahead, chatting like it was just another day. Elizabeth walked alone behind them. We had three blocks before the meetup point with Orlinsky and Cote.

"You jogged?" I asked Aharon.

"Yeah. Keeps me sane," he said. "Try it."

"Were you in the Army over there?" I asked.

"Something like that," he said. "Can I ask you something?"

"Shoot."

"Why are we eating, breathing, and sleeping WenBooks? How did this happen over here? This isn't even his place," he asked.

"Same as over there, I'd think. You have them, right?"

"We were distracted. We were fighting for our survival. I remember they distributed them, but we were more concerned with working guns. Why do they worship WenBooks here? Was it like that where you grew up?"

"WenBooks were huge back home," I said. "They replaced college in most of the world. Slick anatonium-215 shell, lightning-fast processing; 538 times the speed of what we were using before it. HIVE-wired, zettabytes of storage. Six-times military redundancy hack-proof."

"Before Elizabeth."

"Yes. Before Elizabeth. But what really was extraordinary was that Wen was giving them away for free. To every young person between the ages of twelve and twenty-one. We couldn't figure out how he could do that."

"There are ways of making money when it looks like you are losing money," Aharon suggested.

"Maybe. They were on every continent within the same month. They had teams of people going through jungles, mountains, crossing streams, the most rural areas, giving them away. Made for great PR clips. Even some of The Religious Ones, who were out on parole, were said to help with distribution. When we were ten years old, in Year 5. And between then and now, I haven't heard of a single problem with viruses or malware for all the years we've had them. Do you know how weird that is? So…a perfect little educational machine. It was a big deal," I said.

"Who paid for it?" Aharon asked.

"Wen. With backers. The United Nations helped with distribution."

"Wow. Maybe they could get one thing done right, huh?" Aharon asked.

"My mother never trusted WenBooks," I said. "She says 'you get what you pay for, and it was free, so it is worth nothing.'"

"Smart lady," Aharon said.

41

Cote and Orlinsky were there on the corner looking wide-awake, unlike us.

"All accounted for?" Cote asked Elizabeth.

"Aye-aye, sir," she responded, moving her angled hand to her head, and offering a military salute.

"Knock it off, Elizabeth," Cote said, turning to lead the way for the rest of our walk.

Elizabeth Warren Middle School was just a half a mile away. I was both tired and awake at the same time, and I was angry, but I couldn't pinpoint why. It wasn't at Aaron, but it didn't go away while I was talking with him. I reminded myself that I'd probably slept less than an hour or two. Though I really didn't know. I had never been in an American school. Neither had any of the others. CAWS was the only one we'd seen.

We started at the principal's office of the middle school. All the secretaries were on phones. We heard them saying, over and over again: "Not here today. I understand and we hope he is feeling better. Please text us a note upon his return." One secretary said, "No, being still asleep isn't an authorized absence…have you tried getting her out of bed?"

When the principal came, he explained that an absence rate of seven to ten percent was average. Today, forty-three percent were absent. "The parents are all saying the same thing; the kids were up all night with the game. We're not going to make a big thing of it, as long as it rights itself tomorrow."

"May we talk to staff?" Cote asked. He and Orlinsky both wanted to see for themselves, they said, how teens were reacting to this stuff, if at all.

"You're the guys from CAWS, right?" he asked.

"Yes."

"Sure. Go ahead. This '*Hell on Earth*' thing, right? Whatever you can do to help." The secretaries gave us special VIP guest passes. Teachers were told to expect us.

One of the security guards, paying close attention to something that was being said through a speaker in his ear, told us, in between pressing the speaker closer, "Yeah, something's up. They're not here, and those who are aren't right. Snarly. Sleep-deprived, who knows? They're not good on a good day, and this isn't a good day. Look around. See what you see."

We split up. I was with Kristina, Rudra, and Cote. Aharon and Elizabeth went with Orlinsky.

My group of four walked in on a Civic Attitudes class. (These had replaced History in Year 1. Nothing was taught that was more than thirteen-years-old.) We were introduced as International Kids, who were here to learn about schools in the Triumvirate and bring back the info to our countries. We had to say where we from. It was clear though, that the teacher was talking even though kids were talking and very few of them seemed to take notice of us at all. It was hard to hear what the teacher was saying. I listened, though, as she tried to get her footing. I heard "People, we're not going to get anywhere like this. One at a time. Where were we? Yes, The New Alignment coming the year of The Filament. This replaced..."

The teacher was drowned out by a sea of voices, but the students weren't talking to each other in an organized way much, either. There were twelve little groups of people catching up with each other and laughing. One of them turned on his wearable to blast 90s music that sounded like the same kind of stuff in *Hell on Earth*. The kids themselves looked scruffier than any of the kids I had seen at the airport, or on the way to CAWS, even worse than tourists looked in Liberia.

Some of their clothes were ripped and stained, it looked like on purpose, and the girls had a lot of skin showing. They were wearing belly shirts, but the top of them were so long and loose they were daring to almost show their nipples. This would've been shameful in Liberian schools. They would've been sent home. Three boys were having a spitting contest in the back of the room, trying to see who could shoot mucous the furthest. The teacher sounded weaker and weaker as the volume in the class got louder and louder. I looked at the pool of mucous on the floor. The boys were laughing. We left.

We checked out a Business Enterprises class. The teacher, a skinny young woman, was sitting turned away from her desk, crying. "No, suck MY dick!" a kid screamed as a bunch of girls laughed. "You WISH!" another boy shouted and a pre-WenBook laptop went flying through the air, hitting a student on the elbow before landing on the floor and clearly breaking. The teacher's head went further down into her hands. She was shaking. As were walking out of the class, we heard the first punch being thrown, obviously by a girl because the boy responded, "Oh, what, I'm going to hit a girl? I don't want to catch any diseases so I won't…"

We were back in the principal's office, waiting for Orlinsky and the others to return. It was hard to believe any of this was because of the game. This school just obviously stunk, and had for a long time.

"Has it been like this for a while?" I asked the principal.

"No. We… I don't know how to explain. We were on an upswing. We had a lot of poor kids, but we were like a family. A family with differences, for sure, but…we were on an upswing."

"You think one night of the game can cause this much distress?" I asked. "It is not credible."

"Yes, it isn't credible, I know," he said. "Not credible, not logical. It's not likely. And you're seeing it."

"There are a lot of possible intervening variables," Cote added. "Correlation is not causation."

Orlinsky walked in with Elizabeth and Aharon. Orlinsky looked upset. Aharon looked shocked and Elizabeth looked smug. "Anyone have anything to say about us being too stuffy on the other side of the pond now?" she asked.

"That's unbelievable," Aharon said. "They have no respect. Even for each other. In my country we respected teachers."

"This isn't a representative day," the principal said.

"Yes, that's what American teachers are fond of saying when anyone walks into their classes and observes them," Elizabeth said. "For years now."

"This is different, Elizabeth. Get off your high horse and just breathe. I don't think you've taken an actual breath or exhaled since you arrived," Orlinsky said.

"They are like animals in a shelter, or dogs in a pound," Kristina said.

"This is with more than one-third of them absent," the principal said. "What's going to happen tomorrow?"

"Do we really need to see the high school?" Elizabeth asked.

"Wouldn't miss it," Orlinsky said. "It'll be nice to see what they grow into."

We walked into the hallway. There were roving bands of kids in the hallway. They had just walked out of their classes because they felt like it. Two boys pushed a skinny boy hard, sending him flying. One of the bullies was from the class we'd just been in.

"Oh, God," Elizabeth said. "I hate teenagers."

That is when she got hit in the head by a lunch sandwich one of them had thrown.

"Go home, you Limey chicken-head," someone shouted.

The principal, who had seen this, held his ear and spoke into his HIVE Connect. "Security, security," but no one came. The kids laughed at this and scattered. Elizabeth was red-faced.

"Get us out of here," Orlinsky said. He and Cote started to walk faster.

"Hold on," said the principal, leaning his head to the side and pressing his earpiece in further. "Hold on. Yeah, I got it," he said into the HIVE Connect. "You are not going to the high school," he told us. "They're sealed. There's been a stabbing. 9th grader. We've been ordered to close early."

We were herded into the Main Office and heard the announcement go out, advising all students to report to their first period class and wait for the early bus dismissal. "Under no circumstances should there be any wandering. Students should be in their classes and wait for the bell signifying dismissal."

No one listened. Within three seconds of the announcement, the halls began to stream with bodies. Several girls were shoved to the ground, but they were laughing, and shoving people back. By the time the buses got there, we saw only a handful of students left, sitting at their desks, waiting.

"The State Ed Commissioner is going live on The HIVE in a minute," the principal said. "They've had the same kind of thing all over. Rough day."

He brought up the feed on his large, school-sized HIVE screen. The State Ed Commissioner looked tired. "There's an old saying; For every complex problem there exists an answer that is clear, simple, and wrong. Such is the case today. If anyone were to associate the problems schools across the state have had today with the arrival of one new HIVE game or another (as some in the media have done), they'd be mistaken. But I'm sure it makes for a good story. The problem lies not with a HIVE game, but with our failure to take responsibility for ourselves. We had a bad day today, people. I am standing by my decision to close schools early, but let's be honest: this is about just about fear, not substance. Let's all go home and get a good night sleep. Let's think a little harder about what kind of schools we want for our children and tomorrow will be a better day."

The principal turned to address us in a quiet voice. "All districts have been instructed to have a community informational meeting tonight. It's going to be here at the middle school. There will be a police spokesperson, the Superintendent, me, and I'd like it if you all could be there. You are computer geeks, no offense, and you aren't that far in age from the kids. It'll help parents see that not everyone has lost their minds."

"OK," Cote said. "See you at 7:30."

"Have refreshments," Aharon said. "Really. I'm not kidding. It makes people happier."

"That stabbing was more than likely completely independent of any of this, you know," the principal said.

"How often do you they happen here," asked Kristina.

"About once every four years. We were due," the principal said.

#

Cote didn't seem to want to talk. None of us seemed to want to talk. So, we walked home, thinking. I kept wondering: were we all seeing the same things in Level One? Level Two? Were the girls seeing a guy in his underwear, stripping, instead of the woman I saw? (It turned out that some did, but not necessarily. The images we saw were somehow personalized around things that were known about us. On every level this game was a quantum leap forward.) But what was the point of us wasting all these hours playing it, as opposed to focusing on the encoding hints? My brain suggested these objections. But that wasn't what I was feeling. I was feeling a mixture of anger, craving and sadness, while still needing to play the game as soon as we were home. Was I the only one? What did Kristina and the others feel?

As we arrived home Cote said something, about him and Orlinsky strategizing without us. He said to get ready for the evening meeting with the parents. "Just tell them how young brains work." As if we knew. None of us felt particularly young anymore, anyway. Not after seeing that school today.

I blocked him out and wasted no time suiting up and resuming *Hell on Earth* right where it left off.

I hated Cote's voice. It irritated me fiercely; it was that of a bleating goat. As the first image of the game came into focus, I found myself wondering what Cote would look like with his head on a pike.

47

Hand Signals

I was staring at a man who was on his knees, wearing an ordinary blue shirt and ordinary jeans, his hands tied in front of him. He was blindfolded, his head tilted towards the ground and he was breathing heavily. Words were in the sounds he was making. Maybe these were prayers. Behind him was a dark-haired boy with a smile on his face. He couldn't be more than ten or eleven years old. He wore a bandana with modern Syriac writing on it, not Arabic. I didn't know a word of it, but I knew what it looked like. We'd studied dead, or dying, languages in high school, in passing. My school didn't have the same prohibitions about history as Triumvirate schools.

The boy held a rifle, unable to level it up properly. I wondered about the right size rifle for a ten-year-old. The boy was pointing it directly at the back of the man's head. For a split second the boy looked up and looked right into my eyes. Frozen in the moment, I was caught off guard by the sudden sound of a gunshot and the sight of him shooting the man in the head, before throwing his hands up in victory and being congratulated by a man who rushed in to rumple his hair and pat him on the back.

Was he a good guy or a bad guy? One of ours? My stomach churned and it felt like some of whatever in it wanted to come up and get spat out. I swallowed it down

The screen switched to a metal cage with three soldiers, still in uniform, in it. It was on a medium-sized green boat. It was being lifted into the air and over water. The men inside were pounding at the locks and trying to slip out between the bars, but they couldn't. Slowly they were lowered into the cold water, their faces panicked, two of them trying to take huge breaths of air, one of them crying and praying. The cage disappeared beneath the sea and the camera lingered on the beautiful blue water, the cage now gone. There were the sounds of water lapping and sea birds flying nearby. There must have been air bubbles on the surface, but I didn't see them. I was immersed in the slick beauty of the peaceful water. The colors were fantastic. Everything looked like a deeper-colored liquid version of reality. It was like diving into a coral sea. Delicious. I don't know how much time went by. The cage was brought up. Three motionless corpses lay on the bottom, mouths open, water gushing around them. I stared at the peacefully lapping water. I didn't look at the cage anymore.

"ERASE ALL WITNESSES"—large triumphant words—were superimposed on everything, but not like a banner. It looked like reality superimposed on reality.

I felt someone next to me. It would be my tribe, I thought. But the touch on the arm was different. It was happening in real life. There were some muffled words. It wasn't coming from the game. "Take it off, Zokaya." I turned my head.

"Take it off." My hood was being lifted off. I was confused.

"Hey!" I shouted.

And there was Kristina, looking at me. With full saucer eyes, boring into me. "Put it down," she said.

I saw Rudra behind her, staring at me. She turned back to him and asked, "Could you give us a minute?" He looked at me, then, her, then gave a little nod and left. The two of them looked less vivid than the world I'd just left; they were almost black-and-white in comparison. Or a bland, faded sepia color. That moment of transition was always strange. It's like experiencing day and night at the same time before the world decides on one. It was day, and Kristina waited for me to focus on her.

"We're concerned about you," she said.

"Who's 'we'?"

"Elizabeth, Rudra, Aharon and me."

"Elizabeth is concerned about me? Hah."

"Because the game doesn't get to us the same way it seems to get to you. I am concerned for you."

"I'm fine," I told her, reaching for the hood to put back on.

Her hand interrupted my grabbing it and she gently pushed it down. "You're going faster than the rest of us."

"Then keep up with me," I said. "Do we have a mission or do we not?"

"You're changing, Zokaya," Kristina said. "*Hell on Earth* appears to affect sensitive people more than the rest of us. You seem to be one of them. The sensitive ones. You are changing."

"You're not?"

"No. Not really."

"Then how are you getting through the levels?" I asked.

"With detachment," she said.

"Not having feelings is the way to be? But that's what I'm doing, isn't it? You should be happy."

"You're angry in a way we aren't," she said.

"I repeat: Then catch up with me! Don't lecture me about someplace you haven't gone," I said, turning away, and walking to the refrigerator in the corner of the lounge to get something to drink.

"My mother used to say I was a sad child," Kristina said, to my back. "But she was much sadder than me because of my father. They sent me to a therapist. And the woman I saw every week told me that it was better to feel angry than sad. But that just sounded like words. Now…this game just seems very sad to me. I wish I could get angry like you. To me it just seems more of the same."

I sat down at a little table, then realized I was being rude. I stood up and went back towards the refrigerator. "Would you like something to drink?" I asked.

"Actually, I would," she said. "What do they have?"

"Zhyga Zap, or electrolyte-infused triple-distilled Rocky Mountain water, or pineapple juice," I read, turning the labels of the small bottles around in my hand.

51

"I'll try pineapple juice," she said. "Never had it."

We sipped in silence for a bit.

"You know there are hidden messages in Level Two," she said. "CAWS Greenland slowed them down and transcribed them."

"Hidden? Like the old Easter Eggs?"

"More like subliminal messages, early last-century."

"Who cares? So what? Everyone knows subliminal messaging was proven to be ineffective."

"Maybe so," Kristina said. "But here's what you've been ingesting, in between everything else," she said, unfolding a piece of paper with printing on it and putting it before me. "The messages alternated at micro-second intervals."

It said:

THERE ARE NO CONSEQUENCES

THE FUTURE BELONGS TO MONSTERS

EAT OR BE EATEN

SURRENDER TO THE SAVAGE

FEED THE BEAST

THERE IS NO SUCH THING AS SEXUAL CONSENT

"How many times do you think you've seen that before? By the end of Level Two?" she asked.

"Five. Five times already," I said, thinking hard to recall the flashes. "Is that what you want to hear?"

"It was three-hundred-twenty-eight times," Kristina said. "The times you remember seeing flashes were just the slower ones. They've programmed it in to match a diversity of brain wave frequencies and…some are slower than other. Some people are. But…everyone who's gotten to Level Two has gotten it, one-hundred-twenty-eight times."

I felt like she was blaming me for something.

"Do you know what it is that is making you so angry?" she asked me.

People didn't speak this way to each other. Maybe they once did, but what she was asking was personal. People are connected to each other all the time but we didn't talk about personal things like this.

"What is it, Zokaya?"

I took a minute to figure it out for myself, and then a wave of disgust came over me. I thought I might throw up. I wanted to. It felt, though, that my body was used to holding it all down.

"Those weren't SCRAPS," I said, finally. "I know SCRAPS. Those were real people dying. In cages. Being drowned. It really happened."

"How do you know?"

"I've spent hundreds of hours with SCRAPS. I was looking into the faces of people dying. Real ones…in a game. Who would put that in a game? Why?"

She touched me. Kristina touched my arm and her voice got softer. "It's nothing new, Zokaya. Each person's death can be another person's entertainment. They started this years ago and called it *news*."

"It's never been in a game. It's always been stylized," I said, fighting back a surge of tears and fury. "Games are supposed to be fun. That was suffering. The end of life. For a person. Not an insect."

"It's Hell, Zokaya. As promised. Nothing more, nothing less."

I felt like punching something, or hurting someone.

"How about a walk?" she asked.

Walks were a big thing out here. They were supposed to detox you so you could be more productive. I didn't want to go, but I didn't want her to leave me, so I said yes. As soon as we were outside, I spotted her bicycle. Kristina was the only person above the age of ten I'd seen with a bicycle, let alone a retro one. It was simple the way only things from pre-Zero could be. And it was hers, like part of her. It was an odd statement to make, I guess, but one that expressed her enjoyment of herself, no matter who was looking. There was something soothing about that.

"Can we walk with your bicycle?" I asked, hoping that I'd get a chance to ride it.

"Sure," she said, straightening it from the tree it'd been leaning against and resting it against her body.

She stood it up and passed it to me. "What color is this?" I asked.

"Aquamarine."

"Can I ride it?" I asked.

"Can you?" she said, smiling and holding the moment. "Do you mean 'may I'? Yes, you may."

I threw a leg over it and tried balancing on it. I set it in forward motion, fast, so as to not fall over. "Like riding a bicycle, as they say…This is a much nicer bicycle than I ever had," I told her. I went out in the road ahead of her, then circled back.

I had forgotten how you can go in a certain direction on a bike just by leaning into that direction and pedaling. I had forgotten how precious the sensation of leaning while moving felt. I turned it around and tried it in the opposite direction. It was effortless.

I hadn't experienced effortlessness in a long time. Not since riding on the back of my Dad's motorcycle and, two years ago, on my own.

I was gliding. I felt like just another animal in the world of California. I thought of the crickets we heard at night, and I was swooping and circling. I thought of all the hawks and bats I'd seen, the bats back home, the hawks here, and I thought of how simple their lives were. They didn't have games full of pain and destruction. Maybe they had their own version of The HIVE or something. I just envied their ability to glide all day long if they wanted to.

But my mind went back to the game. I couldn't stop seeing the face of the mother who was being asked to dig her own grave. And then the sight of her baby, before and after being shot in the head. Her howling. What was *Hell on Earth* doing to me? And why did I still crave it, want to get back to it? I heard the cry of a hawk in a nearby tree and came back, mentally, to awareness of where I was. On a bike, gliding.

I pulled the bike up to Kristina and said, "Your turn."

She smiled. I got off it and handed it over to her. She leaned it and threw a long leg over it before settling down on it. She started doing the same things I'd just done on it…swooping and gliding. Then she surprised me by popping a wheelie and laughing loudly. I ran behind her as she did a few figure-eights, clearly showing off, and pulled up in front of me, smiling. We were near the school's frisbee field now and she got off the bike and sat down, next to me. For a half-second she looked like a little girl. Then she was back to looking older and much wiser than me.

"How did you end up here?" I asked.

"I ask myself that a lot," she said. "I never liked computers, I hate The HIVE. In a way, I couldn't care less about any of this."

I let this sink in before I laughed.

"Yeah? Why the laugh?" she asked.

"I've felt that way for years. But it's like hating oxygen or sunshine," I said.

"Or chemical rain clouds," she said. "Do you want to say anything about the game?"

I was going to say no, but I just let myself be quiet instead.

"It was inevitable, *Hell on Earth*. It is just more of the same, just streamlined."

"I thought I was the only one who felt this way," I said.

"Are you joking?" she asked. "A lot of people feel this way."

"You mean No-Pointers?"

"No. Regular people," she said.

55

"You know those crickets we hear? At night?" I asked. "Did you know they don't live longer than three months?"

"They don't know they have only three months," Kristina said. "The ones you hear are looking for a mate."

"Are there other ones? Quiet ones? That just die off?"

"Maybe they find each other after the loud ones do," she offered.

We held the silence.

"When we were kids, how come no one ever asked us if we like doing the things we were good at?" Kristina wondered.

"That's not part of things anymore," I said.

"It should be."

"It isn't," I said.

"Let us catch up to you on the game, Zokaya. I'm not kidding. We can't lose you. There's more to what's going on than you know."

"It's not...real, right? The killing that is happening in it? It's not tied to real-time events, is it? It's really a game?" I asked.

"It's a game, Zokaya. A twisted one."

"What do you mean by more to the story then?"

"We all have a purpose," she said. "I'm not talking about being bees in a hive."

"A career?" I asked.

"Nothing like that," she said. "It'll become clear."

Suddenly afraid, I asked her, "Are you one of The Religious Ones?"

She laughed. "No, I wouldn't say so." She was quiet for a good minute. We could hear the crickets now. "Sometimes it feels like we are experiencing one-one-hundredth-thousandth of one percent of the world. We are supposed to accept that and then get old and die," Kristina said.

I couldn't think of anything to say.

"Can I teach you something?" she asked, looking at me with a softness I hadn't seen in her face before.

I nodded.

She took my right hand and squeezed four of my fingers shut, my thumb beside them, holding my hand up. "This is 'A.' "Then she unfolded the fingers so they were straight up and tucked my thumb into my palm. "This is 'B.'" She curled my hand in a semi-circle angling my thumb towards the others, leaving an open space. "This is 'C.'"

"Why?" I asked.

"It's just another way, Zokaya. American Sign Language. From when there was an America. I'll show you the rest later. Here's the most important ones, though." She shaped the 'B' again and followed it with fingers closed into the hand, my thumb touching the far-away pinky. "'E,'" she said. "BE." And she put her hand on my chest, touching with some pressure. "Look beyond the game, Zokaya. Being sensitive only helps sometimes. It's a real handicap most of the time. Keep us at your side and don't leave us. Look beyond these things. We will, too."

All I knew was the feeling of her hand on my chest.

I couldn't see it yet, but knew she brought the way out of here.

Meine Mutter

The school auditorium was at capacity by 7:20 p.m., with parents lining the aisles that were supposed to be kept clear for safety purposes. The reason for these meetings, statewide, was – apparently – to calm the parents. When even more parents than they expected came, they shuffled them off into the cafeteria for seating (the auditorium aisles were already crammed with people blocking the exits) and set up cameras, microphones, and a HIVE link so the cafeteria people could participate, too. The A/C was on, but it was hot in the room, and kind of stale already.

It being school, the principal asked everyone to stand for the Pledge of Convergence first. Maybe they would hand out milk and cookies next.

"Before I forget, I want to mention that we have refreshments provided, both in the back of the room and in the Cafeteria, including bottles of water and some delicious cookies. I hope you'll avail yourselves of these either at the conclusion of tonight's meeting or while we're meeting, whatever you need. Please help yourselves. I am Principal Zerwicky, this is Captain Blanca, of the California State Police to my right, and Asst. Commissioner Chris Dana of the State Ed Department, next to him. They are running things tonight. The only thing I want to say is that for those of us who do this for a living, and I have done this for many years, know that kids are kids. We often don't like what that translates down to –"

He was interrupted sharply by someone shouting, "You mean, like when they stab each other?"

"Excuse me, I'm talking right now. You'll have your turn later. As I was saying, we don't always like the consequences of kids-being-kids. But your children are in the safest place they could be. Statistically they are actually safer in school than they would be at home. No criticism intended," Zerwicky said, shuffling some papers in front of him, readying to leave the podium, and seeming to look for a quick laugh. "Captain Blanca?"

"Good evening," Captain Blanca said, stepping forward and referring briefly to an index card. "Today, at approximately midway through the 0900 hour, an incident of solitary student assault was reported at Cory Booker High School. The student who was assaulted was taken to Dawkins Hospital, where he is recovering and is in satisfactory condition. The assailant was quickly identified and taken into custody, where he, in the presence of his parents, admitted his guilt after being read his rights. That student, I am told, will be facing both a suspension from school and criminal charges. Without trying to prejudice the results of a superintendent's hearing I think it is fair to say that that student won't be back anytime soon. Schools were closed early yesterday and dismissal was held in an orderly fashion without further police involvement or incident."

"Bullshit," someone yelled. "They were running out of the building, hitting each other, running wild through the streets, and stealing from stores."

"Please," said Zerwicky. "Let us be respectful of the speaker; there will be a time for public questions and comment after the facts have been presented. Commissioner Dana?"

A weak-looking balding man with three notecards in his hands walked behind the podium. "Hi, everybody, I'm Chris Dana, from State Ed. Superintendent Keys wanted to be here tonight in person, but meetings like this are happening in many school districts at once. He expresses his regrets, and I am here in his place."

"Doesn't that tell you something?" someone in the audience shouted. "This is happening all over."

Mr. Dana chuckled lightly. "These meetings were actually something Superintendent Keys and I discussed doing anyway, as part of our K.I.T.W.A. Initiative (Keeping in Touch with All), kind of a series of 'water-cooler discussions' with all the players and consumers involved in K-12 education."

"Talk about the Game," a woman called out.

"Let me say this about the Game," Mr. Dana said. "We didn't make the decision lightly to close schools early. We have one-hundred-eighty days to get in, and this has remained unchanged since before Year 1. We made the decision based on a preponderance of reports from across the state that told us that students were responding to unfounded rumors that so-called wild behaviors would be caused by their having stayed up late playing a new HIVE-based game called *Hell on Earth*. Unfortunately, rumors have a way of generating larger rumors and getting out of hand, and the next thing you know someone is very, very upset, as if some real cause/effect had taken place. Nothing took place yesterday that doesn't always take place in schools on any given day in any given school year in any given community. Schools remain the safest place in your children's lives, as I believe has been mentioned, and that isn't changed by a bunch of sleep-deprived kids acting on rumors and being rude to whomever they encounter. Look: we had a bad day. And, at the end of the day, a game on The HIVE is just a game on the HIVE. There's never been any evidence linking games to violence."

"A child was stabbed," a father yelled out.

"I would like to tell you that that never happens, has never happened before, but the truth is that things like this do happen. Is it acceptable? No. Are we doing everything we can to prevent this from happening again? Yes."

"I don't believe you," screamed a mother.

"Neither do I," said another.

"Maybe it'd be helpful for you to hear from someone who works with these young tech-wizard kids, or from them, themselves, at this point," Zerwicky interjected, looking over desperately towards us. A wave of angry voices continued to burble over each other, but was silenced by Zerwicky's voice. "People, please? This is a school. Mr. Cote?" he asked, gesturing for him to come over. "Mr. Cote is from the Center for Advanced World Studies."

Cote more or less dragged himself up there, with Orlinsky watching him coolly from the sidelines, standing with the rest of us. Cote looked at the audience, which was suddenly quiet. He looked from side to side and asked, "Any questions?"

"Where did this game come from?" a man eagerly asked. Someone else was shouting over him, at the same time, "How long does the game screw kids up for?" Someone else was shouting, "Just help, o.k.?"

"We don't know," Cote said. "But we're on it." It wasn't clear which question he was responding to.

A woman walked up to a microphone stand that had been placed in the Cafeteria aisle.

"Is this the questions-and-answers part?" Cote asked tersely. "Is that what we're doing?" Zerwicky nodded yes.

"Is it true that this game is having no effect on our kids? They are constantly saying that it's just a game."

Cote looked at Orlinsky and gave a nod of his head, urging him to answer it.

"We have no idea," Orlinsky said. "We're not sure what we're looking at. We're working our way through the game ourselves," he said, pointing to us.

"What do the students you brought say about it?" someone asked.

"They can answer that," Orlinsky said, motioning grandly for us to approach the podium.

Elizabeth was, naturally, the first to the podium. "Kids aren't stupid," she said, strongly.

"What does that mean?" a father asked.

"It means kids aren't stupid," she said. "Do belt up, please!"

Kristina followed her up to the podium, took the mic, and said, "Kids are sometimes stupid," glaring back at Elizabeth. "But that's not anything new."

Aharon took up right after her. "In fact, all of these inventions you are upset with, all these innovations that may or may not be changing us, were invented by you adults, not kids."

Rudra took over. "And we are willing to forgive and forget," he said. "But in the meantime, we want you to understand. We hope you will be patient."

Just then a police call came into Captain Blanca's HIVE-NOW connection, evidently, because he scrunched up his face and held his arms out as he walked towards the podium. He said out loud, but not to us, "Roger. Got it. Will do." Pushing Rudra to the side, he announced, "At this point I'm going to ask everyone to leave in orderly manner, and ask to you avoid Daniels Street on your way home. There is police activity going on there and you WILL be tied up in traffic for hours if you take Daniels Street."

"We weren't done," shouted several people at once, offering an outcry.

"I've been asked to facilitate your orderly departure in a timely fashion now," he said. "Let's start with the back rows, exiting through the back of the building. The right side—that is my left, your right—please leave out those Exit doors. Please do so now. People on the left—your left—just follow the others out in a quick, quiet manner. Thank you for your cooperation."

Several people were angry enough to kick over chairs or throw food wrappers and cookies onto the ground as they were leaving.

Orlinsky and Cote walked out with us and we walked together as a group for three blocks, observing the small, disorganized riots in the streets. Gangs of teenagers on Daniels Street were screaming at the top of their lungs and throwing garbage cans through shop windows, having already run through the Retro Mallmart, stealing whatever they could fill their pockets with. Several customer service associates at Retro Mallmart had been beaten, a laughing kid on the corner told his friend. The crowd was now headed this way. Following Cote and Orlinsky we piled into the school's van, and saw a raging fireball-blaze in the rearview mirror. The numbers of kids streaming down the streets was increasing. We listened in with the car's environmental audio monitors and heard screaming. The kids were turning on themselves, singling out students to get attacked by five or six of them. We heard "Faggot!" and "Mexican" (even though there was no Mexico anymore) and could see fists flying. Now there weren't hundreds of violent kids anymore; there were thousands. Several couples on the side of the road, obviously turned on by the scene, seemed about to have sex, not evening going into one of the Sex Cubicles. Several other kids were peeing in public. This wasn't even funny.

I wanted to return home and I wanted to start playing the game again. Even if I stayed up all night.

Cote spoke first, saying, "This is bad. The hack, now this. They're either the same, or different. We're running out of time to figure out which. Some of you sleep, others work the game. Orlinsky will work the small stuff with me, looking for breadcrumbs in the observable programming cues. Under no circumstances are you to leave the campus. I don't understand who unleashed this and you've given me nothing, Elizabeth. I don't see the 'game' in this game."

Orlinsky said, "Get to us with any leads, however small. Play the game but don't get lost in it."

We got home. Rudra and Elizabeth quickly suited up into their VR body-hookups. Both had worked their way through most of Level Three. As I was putting on my body-suit I wondered some more about whether we were seeing the same things. We still hadn't talked about it. Kristina had said that I was just more sensitive to what was being shown than the others were, but no one knew what went on in our individual games or what we made of it. How personalized was this? And how did the game have the metrics to do that? How did it know you weren't gay when they showed you nude women?

Level Three began solo; the instructions were to walk into a bank and ask the young security guard who to talk to about a loan. His name was Clark and he started telling me about his family and that it was his first day on the job. "BLUDGEON USING CROWBAR," were the instructions. "TO DEATH."

I took the crowbar out of the back of my pants, reminding myself that this was a game, from under the long jacket I wore, and paused for the briefest of seconds before I smacked him in the upper left part of his skull, crushing it with the sickening sound of something breaking. He fell to the floor and went into convulsions, but not before looking at me and asking "Why?" with his eyes. My head filled with the sound of laughter. I searched for a mute button and there was none. All I knew was this was a game and it wasn't going to be me getting killed anymore. I had to get through it.

Other people appeared, around me—girls and guys (it wasn't even clear if these were ERASE ALL WITNESSES people anymore), and I was told to TRAVEL WITH THEM BUT THERE WILL BE BETRAYALS. We watched as two of them strangled a soldier/driver they'd asked for directions and stole the Zhyga Troop Transport vehicle he'd been driving. We hopped in. It seemed like we'd suddenly been driving for hours—like a movie, somehow cross-fading—and I was deeply tired. But I couldn't sleep because I didn't trust any of the people around me.

Suddenly we arrived. Without words we spread out like a military action. Someone broke the front door in. It was a childcare center of some kind and the command said to ROB ADULTS TAKE A CHILD HOSTAGE AND FLEE and that is what we did. We got them down on the floor and took money from twelve of them before one of them did something that sounded an alarm. The alarm was loud and we grabbed the first kid we saw—he had a name-tag on that said his name was Gary—and fled as he started sobbing. His sobbing was increasingly annoying and loud as we piled into the Zhyga. CONGRATULATIONS it said after we got five miles away, HOSTAGE NO LONGER NEEDED. There was confusion about what to do next. Before anyone talked about killing him (which I knew was on their minds) I opened the door of the vehicle, which had been slowing down, and pushed Gary out the door. I pushed him hard, hoping he'd make it to the shoulder of the road. I didn't want the others to kill him. I don't know why. I'd beaten Clark to death.

SEX AT RANDOM was the command and the vehicle pulled over to a city's central square. UNPROTECTED was the command. MUST HAVE FIVE ENCOUNTERS BEFORE NEXT LEVEL.

Sex always followed violence. VIOLENCESEXVIOLENCE. It felt all one. Just Do It. It Just Works.

Everyone was looking good. CONSENSUAL OR NOT was the command.

I balked. The game sensed it. CONSIDER DRUGS: LEXY D OR OM?

A beautiful young girl appeared before me, looking at me fearfully. Before I could do or say anything, she started unbuttoning her blouse, trying to appease me so that a violent rape could be avoided.

And that is when I finally threw up. I whipped off the hood in enough time to get most of it in the garbage can. Rudra already had his hood off and was sitting there, staring at me. "Hello, brother," Rudra said. "Not for me, either."

Elizabeth and Kristina were still playing. "Let's take a break," he said, "and let's get them to, too. We need to talk."

"I don't even know what we need," I said, wiping the vomit off my mouth with a napkin.

Rudra tapped Elizabeth on the shoulder. "Take a break," he shouted. Elizabeth shook her head. He shouted louder, "Take a break. NOW. We need some leadership about this." That got her to reluctantly do it. She stopped and took off her hood.

"What about Blondie over there?" Elizabeth asked, as she looked around the room squinting, seeing Kristina still playing.

Rudra tapped Kristina on the shoulder next, giving her the same message. Kristina immediately stopped. When she pulled off the hood, though, I thought I saw a tear running down one of her eyes. She quickly wiped it away. She, too, squinted, as she adjusted to the reality of the room around her. And to us.

Rudra was the first to speak. "Did everyone have a robbery at a day-care center? And had to take a hostage-kid?"

We all nodded.

"I threw my hostage-kid into the line of live gunfire when I was being chased by police," he said. "And I fired back, hitting civilians who had nothing to do with it. It's not that I feel sick," Rudra told us, "it's that I don't have any feelings at all anymore. I have some thoughts about all of this."

"What are those thoughts?" Kristina asked quietly. "We could use them."

Elizabeth interrupted, "We need to get operational bearings." Then, after a second, she said, "I had to shoot a dog."

I looked at Kristina and I was worried for her. I didn't want her to have to play the game anymore.

"I think most people will be able to play this game and do the fusion of violence and sex with pleasure, even though it involves hurting others all the time," Elizabeth went on. "They will get used to it in no time. I think it is for the crowd that says 'Oh, well, it is what it is', all the time. I think people who are the most sensitive will struggle and balk. How many of us went on to finish Level Three, the RANDOM SEX part?"

He paused and looked around. Elizabeth was suddenly quiet and Kristina looked at the floor.

"This isn't what I came to school here for," Elizabeth finally said. "And I don't want to get into detail, in terms of talking. There's no need for that. I've already wasted too many months of my life on vicious, wanker 'games.' I could've stayed home and done it in my sleep," Elizabeth mused. Her voice rose as she ranted now. "This is a matter of horses for courses. Some foreign plonker throws a spanner into the works? Ruins something I don't care about anyway? And we're supposed to go running every time a knobhead does something dodgy? I didn't choose a profession in Violent Wankers Anonymous, or the Retro Mallmart Repair Desk."

This woke up Aharon; he sat up, staring at Elizabeth trying to decide if this were a dream.

"Could you translate that into English?" I asked her.

"It IS bloody English!" she screamed. She was raging now. "When are you and the rest of the world going to learn it? Must you live in the Religious Ages? Do you want us all to speak 'American'? 'Sure, yeah, dese guys are, y'know, 'y'know, f'in' this, f'in' that, why do we gotta go running' to try to put this shit together again, y'know, just cawz sum third-world-African/Asian software-moron spreadin' sum virus-y, motherhumpin' boolshit and people gotta play it?' Does that work for you?" she screamed, her American imitation over.

I couldn't take any more of her. I was still angry that she'd interrupted Kristina a minute ago. I walked really too close to Elizabeth and got in her face. "You know what? You have real problems. I don't give a shit how smart you are or think you are. I have news for you: your country? Your Empire? It's over. Had its day. Gone, hundreds of years' worth. You accuse us of living in the Religious Ages? Who is here who sounds like before the Year 1? Us? I don't think so. The world is mainly Indian and Chinese and African now. Do you know that?? Your country hasn't even had a replacement rate of population for sixty years now. You should rent out empty castles to the Chinese, finally get some good take-out food in your piss-poor excuse of a country. There is no one left in the world, Elizabeth, who thinks the way you still do! We've moved on and we are happy. We don't cry ourselves to sleep at night for the old British Empire! No one remembers it anymore. So just lose it and stop yelling at us and treating us like your lackeys. We're not."

"Hear, hear," said Rudra. "He speaks the truth."

"*You* are yelling at *me*," she said, backing down a bunch. "What is THAT OK? Because you are a *minority*?"

"No, my *luv*," I said, using her word as sarcastically as I could make it sound. "I am not. I am a majority. Do you understand what I am saying? You make people yell because you won't listen when we speak to you quietly."

She looked defiant and lost, at the same time.

There was a knock on the door. This was weird; we knew it wasn't Orlinsky, because he always just walked in. The knock repeated. It was a slow knock, like in the old retro monster movies. Kristina went and opened the door.

It was another student. We'd seen him in passing before. He was tatted up. (Tattoos had come back into fashion in Year 1.) But even though tattoos weren't so unusual to see on kids, there was something really, really off about him. His hair was matted in places and his body odor was pronounced. It wasn't really clear which one of us he was looking at or talking to, and he was taking way too long to say anything. He was sweating and it looked like he was caught in a very bad predicament, being pulled to another place while staying exactly where he stood. Even though his eyes were blazingly wide-open and we could feel the pressure in him, he spoke unnaturally slow and calmly. The overall effect was more than a little frightening.

"May I come in?" he asked. He had a German accent.

We mumbled a welcome and he came in and looked around.

"Are you playing The Game?" he asked.

Was he a spy? I asked him, "Why do you want to know?"

"You are, aren't you? Playing the Game?"

"Yes," said Elizabeth.

"Good. How far? Have you gotten to Level Five?" he asked.

"Nope. On Levels Three and Four," Kristina offered.

"Level Five," he repeated.

"No, we are on Levels Three and Four," I said, louder. "Why?"

He didn't say anything more at first, then said, "My name is Gottlieb Drescher. I am from a good family. In Dusseldorf. My family is a good family. *Meine Mutter war eine gute Mutter. Mein Vater war ein gutter Mensch. Ich mochte nach Deutschland zuruckkehren, wenn dieser Traum ist vorbei.*"

"English?" asked Elizabeth.

He looked confused. He was just standing there. We pointed to the chairs, but he wouldn't sit.

"Have you gotten to Level Five?" he asked again. He struggled to process something, then, with a lot of pressure, said it again, "Level Five?"

"No. *Nein.* Negative," I said. "*Nein* Level Five."

He looked up, looked around like he'd just been placed in our room while sleeping and woke up, knew it wasn't the right place and, with sadness, began to leave.

"Why did you come here?" Elizabeth asked him.

"I was on Level Four. Then I went to Level Five," he said. He looked for the door, found it and walked away, towards it. He looked back at us, as if trying to remember our faces. Then he left.

We looked at each other in confused silence. "Was he stoned?" Rudra asked.

"Or are we?" Kristina asked, laughing nervously.

Elizabeth looked concerned and suddenly very adult-ish. Finally, she said, "Let's stick to the plan. Aharon is on; the rest of us sleep."

An hour and a half into it, something like 5 a.m., Aharon woke us. He was watching HIVE News.

I focused my eyes on scenes of cement blocks being thrown through bank windows. The riots were getting worse, not better. People with hammers and any tools they could grab were smashing Retro Mallmart windows, people were driving their cars through Mallmart store windows, and crowds were running off holding stolen things, celebrating. And they were worldwide. The news we were watching was about India.

"...all morning," said HIVE News. "Authorities are expected to get things under control within hours, but, for now, events on the ground remain very fluid."

"Is that near where you are from?" Kristina asked Rudra.

"No. I'm from the South," he said. "The people from the northeast have always been like that."

"Then why is it news?" Elizabeth asked.

"Because people love violence," Rudra said. "The media knows that."

But Rudra got immediately quiet when the camera switched to Myanmar, Budapest, and Birmingham, England. The streets were full of streaming hordes of teens, all similar scenes. It wasn't just violence and theft; it was happy violence and theft. And it didn't look like SCRAPS. What was in common in all the clips was there were no middle-aged people, or older people, involved at all. It was all kids. Lots and lots and lots of them.

Orlinsky arrived, walking in again without knocking, sipping from a large mug of black coffee. "I couldn't really sleep," he said. He sat with us as the scene on HIVE News switched to Mr. Wen, wearing white, standing in front of a field of flowers. "We need Quiet Mind right now," he said. "This is time for reflection and meditation. We are close to fixing WenBooks but this behavior has nothing to do with the game. This is bad

71

behavior. It isn't what happens to you in your life that determines who you are; it is what you *make* of what happens to you that determines who you are. The same is true of The HIVE. We ask all young people to use their Quiet Minds right now so we can find harmony and balance."

The cameras flicked back to lines of soldiers standing by, in the Ukraine, as students threw burning bottles in the street. When one crash-landed on a soldier's leg, setting his pants on fire, a huge roar of approval and laughter came from the crowd.

On screen there was a long-haired professor-type, sitting behind a desk next to a smart-looking Indian woman. He said "…self-fulfilling prophecy. The HIVE creates a lot of chicken-egg situations, wherein rumors about things can be as powerful as if they were real. What we may be looking at here is a case of what they used to call simple hysteria. Think Salem Witch Trials, for those of you versed in antiquity.'"

The news host jumped in with "Well, we had that all centuries ago, and more recently during the early Religious Times, so I'm not sure that frame of reference is valid. This is The Instant-Knowledge Age now. It's not the Age of Belief. And in the I-K era, the question is: is there any hard information to link the playing of the game to any of these antisocial behaviors? Not what you believe, what you can PROVE. In other words, what does evidence-based research tell us about what we are seeing?"

The Indian woman said, "I agree. It isn't a question of belief. We don't want to go back there, none of us do. It is a question of perception. And the evidence does show that perceptual distortions can, and do, occur after as little as eight hours of uninterrupted HIVE gaming participation. Looking at things differently, combined with lack of sleep, poor nutrition, could easily explain what you are seeing."

"Along with a contagion effect," said the long-haired man. "Parents should be parents here. And it would be helpful if the media wouldn't amplify this whole problem by repeatedly showing images of tired people exercising distorted judgement, based on poor perceptions, just because it seems like 'news.' It's not news. It's Fake News. There have ALWAYS been things like this. The jails are full of people who saw situations differently and proceeded from there. Bad decisions are bad decisions, you can't blame technology."

The screen filled with a replay of the rioting in the Far east, then the scene in Budapest against, switching to a tense standoff in Birmingham as the voice of the newscaster continued over it, "Thank you both. HIVE News is going to continue our live coverage of 'YOUTH AT THE CROSSROADS,' after these commercial messages."

When they came back there were scenes after scenes of laughing crowds gathered in front of different American schools, in front of the main doors. The schools weren't open. The main doors were surrounded by police, who tried to look casual, even as the crowds got rowdier. A few had signs. HIVE News cameras showed them briefly, before cutting away quickly: "END EDUCATION," "Thanks, But No Thanks," and, "No."

On split screen was a city where the crowds of students were even bigger. They were swarming forward, enormous numbers of them, looking unsure of their final destination, but moving in unison. At least a dozen signs said the same thing: "NOTHING."

"Where are you with the Game?" Orlinsky asked Kristina.

"Almost done with Level Four" she answered.

"Switch off with Rudra," he said. She stood up and rubbed her face. Rudra sat down.

"Why are we even working on this game with these things going on in the streets?" asked Aharon. "You think they are related?"

"Well, before the hack: no protests. The hack came, the protests came, starting with Level One," said Orlinsky.

"Isn't that a wee bit reductionist?" asked Elizabeth. "Intervening variables? As Cote was suggesting? Maybe the game is correlated, not causative. Some other factor? Have you considered that?" she asked. "Schools have been terrible for a long time."

"Wen went live on the HIVE, asking people to *not* play and, guess what? There is an astronomical *increase* in the rate of playing. And progressing through the different levels," Orlinsky said.

"Because it's not just people, we are teens," Kristina said.

"Exactly. Like he knew that would happen?" asked Rudra.

"Yup," said Orlinsky. "Teens do whatever they're told not to. And Wen played to that. He played it. Keep working on this. Do me a favor and don't sleep, o.k.? Push past being tired. And all of you stay here. Consider yourselves invaluable. If you need relief in an hour and a half we'll send in a different Affinity Group. But I prefer you be the ones to crack this. I'll be out in the streets, sniffing around."

Orlinsky left and I felt just a little more helpless. I liked it when he was around.

"What was that German kid saying before we slept?" I asked. "Or did we dream it?"

"He said he was from a nice family. And that he was up to Level Five," said Elizabeth.

"Was he sleepwalking?" asked Rudra.

"I don't think so," Kristina said.

"Then why did he say what he did?" asked Aharon.

"You mean asking about Level Five?" Elizabeth said.

"No. The last thing he said, in German," Aharon said. "I know enough German to get by. Do you know what he said?"

We shook our heads.

"He said he wanted to return to Germany when this dream was over."

After a pause, Kristina said, "I think he was sleepwalking."

Sleep Beckons

Kristina suited up to relieve Aharon on the game.

"I know no one wants to talk about this. Because it brings it all back, what we saw. I saw an autopsy in progress. And there was a laugh track to it. But what happens if we don't talk?" Rudra asked.

"I don't want to talk," Elizabeth said. "I want to think. I hacked WenBooks. Someone followed that up with *Hell on Earth*. It wasn't me. I want to understand the vulnerability in the system, and I want to plug it."

"That's technical stuff," Rudra said.

"Isn't that what we are here for?" Aharon asked. "To revise and improve technical stuff?"

We looked over at Kristina. She sat there in quietness, playing the next level of *Hell on Earth*. She was well into Level Four. Why did we *all* have to play it? I suited up again, in solidarity with her and would resume playing, whatever it took us. I didn't want her going further alone. Even though we were both alone in the game. All of us were alone.

The same sexy young woman in the game was staring at me. Four buttons on her blouse were open now. Though she was looking straight into my eyes, she didn't look less fearful. She looked even more afraid than I remembered.

The prompt appeared: CHOOSE DRUGS: LEXY D OR OM?

I didn't want any drugs. I turned to leave again.

A blast of visual flash, it must have been hundreds of subliminal messages, filled my vision as static for three whole seconds.

There was a crowd of people gathered and a man with a bullhorn was screaming at them to return to work. They looked like factory workers. They wouldn't budge, even though he was threatening them. "Last warning," he said. An old truck with an industrial crane attachment pulled up. "Go back to work." They didn't. He then pointed to one man in the crowd, chosen at random, and said, "Him." Two uniformed thugs with guns went into the crowd, which parted for them with ease, to drag him over to the truck, where he was lifted to the truck bed. A noose appeared, attached to the crane and he started crying. "I'll go back to work. I'll go back to work."

"What's your name?" the larger thug barked.

"Andrew Winship," the man half-cried.

"Children?"

"Three."

"Ages/names?"

"Claire, Brittany and Stephen," he blurted in between sobs.

"Say goodbye to them."

It was too late. They tightened the noose around Andrew Winship's neck and started hanging him, lifting him off his feet as he choked and cried. The crowd was silent and after he died, his feet rotating in north, south, east, west directions slowly, they went back to work.

I ripped the hood off, fast. Playing this game, for me, was like trying to eat two pounds of ice cream. It was possible to do and a strong part of me really wanted to, but another part was disgusted and made me nauseous.

I was breathing heavily. It was possible I was going to throw up. That's when I heard Kristina making noises. Kristina, talking through her hood.

"That's weird. The game changes," she said. "Rudra: take note. In Level Four it switches from virtual command/control to touchscreen control on the WenBook. I'm working directly through touchscreen now."

Rudra and I walked closer to her, and I remember what happened next very clearly.

She continued to narrate. "It is saying type in the following code to verify you wish to continue. It is a mixture of letters, numbers and punctuation, on-screen keyboard. This is old-school stuff." The way she was talking made Elizabeth and Aharon come over to her, too. We were now in a little semi-circle, with her still working.

Something began to happen and as soon as we heard an ominous hum, three enormously bright blasts of light came shooting out of the WenBook. The light shot through the hood, it was so bright, but Kristina must've seen ten times what we saw on the outside. Rudra ripped her hood off and we saw her fingers frozen on the WenBook, pressed down all at once, as her back straightened and her mouth shot open.

The humming continued even after the lights stopped and all her energy seemed focused in her fingers. She made a small sound, like, "Oh." Her arm muscles quivered and she stopped blinking. I wondered for a second if her heart had stopped. She leaned forward a little, back still straight, peering in further. Her fingers were still pressing down ten keys at once with no response from the screen, no error message. She was riveted to whatever she was experiencing, and it couldn't be seen by me.

"What is going on?" I asked.

She didn't even seem to hear me. She nodded a little bit, then lifted her fingers up all at once and, most bizarrely, licked her fingers one by one.

I shouted at her, "Kristina, talk. What is going on?" and she looked at me with a long, blank stare. Everything was missing from her face except her physical features. Her eyes were blank. She looked like a simplified imitation version of herself. "So tired. I'm going to go to sleep now," she said, walking away. "Getting enough sleep is very important." She walked over to her rucksack, removed an item or two, left her rucksack behind and was gone. Gone from me and gone from us.

"What just happened?" I asked.

She walked out, in the direction of the dormitory. We let her go.

"That's it? We let her go?" I yelled. "What was the whole point of playing along with the game? We put her out there on the furthest level of the game. And we don't even care now about each other? WHAT JUST HAPPENED?!"

I grabbed my hood and put on the set-up. I would follow the game through to whatever she'd just seen, in solidarity. I would not leave her.

The game picked up with another woman appearing about my age, about eight feet away from me, on all fours, hips back, ass arched up, jeans already pulled down, only a pair of thin pale-blue satin panties separating her privates from me. FIVE RANDOM SEXUAL CONQUESTS REQUIRED: CONSENSUAL OR NONCONSENSUAL ALL COUNT. In the moment that I paused to look at this woman in flagrant surrender-offering. It wasn't sexy. It was sad. She slowly turned her head to look back at me. It was Kristina.

I looked away, angry—this game was using things in my head?—and ran to the right. Stopping me, inches away from me, was Akeelah, my old girlfriend from home. "I can be one of your five," she said, in the exact voice I remembered.

This was a mind-fuck. I turned to run again.

ALTERNATIVE TO LEVEL THREE COMPLETION: SHOOTING ESCAPE presented itself, and I grabbed at the option. I was aware of breathing very rapidly, and I could feel my blood-pressure rising. And suddenly I had an automatic-firing PID (Physical Integrity Disintegration) gun in my hands, loaded for a hundred and six rounds. I was running towards an alleyway. I could hear footsteps behind me, gaining on me, running. I tried to run faster, but they were faster than me, and I felt people grabbing me and ripping my gun away. Two enormous guys who looked like beasts—no tribe-affiliation I could see—dragged me into the alleyway, handed me back the gun, while holding my arms stiffly in a safe position for them and pointed with a nod of their heads to the two people at the other end of the alley, crying, hands tied, their heads down.

"Look up!' they shouted. "Choose one," they said to me. "Kill the other."

It was my mother and my father. *My mother and my father*. I looked into my mother's eyes and there was love. I looked into my father's eyes and there was love.

I tried to whirl on the guys controlling me, to shoot them, to shoot them in the head, the gut, to endlessly kill them, disintegrate them, but I couldn't. I didn't care if they shot me. So, I screamed. As loudly as I could, a rageful scream from the tips of my toes to my nose, growing in intensity as it passed through my legs, stomach, lungs, and throat.

I ripped my hood off, ripped the VR setup off me, still screaming, throwing it all on the ground, after ripping the hood in as many pieces as I could, screaming in real life what I started as screaming in virtual life, unless I had been really screaming all along in both places, barely noticing the others in the real room as I shoved chairs out of my way, slammed a desk over and ran to the door, running fast now, a student no more, a game player no more, a known entity no more, the first day of my life beyond virtuality in many ways.

I left CAWS.

Jerry Sander

Nothing

"Where are you going?" a voice behind me called.

"Somewhere beyond these things," I remember saying.

"We can't go out. Cote was specific about that, Zokaya!"

I was outside. Having air to breathe—air that wasn't under a hood—made a big difference. It felt like a rush of energy. And I didn't care anymore about what happened inside, on computers, on The HIVE. I didn't even care what happened back home in Liberia.

The more I walked, the more energy I seemed to have. I wasn't nauseous anymore. I was angry.

I walked into town, and it wasn't long till I saw that there were bunches of other people doing the same. Not from CAWS, but young people.

I went to the very school we had been at before. And I stood with about a thousand other people my age, shouting. Maybe there were several thousands of us. I'm not certain what we were chanting. I tried to sound it out and join in. It felt good, like a thousand motorcycles starting up at once. It was blind rage.

Fuck Hell on Earth, Fuck this place and The Triumvirate and The HIVE!

Nothing.

I found a crowd, surging forward, leaving a schoolyard, walking towards stores. We walked as one, breathed as one, and shouted as one. I'd say we thought as one, but we weren't really thinking.

We pushed over seven Sex Cubicles without even making sure they were empty. We threw tree branches and trash through the windows of the bank and bakery. When security guards or other adults tried to stop us, we punched them out until they dropped. Some kicked them.

I ran into a drugstore with about a dozen others, and I shouted support as they ripped things off the shelves, stuffing their pockets with whatever they could. I took four packs of chewing gum. No police responded, even though we could see the manager on his wearable.

I saw employees fleeing fast-food places as kids ran climbed over the counters, ripping display counters and the dispensing area apart, throwing everything into the air. We turned towards the center of town when we heard the mechanized roar of public safety vehicles, unloading dozens of policemen. Another *BOOM* went off, and in the next moment, all sorts of things were in the air, either having been hurled at the police, or coming back at us. It didn't seem like there was even ten seconds before the tear gas was on the ground, hissing out all around us.

The sting to my eyes was like having your face smeared with lemons and hot peppers. You couldn't stop yourself from choking and coughing. I stumbled around in the gray, rancid mist and could feel the crowd thinning out as it ran in all different directions. I ripped up some plants and rubbed them on my eyes and face—I wasn't sure if this was going to make things better or worse—and turned back in the direction from which I came. I didn't know if it was day or night anymore.

I went back to CAWS to take Kristina away with me. I washed my eyes and the rest of my face. When I looked around, I was startled to see Elizabeth crying, her hands down by her side, not touching the WenBook or her VR set-up. I guess she had continued the game after I quit.

"Where is everybody?" I asked. "Why are you crying?"

She slowly realized I was in the room and looked at me, not even attempting to talk.

Aharon and Rudra burst in, with Aharon yelling, "Holy shit. Holy SHIT! HIVE News! They are all crazy, it is every man for himself out there. All you need is the bad music and you are back to before the Year 1 again." He noticed Elizabeth. "What's the matter with her?" he asked me.

"I don't know," I said. "Something about the game. I guess."

"You came back, huh?" Aharon asked. "Smart. I'd rather play the game than get shot or crushed by thrown bricks out there."

"Where's Kristina?" I asked.

"Sleeping, I guess," Aharon said.

If only he'd known where I'd just been and what I'd just done. I was getting better and better at keeping the most important things to myself. I didn't tell him I was going to take Kristina with me and leave. Part of me wanted to convince the rest of them to leave with us, too.

"No one is getting shot," Elizabeth said, finally talking.

"Oh, yeah? Wake up, Queenie," said Aharon. He turned on HIVE News:

"…twenty-six confirmed casualties, with great uncertainty as to the condition of hundreds of others. That's twenty-six nationwide, mind you, not just local, but this thing shows no signs of ending soon. Four policemen have been hospitalized, and pockets of activity are reported amongst The Religious Ones, who argue, of course, that these events, which they insist are taking place in 2034, represents the End of Times."

Aharon clicked it off.

"Elizabeth, have you had anything to eat? Have you slept?" Aharon asked her.

She looked up, confused. "What? I don't… No, I don't think so."

"Let's go get something," he said, offering her his arm.

"I can't. The Game," she said, pointing to the screen.

"I know," Aharon said.

"You don't know," she said, then started weeping again. "Can you call for Cote? And Orlinsky, I guess?"

Rudra came over and actually touched Elizabeth on the arm, then shook her lightly.

"Elizabeth. Can you come back to us? You're back with us now, everything is safe," he said.

"Nothing is safe," she said.

"That's a feeling. Feelings aren't facts. We are experts in things related to facts, and we need you now."

She looked at Rudra slowly.

"Something happens at the end of Level Four. You didn't go that far, did you?" he asked.

"No."

"Well, we need to replicate it and understand it, fast," Rudra said.

"What about the others? It's not just the four of us. They are likely to be further along, right? Because we stopped after what happened to Kristina," Aharon said

We moved as a group into the dorms. There was a clutch of four students sitting in the hallway in front of one person's room, playing the Game. They all had their hoods on and didn't take them off as we spoke with them.

"Hello, I'm Elizabeth, and these are my friends, Rudra and Aharon. Our Affinity Group was assigned by our advisor to observe the gaming process. Do you have any problem if we watch?"

It sounded weird, like some sort of come-on-line from a child molester. But they just nodded, so entranced by the liquidy visuals it barely registered that we stood behind them, looking over their shoulders.

"What level are you on?" Elizabeth asked the first one of them.

"Four," the student said.

"Perfect," Elizabeth responded. "Could you tell us if anything unusual happens?"

The hood nodded again. Then a voice in it said, "It's switching to touch screen now. You have to enter a code by hand. You can't even cut and paste. Wow. Old-school."

And there was the same loud hum we heard with Kristina. Three huge blasts of light filled the room, coming right through her hood. We ripped the hood off her and saw that her fingers were rigid and her jaw hung open for the briefest of milliseconds. There was a startled look in her eyes.

And she, too, oddly licked three of the fingers on her right hand. Finally, the girl stood up, looked at us, refocusing her eyes with purpose, and said, "I've had enough. Time for sleep. Getting a good night's sleep is important."

"What just happened?" Elizabeth asked her. "What happened to you just now?"

She didn't say anything. She just walked away.

"Get her WenBook and check it," Rudra commanded.

I did, and I also put on her hood. There was nothing. It was frozen on a blank screen. I touched the screen briskly to make sure there was no electric shock. It was bricked.

Before we could talk about what to do next, the room filled with three more blasts of light. Then three more. And three more. We watched as the three other students removed their hoods after a moment, licked their fingers, focused on us, stood and took turns saying the same words, "Time for sleep. Getting a good night's sleep is important," and left.

Hell on Earth was never intended to go to Level Five. It was only later that I learned that Level Five was an exit from the game and an entry into a new way of being. And that everyone who *went over* were forever known as Fivers.

The Light and the Liquid

I let myself sleep for a few hours and in the morning everything looked different. The light of day just had a yellow and blue tint to it, replacing last night's deep darkness and making it seem like I had dreamt it. Kristina wasn't in her dorm room and she wasn't with us. No one knew where she was and I was worried. She'd left her rucksack behind. I had never seen her without her rucksack. It had tissues, gum, and lip balm in it. I took it and would give it back to her when I found her.

We guessed that increasing numbers of people had become Fivers overnight. And the rest were in the process.

Kristina had left her bike, behind, too. I took it and moved it into my dorm room.

Governor Higgins was now live on HIVE News, saying, "I think we all could use a little cooling off period, a chance to recoup. Let's think about the things and people that are important to us. Let's try to bring our best selves to school tomorrow, and I'm talking to the kids AND the teachers out there, and have a better day. Thank you."

The news cameras showed things getting quieter. There were pockets of kids still shouting, looking very tired, and even a few throwing things, but it was starting to look like things had played out

Orlinsky returned, joining us in front of the TV and, pointing towards HIVE-News, asked, "What do you make of this?"

"What do YOU make?" I asked him.

"I think there are large numbers of very lost people out there. Just as before," he said. "I'm not sure this 'wildness' changes anything. People are still self-centered, ignorant, and nasty. You could say it could be an ordinary day at an average school, just a little more sleep-deprived and media-saturated. Or this could be much more."

"You can't say you've seen this before," I said. "Do you understand that the game ends at Level Four? There's a process that happens. Bright lights and something on the fingers. And people are changed."

He laughed. "Sure," he said. "Why not? Like a movie? Or the programmer just nodded off after pranking people for four level's worth, gave the user a cheap thrill."

"No. This is real," I said. "Why do you think it is starting to calm down?"

"Because things always do. After having their moment in the sun."

"You are misreading the situation," I said firmly.

He seemed to respond to this on a different level. His interest was piqued. "They're calling a big meeting. We all have to go. You know, this isn't the kind of semester you all were supposed to have."

"This isn't the kind of world I was supposed to have," I said, truthfully. "What kind of semester were we supposed to have?"

"You were supposed to extend the HIVE. Give it greater powers," he said.

"That's the first we're hearing of that. In those terms," I said. "What did they want done?"

"Overrides. Of the built-in-defaults."

"Isn't that limited by law?" I asked.

"Yes. That's what we all thought," Orlinsky said sharply.

I realized, at that moment, how little I cared about HIVE functionality; I wanted to be riding bicycles with Kristina, whom I hadn't seen since her face went slack before her sleep, and disappearance.

#

Rudra was resting on the floor, with his knees up and his head on a pillow, and Elizabeth was stretched out on the couch, me sitting on a cushioned chair with my feet up on another chair, all of us exhausted when the news of the first suicide-explosion came. A kid ran in, saying, "Someone blew up the Governor...and himself," and we put on the monitor fast, catching a breathless HIVE News announcer, mid-sentence: "…just in. Again, Governor Higgins has been confirmed killed, along with Lt. Governor Sean Malcolm in an apparent suicide attack."

The usual "pings" were heard, signaling the large mandatory assembly to start. We walked towards it, Aharon joining us just in time.

Finally, after almost everyone else, Kristina appeared. She calmly walked the aisles choosing a seat in a row by herself, across from the rest of us. Her hair was different, brushed to one side, and she wore a completely ordinary, mousy-looking blouse, buttoned high-up. Since the rest of us were seated together, I felt it would've looked too weird to move to sit next to her. I looked at her several times and couldn't figure out a thing. She looked like it was just another day. I would talk with her the first chance I got.

All of the students at CAWS were gathered. We hadn't really been like this since our first day here, since before our own Affinity Group had been set. I scanned around. The others looked smart, but it was true that we looked like the smartest.

Elizabeth took turns checking Kristina out, too, then looking at me with a questioning look. Cote strode in with authority and took center stage. "This is a tough day. Let's start with a moment of silent intention for Governor Higgins and Lt. Governor Malcom."

We were quiet. Thinking of good wishes for their families.

"We have some additional bad news, I'm afraid," Cote resumed. "Bad news for the entire CAWS family. Early this morning at approximately 6:30 a.m., we lost one of our best and brightest. A first-year student, from Germany, Gottlieb Drescher, unexpectedly died in his dorm room. All indications are that a drug overdose of some kind may have been involved. His family has been notified and we ask that you send them your expressions of support at this difficult time. Ways of contacting them will be distributed to you and there has already been a Scholarship Fund established in his name, for those of you who feel you wish to contribute."

We were stunned. I looked at my friends, and we each looked like we'd been smacked across the face. Except for Kristina. She looked cool and like she didn't care.

"Without judging any one particular person's habits or decisions, I think it is important that we take this moment to remind ourselves that this is a drug-free community and that drug-abuse kills," Cote said. "As for events in the street, and events in general, as they affect our curriculum, we will have more information later. That is it. Please dismiss to your regular 11 a.m. schedule. And…stay safe."

There was some murmuring but nothing too big. That is when this girl walked up to Elizabeth, eyes full of tears, brimming. "He wasn't that kind of guy," she said, grabbing Elizabeth by her shoulders, and whispering. "I knew him…well. We were together, I knew him WELL, he hated kids who took drugs or got lost in HIVE games. Do you understand me? He couldn't have done it. He was no drug user, EVER."

Elizabeth looked shaken. "Who are you?" she asked.

"Selena Portilla. Do you…"

"How long did you know him for?" Elizabeth asked, almost coldly.

"Since we arrived here," Selena said.

"Well, people are full of surprises, aren't they?" Elizabeth asked. "Particularly guys whom you've just met."

"You're not listening…" Selena said, pushing off from Elizabeth and searching out Aharon's eyes. "Do YOU understand? Do you speak Spanish?" she asked.

"I'm Israeli," he answered.

She looked confused.

"From The Protectorate," he explained. "But I understand Spanish."

"*Todo esto no se siente bien. Él era mi amante, que lo conocía como nadie lo conocía. Alguien lo mató. Alguien lo asesinó.*"

"*¿Qué pruebas tienes de eso?*" Aharon asked.

"*Mi corazón. Mi cabeza. Mi alma,*" Selena whispered, drawing even closer to him, and holding his gaze with intensity.

"What is she saying?" Elizabeth asked.

"I'll tell you in a minute," Aharon snapped.

"Ask her when she last saw him and what they were doing, though I bet I know the true answer to that one," Elizabeth said.

"*¿Cuándo fue la última vez que lo viste? ¿Qué estabas haciendo juntos?*" Aharon asked.

"*Estábamos riendo y jugando el juego hasta que se fue a ir a verte,*" Selena said.

"*¿Qué tan lejos en el juego te metiste?*" Aharon asked.

"*Yo estaba en el nivel cuatro. Acaba de llegar al nivel de seis. Y ocurrió algo. Dejé de ir a orinar, regresé y él estaba de pie para irse. Él era diferente. Nunca lo volví a ver,*" she whispered. "*Nada es lo que parece, no estamos seguros,*" Selena concluded, eyes brimming over. She looked at us each in turn, uncertain, and ran out.

"Well?" Elizabeth asked again, annoyed.

"She said nothing is what it seems, and that she didn't feel safe. She was playing *Hell on Earth* with him, got up to go pee, came back and he was different. That's when he left to come see us and she never saw him again. She thinks…he was murdered," Aharon said. "He wasn't capable of any sort of drug overdose; he wanted to live. Always."

Elizabeth snorted. "Does she have any proof of that?"

"No," Aharon replied. "Well…actually, she said she knew it in her heart, her head, and her soul."

"Her what?" Rudra asked.

"Her soul," Aharon repeated.

"Oh, great, she's a Religious One?" he asked, smirking.

"I don't know," Aharon shot back. "She just said she knew him and knew he wasn't capable of hurting himself, or anyone else. Something else happened."

"Yeah, she knew him for a week and a half," Elizabeth said calmly. "How many times have you ever heard of a young girl being surprised by a young boy's stupid decisions?"

The question hung in the air.

#

I went to Kristina's room to return her rucksack. And to find her. To connect.

I went back to the dorm, to Kristina's room directly, and she was there, sitting bolt upright at a desk, reading an old pre-WenBook E-reader. She seemed well-rested and very, very focused. She frowned when she saw me wearing her rucksack, though.

"Why are you wearing that bag?" Kristina asked. "It's old."

"This is your bag," I said. "I bought it because you left it. It's yours."

"It's silly, really," she said, taking it from me and stuffing it away in her closet. She stared at me, waiting for me to speak. She seemed so different I couldn't think of what to say.

"Yes?" she asked. "Is there something else?"

"Your bicycle," I said.

"MY bicycle?" she asked, laughing.

"Yes. Retro pre-Zero," I said, reminding her.

"That's ridiculous. I'm not a child. I don't need, or use, playthings. If you thought you'd get in good with me, or something, by buying me a bicycle, forget it. I don't go for antiques."

I stood staring at her. I decided to take what felt like a huge risk, and I walked towards her. I stood a few feet away, and I turned my palms over to her. I wanted to show her that I'd learned the entire sign-language alphabet. I hoped we could talk better that way. I got as far as showing letters A through G, my hands moving quickly.

"What is that supposed to mean?" she asked, scrunching her brow and frowning. "Is there some reason you came here right now?"

"Elizabeth, and the others wanted me to go get you and bring you back with me to Rudra's room to talk. Is that OK with you?" I asked.

"Is it really necessary?" she asked.

"I believe it is," I said.

"Well let's go then," she said crisply, turning off the E-reader in front of her. We walked there in silence.

"Are you reading anything good?" I asked.

"'*Sleep Hygiene*,'" she said. "Norwegian author. Written six years ago. Holds up well."

We walked into Rudra's room, where he and Elizabeth were waiting. They looked up sharply and stared at Kristina in a way that could only have made her feel more uncomfortable.

"Hello," Kristina said, formally.

"Why are you being so weird?" Rudra asked.

"What are you talking about?" Kristina asked.

"You are just…being colder than usual. Which is saying something," Elizabeth offered. Kristina didn't say anything back, which was not usual in, and of, itself. "We have some questions we want to ask you," she said, sounding so adult.

"OK," said Kristina. "Shoot."

"You were playing *Hell On Earth* and finishing Level Four, right?"

"Right."

"Then you went to Level Five."

"Is that a question?" Kristina asked.

"Did you go on to Level Five after finishing Level Four?"

"What other Level could I go on to?" Kristina asked.

Just then Aharon walked in, looking sweaty and strange. "Um, I hate to interrupt. But that girl?"

"Yes?" Elizabeth asked. "The Spanish one?

"She wasn't Spanish, she was Mexican. She was speaking Spanish. Not everyone speaks English," Aharon said.

"Fine love, fine. What is her name again? Sonia something?"

"Selena. Portilla," Aharon said. "They don't have any record of her. They say she doesn't go to this school, never did."

"She was first-year," Elizabeth said.

"They have no record of her," Aharon repeated.

"Who was she then?" I asked.

"They didn't know who I was talking about. No one said they knew her and the administration had no record of her, even of withdrawing from school."

"Well…I knew it was a bit dodgy, but, I mean, we were HERE and we saw her, we talked to her. She exists. The question is who IS she?" Elizabeth was almost sputtering in anger. "And *where* is she?"

"I don't know," Aharon said.

Kristina pursed her lips together slightly and asked. "Is there anything else you need me for? I have work to do."

"Don't leave," Elizabeth spat out sharply.

"What is wrong with you?" I asked Kristina, directly.

"I'm tired of wasting time, of having days off from school. For a game! "Just how much time do you intend to waste on all this?" Kristina asked. "An entire semester? School is important, and we have been greatly distracted," she said. "We need to get a good night's sleep."

"OK, you can go, Blondie," Elizabeth said, dismissively. "Attend to all the important things."

Kristina's eyes narrowed as she looked back at Elizabeth. As she left, she turned back to us and said, "Put your energy where you can do the most good." Her voice was lilting and younger than I'd ever heard. "Be a good student and you can learn something new each day," she said. Her voice wasn't hers. Yet she was standing right in front of me, talking. She gave a fast smile and exited.

The moment Kristina was gone Elizabeth said to us, "I want another control group. Level Four going into Level Five. Aharon and Rudra see if you can get that together? Mixed females and males, at least five of them. Just set it up and get it going as fast as you can. Don't wait for me. Do it in the same place."

"Sure," Rudra said.

"I want it filmed," she said, as she took out of her pocket a recorder chip.

"There's something you should all know before we go," Aharon said. "Before you go, I want you to know what is going on. When I was looking for Selena, I ran into a very nervous student, a fat kid—Harvey Steinbecker— who gave me a recording on an old disc-chip and told me not to watch it on anything that could be monitored, only on an air-gapped computer. He was whispering to me and saying stuff like, 'This is the last time you talk to me in person, OK? Air-gapped computer.'"

We all looked at him with confusion.

"One that's never been on the HIVE," Elizabeth explained. "They are very, very rare, but they exist. I think it is time to update Cote and Orlinsky. Maybe start with Orlinsky. Too much weirdness going on. He might be helpful; he is weird, himself."

"I can get him," I volunteered.

"Good. Go," she said.

I found him not far away staring at a crowd of kids on the "commons" area, as if he were looking for something. He grunted hello, and went back to scanning.

"What do you see?" he asked.

I looked around and saw kids hovering over books, reading them on the same pre-WenBook 12th-generation e-readers that Kristina had, quietly absorbed. They looked unusually clean-cut. I didn't want to give Orlinsky a stupid-sounding answer, so I said, "Not too much. Just quiet."

"Right. They are all reading. When is the last time you saw that?"

Almost on cue a whole bunch of them turned towards us and stared. It was completely creepy. The ones I stared back at turned up the corners of their mouths in a sudden smile, as if they knew me.

"Can we get out of here?" I asked him. "We really need you back there."

"Um-huh," he said, his eyes still scanning the crowd. He walked with me, but I wasn't sure where his mind was. "What do you think is going on?" he asked.

"Level Five," I said. "I told you. This is Level Five. Game Over."

He looked at me skeptically. His eyes searched my face for clues.

Orlinsky came into the dorm area with me and when we arrived Elizabeth was sweating. "Rudra has a group he is working with right now, filming; Level Four into Level Five. We're going to see whatever this is in slow motion. We waited for you, Mr. Orlinsky, so we could see what this kid Steinbecker gave us, together, in case he formatted for one viewing only."

"Like in the old spy movies?" Orlinsky wondered.

"No, I've just been staying here working, trying to figure out what's going all arse-over-tit here. So sorry, can't sleep anymore or eat," Elizabeth was shouting now. "Maybe I should just give it a sweet Fanny Adams, like the rest of the wankers."

"She gets like that when she is upset," I told Orlinsky. "Needs a translator."

"I'm sick of you saying that!" she screamed at me. "You think I want this whole everything going all barney when we we're supposed to be working together? Well, alright then, let's work on this together, OK"

"Play it," Orlinsky said.

"Before you do," I asked, "Could you tell us how you have access to an air-gapped computer? How you got one, so far away from your ancestral home?"

"Of course, Zokaya. It turns out that the network of people you derisively regard as 'hackers' are uncommonly generous with each other when it comes to things that might help disrupt the supposed status-quo. Miles from home has nothing to do with it. I'd return the favor back in the U.K."

"Could you just play it?" Orlinsky asked again.

She popped the chip into her air-gapped computer and we saw a sweaty-faced kid with long-hair briefly in front of the camera, with a blonde kid in the background on a WenBook. It was a little out of focus for the first five seconds as the sweaty kid said, "My name is Harvey Steinbecker, this is September 16th, Year 13, this is recorded at CAWS with my roommate Daryl Green. He is going from 4 to 5. He's been playing *Hell On Earth* nonstop for 36 hours. I don't think he's eaten anything. He's a good kid, but he's getting weird. I've seen this all around me; for the record I don't give a shit about gaming I'm at CAWS for security technology innovation, and something is happening that is just like…nowhere near normal." He stepped aside, obviously picked up the camera and closed in, in perfect focus, on Daryl, in the hood set-up. "He let me rip a hole in the back of his hood and peek in the left part of his visor so I can see what he is seeing."

We watched, with a close up on Daryl's head, the visor pulled aside a bit to allow for filming. In the foreground and in the background was the prompt asking him to switch to touchscreen on the WenBook, followed by the code he was supposed to type in. Harvey maneuvered the camera enough to show his fingers doing that, and then we heard the hum and the screen was blasted with bright white. When the blasts subsided, we saw Daryl's fingers stuck rigidly on the WenBook. The camera swung to show veins pulsing in his neck, a rigid posture, then a slacking as he relaxed. The hood came off (it wasn't certain whether Daryl took it off or Harvey did) and the camera went to his face, which was suddenly relaxed.

"Replay those light blasts," Orlinsky shouted.

We did. "What are you thinking?" Elizabeth asked.

"It's a HIVE-encoded trigger," Orlinsky said. "We knew it was very possible. It's just that no one's used it yet."

"They have now," Elizabeth shouted. "Stop Rudra. Tell him to stop. Call it off, right now, whatever he's getting himself into. We already know."

I ran out and went to the room where Rudra had fifteen people in seats, filming them as they made the transition into Level Five. "Stop it now!" I shouted. "Elizabeth is calling it off."

Rudra looked up at me in surprise.

"Don't do it!" I shouted. "It's poison!" I couldn't think of anything else to say that would grab their attention immediately.

At that same moment most of the group went over to Five as a roomful of triple-blasts of light, like little atom bombs, went off. The hoods came off, and I saw their faces, all neutral. They all licked their fingers. Within seconds the entire group was staring at me, their heads having turned to looking at me at the same time. I ran back to Elizabeth and the others.

"Too late," I said. "They went over."

Elizabeth was hammering at a WenBook, with any tool she could find. The machine seemed impervious to being opened. She was practically clawing at anything like a seam, near tears with her frustration.

"You won't be able to do it," Orlinsky said, calmly. "Proprietary tools are necessary. Started in the 20th century. The old Apple company, non-removable batteries. Here," he said handing her a gleaming, new pointy tool that he removed from his pocket. "Try this."

Elizabeth looked at him hard before taking it. "Where did you get that?"

"I specialize in hard-to-find information and tools," Orlinsky said. "It's kind of a hobby."

Elizabeth did something with the tool and her wrists and the WenBook literally split in two. She dug around, scooping out the guts of it, pulling apart electronics that had been carefully assembled, in one case holding one part of something with her teeth while tearing apart with both hands. She was mumbling to herself, ferocious, "C'mon, Elizabeth, no time for a cockup, it's here, it's here, don't be a numpty, check the inseam, under the ambient noise sensor." She froze and picked something up in her hands. "It's NOT an ambient noise sensor. I mean, it IS one, but that's not all it is. It's also some sort of high intensity light projector." She squeezed it. "Advanced bulb."

We all stood around staring. "How can that be?" Rudra asked.

"How can it BE?" she asked. "How can that 'BE'? Here it IS, Rudra, it is frigging HERE, Rudra. It has done what it is supposed to do, all over the world, love, not just here in sunny California." She was ripping the machine apart now, digging and throwing parts.

"That can't explain it. What, mystery-light? From a computer? And people change? I wish," Orlinsky said. "Why do they lick their fingers?"

"There is a type of small bladder in these things, too," Elizabeth confirmed, still digging around the guts of it. "Some drug?"

"That explains personality transformation?" Orlinsky asked.

"That's not it. It's not it alone. It's a combination of the days and nights and days of getting worn down, of not even caring, of not eating, of watching people die, of helping people die, shooting them, cutting off limbs and laughing, of betraying each other, betraying ourselves, WHO EVEN CARES ANYMORE? You're seeing the signs all over, literally, there is NOTHING to believe in anymore and that is BEFORE the Mystery Light, the light blasts, the goo on your fingers, whatever THAT HIVE-poison is, that is BEFORE LEVEL FIVE, it's just who we are now. The light and the liquid, they just sealing the deal, freezing us in place. We have no feelings, no real ones, we have our 'been-there-done-that' bullshit." She was screaming and crying at the same time now. "I don't want to even be a teenager anymore, I hate teenagers. I don't see any reason to grow up, not in this shithole of a world, where the person next to you is going to kill you for amusement, laugh at your dying corpse, then post it on The HIVE," she half-cried.

"I think you're going overboard, Elizabeth," Orlinsky said.

"It's your fault" she said, whirling on Orlinsky. "Your generation!" She pounded the desk in front of her with both fists now, raging. "War, war, war, the Religious Wars—we can't even get the straight story about THAT now, can we? It's just stuff we'd all rather not talk about, best left unsaid. Then you invent all this shit that tells us who to like, who to be, what to listen to, you IMPLANT it in us, and you have no problem with that, no problem AT ALL. I don't even know if I am fully human! What does that even MEAN anymore? So, these little alien-light-blasts up from the depths of this monster-machine, it's not THE THING, do you know what I mean? Even if it is The End, it wasn't THE THING. Not THE THING that 'did it,' give us that, OK?"

She had been building and building up at the same time she'd been screaming but no one expected her to swipe a study lamp sideways, hurtling it across the room, where it smashed loudly. Orlinsky walked towards her obviously wanting to put his arm around her.

"Don't touch me!" she screamed. "Do not touch me!"

"Let's get out of here," Orlinsky said to all us. "Somewhere we can talk."

"Why can't we talk here?" Rudra asked.

Orlinsky looked at us, seemed to begin saying something, then stopped, turned, and walked away. Rudra, Aharon, and Elizabeth, and I followed him.

"Should I get Kristina?" asked Aharon.

"No," Orlinsky said. "Just get in my car."

"Can we talk now?" I asked.

"No," he said. "Wait."

We drove in a silence that felt conspiratorial; we all knew that a dam had just broken. And I was strongly aware of the fact that Kristina was not with us. That she seemed lost to me, having more in common, suddenly, with the room full of grinning strangers than with me. Seeing Elizabeth's descent into fear had forced me to recognize my own. I didn't know what was happening, and I wanted to be at Kristina's side. I wanted to see her face; her old one.

We came up on a house, about forty mins. away from CAWS, parked, threw our things in the house, and followed Orlinsky towards a stream. The sun was setting, and the light seemed sparkly, almost like a liquid substance. We looked at Orlinsky, knowing something weird was going on.

He looked different. "I'm not who you think I am. I am Orlinsky, but I'm not a teacher. I am TriSec. Been with them since we made the transition from Homeland Security, undercover—since Year 2. I can't tell you more of my assignment beyond that. I can tell you that CAWS is only one of the places we've kept our eyes on. There are people out there who have been very unhappy with a lot of things. Feathers have been ruffled. Wen and the WenBooks were a wild card, we didn't really know what we were looking at. We still don't, really."

"So, you could've stopped this?" Aharon asked. "And you didn't?"

"No, I couldn't. There are still a number of freedoms accorded technologies—we seem to have a weakness for things from the East—and all we're allowed to do is monitor until we have evidence that something threatening is imminent or warrants further investigation. Wen seemed interesting. We don't think he's a bad guy necessarily. But we wanted to watch close-up. That's why I'm a teacher at CAWS. And remember: CAWS isn't Wen's. It's his rival's, WhoozHooz."

"Well, what do you think now, Teach?" asked Elizabeth, still sniffing back tears and wiping her nose. In a clenched voice she asked, "Still think Wen is a good guy?"

"I don't think we know what we're looking at. You breached Wen's system. That's how this started, right?"

"But he'd already modified the hardware," Elizabeth said. "And distributed it to every young person in the world."

"Like he was waiting for this day," I said.

"Why would he want this day?" Rudra asked.

"Maybe for what follows it," Aharon said.

"Level Five? Unclear," said Orlinsky. "So, they go back to reading and clean up their act, style-wise? Dress nicer? Is that it? That's the payoff? Look at Kristina. She went over to Level Five. There's got to be more to this. And we have to crack it fast."

"She's not the same," I said, quickly.

"How?"

"She's lost…her beauty," I said, immediately regretting it. The others quietly laughed. "I mean, she's not riding her bicycle, and gave up her rucksack."

"How bad is that, really?" Orlinsky asked.

"Come on, Mr. Orlinsky, or Secret Agent Orlinsky or whomever you are," argued Aharon. "You're the one who is teaching all the outdated classes, the liberal-artsy stuff from before Year 1, right? You're the one who tells kids to dig deeper. And you don't know why it is sad that Kristina gave up her rucksack? Are you that much of a government agency spy?"

A Nest for Their Young

Orlinsky told us he needed time away from us. "Take the car," he said, tersely. "The only way I can parse this out is alone. I can't babysit you." This seemed harsh, and I wondered if he'd been genuinely upset by Aharon's verbal challenge. In the absence of hard facts or knowledge about how we fit into all of this, we decided our safest bet was to return to CAWS. We could seem to lay low but also could observe the crowd of kids who had just passed over to Level Five. We found them, fast, in a neighboring dorm.

When we walked in we were smothered in silence. The group was just sitting there, and I had the feeling we had abruptly interrupted some conversation. They turned their heads and stared at us, almost in unison. Then, perhaps aware of the creepy effect they had just transmitted, one of the Fiver students tried to sound "casual," making the adjustment of looking more relaxed, and said to us, "How's it going?" he asked. "How far did you guys get with the game?"

We hadn't figured on having to answer that. "Everyone is going at their own pace," Elizabeth said, biding us time.

"If you want some tips or help with Level Five, we could walk you through it, just join us. Where's your WenBooks?"

"We've got to check up on things back at the dorm," I offered.

"Just stay with it through Level Five," the same boy said directly. "It's really worth it."

"It's really awesome!" a girl volunteered, sounding too chipper. "Stay with it through Level Five," she said, echoing the boy. "It's really worth it."

Rudra recommended sitting outside. We found a good tree and the three of us considered what was occurring, even at CAWS.

"We're going to be in the minority, if we're not already," Aharon said. "Because we haven't passed over."

"So what?" Elizabeth asked.

"Well if there is something big shaping up we'll stand out like fluorescent phlegm," Rudra offered.

"Are they going to call off the semester because of this stuff?" I asked.

"I think this *is* our semester," Elizabeth advised.

Orlinsky returned; we saw him walking from almost a half mile away. "Kind of stunning" Rudra said to him, by way of a greeting.

"What's your take, Rudra?"

"Do you know cobras?" Rudra asked, responding to the question with a question.

"Just enough to not pet one," Orlinsky said.

"Well there are cobras, and then there are king cobras." Rudra paused. "Much of the time they are peaceful. Pretty, even. They like to stay under the radar."

"What are you saying?" Elizabeth asked.

"Our friend, Mr. Wen, the peaceful one. The man who made these machines."

"He's a cobra?" I ask.

"Do you know how king cobras survive? What they eat?" Rudra asked.

"Rats," Aharon ventured. "Rats and mice."

"No. Other snakes. They eat them head-first. They eliminate their competition. They see farther than other snakes. They also do something else that no other snake is known to do. They actually make a nest for their young and stay with them until they are hatched. They guard them ferociously. It's as if they know their own future is dependent on their young. You find them in forests, lakes and streams. They've been known to drown other snakes in a beautiful river before eating them."

We just looked at each other and heard the wind blowing outside.

"*Hell on Earth* wasn't a game," Rudra said. "It seems to fit in seamlessly with the hardware that was designed and distributed by our friend, Mr. Wen, for the very purpose of creating what we've just witnessed.

And, by the end of today, I'm guessing, we'll be the complete outliers if we've not gone over to become Fivers."

"What are you suggesting?" I asked.

"I can answer that," Elizabeth said, "Because if you're not, I am: I suggest we get with the program and go tumbling arse over elbows into whatever Asian mind-melt the good Mr. Wen has prepared for us in our new lives ASAP, right?

"You're not serious, right?" I asked.

""So just lose our minds and personality and become part of this weird herd?" Aharon asked.

"Well it IS the Year 13, isn't it? It's not like we have too far to go," Elizabeth answered quickly "We've been part of The HIVE for years now, what is so different?"

Rudra stared at her. Before he could say anything, Elizabeth said, "Don't insult me. Look, I am figuring that they are monitoring each WenBook's progress through the levels of *Hell on Earth*. They probably have a register and that they have to see that each of us has 'gone over' to avoid being identified as some sort of freethinking weirdos. We have to show that their Eastern computer laser-beam has shot its wad right straight through our eyes and impressionable young brains. We'll just close our eyes and look away for the light blasts. Also keep your fingers off the wad of goo that spits out. And then…act the part. Enjoy Happy Land. Only undercover. Find out what they have planned and unite with others who might be refusing this crap. There must be others, because there always are others. Take it from there."

"I've never done anything like this," I volunteered. "Should we be scared?"

"I'd say so, yes," Elizabeth said. "I think we should be very scared. That will actually help us now, I imagine."

The Freedom Dome

The next day began the biggest series of lies in my life. Lies that led to the truth.

We all faked "crossing over" into Level Five, eyes shut, having known exactly how many seconds before the blasts of light were emitted. Our retinas and brains were protected; we just looked away from the screens at the moment of going over. We also painted liquid-skin on our fingers to act as a repellant/protectant to whatever the liquid goo was that came out the WenBook .25 second after the light. And we all licked our fingers at the right moments. But we weren't licking anything other than the regular everyday germs on all of our fingers.

We saw the confirmation that Level Five had been achieved for each of us. We felt nauseous but were still the same. Now we had to fake it, 24/7.

We were able to get two and a half hours of sleep.

We decided, after seeing some of the others, to dress in muted colors and remove all of our jewelry. It's just how it was done, apparently, post-Level Five.

And Kristina? She, apparently, had genuinely "gone over." I couldn't seem to attract or engage a moment of connection with her.

The hallways of CAWS were quiet and the classroom was silent but for a few whispers. A voice came on, making an announcement, something unusual for CAWS, which prided itself on a more freewheeling structure. It was a soothing female voice and it was one we hadn't heard before.

"Good morning," it said. "I hope you've all had a good night's sleep. It's important to get a good night's sleep. Nothing puts you in a better mood for learning than a well-rested body. Your WenBooks will be HIVE-restored to healthy functioning at 11 a.m. today as their BIOS will be refreshed and enhanced, post-Level-Five."

This was a good time to look around and that is just what I did. The look on everyone's faces was, unnaturally serene. "Morning schedule will be changed slightly to allow for twenty-five minutes of post-religious training and review. Post-religious thinking makes us clear-headed and virtuous. On 'A' days, we will survey each of the world's major and minor religions, looking at the logical fallacies and poor thinking in each. On 'B' days, we will advance our understanding of the ways to build a new society in the wake of their narrow-minded failures."

I tried to make eye contact with Elizabeth without reacting obviously. Everything was different. Studying *religions*?

We left class in an orderly fashion—the first twenty-five minutes had been on the primitive peoples of the ancient world thinking that there were gods all around them controlling rain, sunshine, fire, and earthquakes. They talked about deer antlers, fox teeth, burying their dead this way to curry favor with mysterious forces around them. "Early men and women simply didn't understand the scientific underpinnings of the way things worked," our teacher said.

No one had tried to teach "history" since the Year 1 and we hadn't heard anything like this.

"Göbekli Tepe, in what is now Turkey, came to be, around 8,000 years before the Jesus cult, the first religious site in the world." More about death; they let their dead be carried off and picked apart by vultures, apparently.

Tomorrow would be a 'B' day, but the next 'A' day would cover Stonehenge, Krishna, and things thirty-two centuries before Jesus, we were told.

Class dismissed. "Let's find Orlinsky," Elizabeth said, as we wandered out together. The rest of us nodded. When we did find him, he was succinct. "Stop writing, texting, communicating on any and all computers, wearables, laptops, post-Level Five WenBooks, anything they give you. Assume it is all monitored."

"Won't that raise suspicions?" Rudra asked.

We pondered this.

"He's right," Aharon said. "It'd make more sense to carry on typical teenage conversations in our usual manner, on whatever technologies they give us, which we keep the 'real' communication off The HIVE and off our wearables and laptops."

"So…how do we communicate the real stuff?" I asked.

Orlinsky looked at me with dismay. "Paper and pen, you hopeless bastard-children of technology. Notes written in handwriting passed directly to the other person. You can tell it has been received when you see the other person's fingers clasp around it and their hand withdraw with it. It is easier than it sounds. It also can be destroyed pretty easily without leaving behind a HIVE presence for eighteen hundred years."

I didn't tell anyone that Kristina and I had already learned how to communicate in American Sign Language. It felt weird to withhold it, but I still didn't want to share it.

"It's not a way of communicating that we need," Elizabeth said. "We need to know what is happening, where this goes, and how we don't become a part of it."

"You mean a strategy?" Orlinsky said. "Because you already are a part of it."

There was a considerable silence as we contemplated this. We were an elite core at an elite school. Whatever was happening had us at its center "I can offer us a place to figure it out, though. Come with me."

We climbed into Orlinsky's car. He'd told the school we were doing preliminary research into using rural sex-booths as a beta project for the exchange of two-way retinal/body looping. We could be in the field and gone for up to two days. He told Cote we would be recruiting volunteers. Then he took us to a house up in the hills, about an hour and twenty minutes from CAWS. There were some scraggly trees and a few rain barrels on the side of the house. A very old, disheveled man opened the door stared at him, and said "What changed everything?"

"Port Huron, 1962" Orlinsky said. Totally weird; this was some sort of code-phrase, like a spy-movie.

The door now swung open widely and the man smiled. They hugged each other, slapping backs. He looked old so old that he might break in half if the hug was too strong. It was unusual seeing men hug each other, unless it was at one of the sex booths.

"Come in, come in," the old man said, his eyes landing on each one of us in turn. "What beautiful young people," he said to Orlinsky. "They still exist," he said with some excitement.

"We're off-HIVE?" Orlinsky asked.

"Yes. Have been for three weeks. I got The Dome."

"The Dome?" Rudra asked.

"The Freedom Dome. Wipes out and redirects any signal related to The HIVE. They can't identify or fix the location because the location of this house is, apparently, the Adriatic Sea. To them, anyway. So just know that your retinal whatchamacallits aren't going to work here. They'll still struggle to, but they won't connect."

"What about your implants? Are they permanently disabled?" Elizabeth asked.

"Never got 'em," he answered quickly. "I went into hiding; I was part of a whole community who escaped getting any implants."

We looked at each other with shock. The HIVE wasn't voluntary!

"This is Mr. Alan Weissman. He is ninety-three years old. He is one of the most important political thinkers of the last century. Alan, these are the students from CAWS I told you about."

The old man smiled and looked at each of us in turn.

"Alan was in the group who wrote The Port Huron Statement. He was about your age when they did it."

"The what?" asked Aharon. "He wrote a 'Statement?'" he asked, smirking.

"The Port Huron Statement. Port Huron is a town in Michigan. A group gathered there, about seventy-five years ago, long before the Religious Wars, long before the Year 1."

"We didn't like what we saw, the world we were given," the old man said. "It stunk. Our inheritance. We knew we had power to change it, if we could organize other people our age. We were almost right. We changed some of it. Then we became fat, comfortable, fearful cowards. Never underestimate human cowardice. We quit. The Religious Ones did a better job of getting people riled up than we did. Then, of course, The Religious Ones were crushed, for entirely understandable reasons. Where we are now, I have no idea. I grow cucumbers now, make my pickles and live off-HIVE. I am telling you this because something big is happening and this is your moment. If you wait, and talk too much, you will be ninety-three years old soon, too, telling your own stories of failure. You will get comfortable and quit."

"What are you proposing we do?" asked Elizabeth, skeptically.

"Unlearn everything they've told you," he said. "And understand that your computer connections, The HIVE, the commands, the planning, the logic, has already killed you, in increments. You are the walking dead, dead to each other. There is only a little part of you that is alive."

I thought of *Hell on Earth*, and what we had done and seen, and I sat down and felt sick all over again. I couldn't understand the feeling. I mean, it wasn't really ABOUT any one thing, it just felt miserable.

"Your friend there, for instance," he said, pointing to me, "he is sad. I can see it in his face. That is the way it should be; the face expresses the emotions. That is not a failing, it is a blessing. And he needs to cry."

He came over and hugged me. I couldn't believe how accepting of this I was. I melted into him. And I started crying, thinking of my father and the

111

last time I hugged him after a Sunday morning motorcycle ride. Before he went away, forever.

"There, there," he said, patting my back. "It's OK Don't stop it…let it flow…it's too much, all too much." He pushed me away for a second and looked in my eyes. "It's too much, isn't it?" I cried again. We stood like that, not caring who was watching, and I felt almost like I was in Liberia again.

"We're not political," Rudra said, "and I don't intend to become political."

That's when Alan started laughing, at first while still holding on to me, then separating from me with a series of strong pats on the back. His laughter got deeper.

"Of course not," he said. "And a fish doesn't know it is in water. Until there is no water anymore. Then he learns about water. I think you are all about to be out of water."

Orlinsky spoke up, after gesturing for us all to sit. Alan sat in a chair, Orlinsky stood, and the rest of us sat on the floor. "Here's what we know," he said. "Wen distributed computers to every young person on the globe, it got hacked, the most screwed up game of all time has been played nonstop since it appeared and millions of kids have 'gone over' to some level of weirdness related to a combination of laser-like light-blasts, subliminal messaging, sleeplessness, hunger and ordinary desensitization to violence. Then, abruptly, they become docile, unquestioning, polite, change the way they dress, and are ready for a new curriculum, which centers around reinforcing the anti-religious methods that surfaced in the Year 1. We don't know who, how, or why this thing was hacked, and we don't know where this is all going.'"

"Of course, you don't," Alan said. "It is asking too much to know where this is all going; all you can do is make a stand. And I don't hear any of you speaking yet of your own right to free thought and actions. Maybe that is because you are connected to the HIVE through your implants and you barely remember a time when you weren't. I'm telling you that ALL is up for grabs, that you can be anyone you want to. Refuse to participate in any culture that destroys your wholeness. But only after you regain your wholeness."

"And how do we do that?" asked Elizabeth, smirking.

"Well...wouldn't it be nice to have your body back? You can't get your implants out, but you could get into your feet, couldn't you?"

Orlinsky told us to stand up and Alan led us through breathing exercises, touching the floor, walking "with your whole foot," adjusting our pelvises, putting our shoulders back, holding our hands over our stomachs and feeling it going in and out as we breathed. Total weirdness. It felt OK, except for being afraid of what the other people were thinking as we looked at each other. No one said anything, we just "went with it," but I was worried they thought that my body might be stranger than theirs, my butt bigger, or something like that.

"Don't compare yourself to anyone, or anything else," Alan shouted, "just experience it. You don't need to justify your own experience to anyone. You don't need to post it on The HIVE, get comments on it, have other people like or dislike it; it is enough to just feel it."

Even Elizabeth started laughing, a good laugh, not her usual sarcastic snorting, and when we sat around afterwards people looked more alive in their eyes.

Alan took out an old folder and started reading to us:

"'We are people of this generation, bred in at least modest comfort, housed now in universities, looking uncomfortably to the world we inherit...'"

Candles were lit, someone started crying—I don't know why—and we fell asleep listening to those words from 1962.

I dreamt about Kristina. I missed her. Was she altered permanently?

In my dream, she and I were both riding bicycles, somewhere far away from California or Sweden or Liberia, leaning into turns, then taking turns being the one in front of each other, then dropping back. We parked the bikes on the field of an elementary school and laid in the sun on our backs. There was a ring around the sun, a subtle one. "This is a good omen," Kristina said. "For our future." We kissed, and I lay my body on top of hers. I could feel a third presence, not hers or mine. It was *us*.

When I woke up, I saw Alan, Orlinsky, and Elizabeth sitting around a kitchen table looking exhausted but arguing with surprising energy. It wasn't clear whether they had woken up earlier than me, or were still up from last night. They were mid-way into an argument, and no one seemed ready to back down or set it aside.

Alan was reading: "The dominant institutions… are entrenched enough to swiftly dissipate or…repel the energies of protest and reform, thus limiting human expectancies." He stared right at Elizabeth and asked, "You don't think that is true? You don't think that's exactly what has happened? Foretold seventy years ago??"

"It's not that it's not true, love," she said, "it's just so…American. It's lovely, really quite lovely, but the implications are…abstruse."

"Abstruse?"

"Yes. Abstruse and the product of hermetic thinking."

"I'm sorry, I'm an old man. But I didn't use words like that even when I was in my twenties. As for being American, I plead guilty."

"Abstruse in the sense of big, theory-of-it-all, etc. Hermetic in the sense of airtight, impervious to outside influence. It's true because it's been thought of as true, has been true, everyone knows it is true…so what? So bloody what? What are we supposed to do with that?"

"I keep forgetting that you aren't fully human anymore. No offense, you are beautiful young people, but you aren't all there.

114

You're…diminished. You were even before the implants. The implants just accelerated it."

"Then why bother with us?" Elizabeth half-shouted. "Orlinsky; why are we even here with this old man? He is exactly the reason they gave up teaching history in the first place. It's curious for about five minutes, then gets into a circle of hopelessness. We're alive now, not in 1962."

"What he's saying is that you aren't even close to alive. Not yet. You are more like sleep-walkers. And they've upped the ante. Whatever little shred of passion you still had—and it wasn't much—someone wants extinguished now and forever. You might be the last young people who ever feel dissatisfied, who are aware of being incomplete. The ones who come behind you will be raised in a different world. Do you understand that?"

I had HAD it. I walked up and interrupted them all.

"This is nonsense. Jabber, jabber, jabber, this is TALK, this is words. You are as bad as the Religious Ones. This is exactly what we don't need," I yelled.

"You're saying we are the same as the Religious?" Alan shot back, tiredly, and with an amused look.

"Yes. Maybe worse. My father, when I was a young boy, and the Religious were still around a lot, he told me a saying, and I have not forgotten it. He said, 'Give a man a fish and you'll feed him for a day. Give him a religion and he'll starve to death while praying for a fish.' That is what you do, you are just talking another old religion, one from the 1960s, you want to give it, spread it. I'm not buying. People need people, not theories. Even Kristina right now. Has it occurred to any of you, maybe you, Elizabeth, that she might be lonely, or afraid?"

Orlinsky said, "If you are saying you want to leave, Zokaya, you aren't allowed to until we give you the green light to do so." He shouted for Rudra and he came in, rubbing his eyes, in shorts and a t-shirt." "Zokaya wants to leave," he announced. "To be with Kristina."

"How are we going to help her?" I yelled.

"She's gone over. She's a Fiver now," Elizabeth said, immediately.

"So, I can't keep her as a friend? Are you my mommy? I can hang around someone who has gone over without going over myself," I said.

"It's too dangerous," Orlinsky said.

"I thought we were supposed to act like we'd gone over, too," Rudra offered. "That's what was discussed. We're all supposed to be Fivers. Why *wouldn't* he hang around Kristina, then? Isn't it suspicious that we're away this long without her? The smart thing to do is to make it look as normal as possible. Let him go, and we should all go back, too. She's a valuable asset, actually," Rudra said. "He can observe her close up."

"I'm sure of that…easy-peasy there…" Elizabeth muttered quietly but loud enough for me to here.

"What, Elizabeth?" I shouted. "No one is looking at you, Elizabeth? Just stop being so jealous. Keep it in bounds. Or, better yet, start being nice to people and someone might want to be with you, 'close up,'"

"Right, Zokaya. All she's got to do is slowly brush her hair out of her Scandinavian face, and you're running around like she's the mutt's nuts. Tell me if I'm wrong!" Elizabeth was screaming. At this point, I just wanted out.

"Let's go," Orlinsky said. "All of us. Except for you, Alan. To be continued. They'll be back."

Alan walked us to the door—Elizabeth was still glaring at me—and he held up the old text one more time to read: ''We regard men as infinitely precious…possessed of unfulfilled capacities for reason, freedom, and love.' That is not Religion, my children. Those are concepts that only those who are fully human can fully grasp."

We rode back in silence.

#

I knocked on her door about 15 minutes before classes and waited for Kristina to answer. I had an explanation ready as to where we all had been since we last saw her: hunting down leads for internships that CAWS wanted us to land for the second part of the year. It was something she would be doing, too, I was ready to tell her, just that we three got a jump on it by seeing an animal control facility about forty miles away that she probably wouldn't have wanted to work in. I was going to tell her the place was pretty bad and the work was nothing that we'd want to do.

But I didn't have to; she didn't ask and didn't seem bothered by the absence of me in her life.

She answered the door and gave a slight, automatic smile, the kind you give the school photographer when he tells you to sit up straight and give a nice big one for the camera. She said, "Hello, Zokaya, how are you? Did you have a good night's sleep? I did."

I said I did and asked if I could walk her to class. Kristina actually did look well-rested, but there was something obviously flat about her. Her spark was missing. Her blouse was buttoned up to the top button and the faraway look in her eyes, combined with the wispy smile, made me want to rescue her. I wanted to take away from her whatever had happened. Like in a fairy tale, or in a movie. It seemed like it had been such a long time ago that we were actually talking and enjoying each other. I felt, now, that I was with this perfected image of her, instead of her. I wanted real Kristina, the one who held my hand in the desert at night, after riding our swooping circles on the bike. But I looked at her and saw someone who looked like a yearbook picture.

"So, what have you been up to?" I asked. "In addition to getting sleep."

"I've been reading, for class," she said.

"I didn't know there were assignments," I volunteered.

"Yes. We're supposed to read about belief in Lord Krishna, one of the prime deities in Hinduism, spread, 3,100 years before Jesus. Oh, and Stonehenge. About the same time. We have to write about it."

"Why are we studying religions? Isn't that the exact opposite of what we were brought here to study?" I offered.

"That's the point," Kristina said, suddenly looking and sounding quite intelligent. "you have to know what you are up against before you can banish it. It has deep roots."

"The wars are over, Kristina; the Religious Ones lost. We're quite safe," I said.

"Of course, we are safe; we are safer than ever before, but the point being made in class, which you missed yesterday, was that the roots of nonlogical feeling (instead of 'thinking') run deep. And you can't grow to the next level with roots pulling you downward."

"So, what are you going to write?" I asked.

"The basics. Krishna: blue skin, a cow-herder, a dancer with butter; married 8 queens. Then 16,100 maidens, ended up with 16,108 wives. To marry them all he took more than 16,000 human forms He either was one with Vishnu or was separate from Vishnu; it is complex. Played the flute, but it might not have literally been a flute. Was said to have lived one-hundred-twenty-five years."

"How did you get all this?" I asked.

"You have to know where to look," Kristina said. "I liked that his skin was different. I can relate."

"So, there is a likelihood people could start worshipping you?" I asked.

"No. I'm no deity, I assure you." She looked at me directly; this is when I used to feel the connection, almost like a live stream of molecules between us. Instead, it just felt empty in the moment. "Why is it you came by this morning?" she asked with what seemed like genuine confusion.

"I was wondering if you started riding the bike again," I asked.

She crooked her head to the side a notch, gave the automatic smile and said, "Why would I want to do that? Are you still talking about the bicycle you found? Ride it if you want to, but, it's really not very interesting to me. Is there anything else?"

I was caught off-guard and said no. As tempted as I was to take her hand and trace letters in it, just as she'd taught me, I just stood there. I closed my eyes and asked myself if I could still feel her in front me.

I could, just barely; the flicker of a presence.

That next day at school was bizarre. We were wearing, of course, the grayest, most nondescript pieces of clothing Orlinsky could find for us. We were Fivers. We would be complete Fivers.

Just as there is a hushed, respectful feeling in a classroom where the teacher is smarter, and more experienced, than the students there is a sound to a classroom where the teacher is as flat and disinterested as the students themselves. It the sound of air getting sucked into nothingness, of words disappearing as soon as they are said, of carbon dioxide being produced for no good reason, of seconds ticking away into the past. Someone, somewhere, might be learning something, but not here. There was a saying-of-these-things in order to be able to say they-said-these-things, and I couldn't even recall them as soon as the sounds of the words stopped. There was no connection, and I suddenly understood that all the teachers, as well as the students, had gone on to Level Five. The teacher stood before us— gray, pleasant, monotoned, and it sound like an instructional workshop for people who had English as a second language.

I looked around and saw this girl, Susan, who, only days before, had regularly worn ripped-up blouses designed to cling to, and reveal, the top arches of her breasts, sitting there in a tightly buttoned-up gray top, her hands neatly folded in attention. She used to look like she was just daring someone, anyone; male or female, to get frisky and wrestle with her, anywhere people weren't looking. Now she looked like she was ready to offer you a mortgage if you qualified. She stared straight ahead, as if she were connected with the unconnectable, the twaddle coming from the teacher's mouth.

"...the birth of Abrahamic religions," he was saying, without emphasis. "1250 B.C...950 B.C...the Torah...800 B.C..." It was all blending into a haze in my mind. "...celebrations of magic, pre-logic...Jainism...563 B.C., Gautama Buddha...living with suffering...the Hebrew Bible is written. We will pick up here tomorrow."

This had as much to do with me, I thought, as a discussion of how many miles Jupiter was away from Pluto. Whether it was 3.187 billion miles or forty-three miles, it struck me as the same. So what?

Everyone picked up their WenBooks and rose in unison. I looked at this wild-haired kid, Andrew, whom everyone already knew was one of the only ones at CAWS consuming any substances he could find, only the week before. I didn't see him; maybe he dropped out? Then I did. He was unrecognizably clean-cut, hair neat and combed to the side, gray shirt buttoned high, nondescript pants. He had a pleasant smile.

I connected with Elizabeth in the hallway; she looked like a museum curator or lawyer, herself. She handed me a note and walked away. It said, "Going to Alan's tonight, all. Talk then." I ripped it into shreds, distributing the shreds in different places, as we'd been told to do.

The next class was Orlinsky's. He was playing along, of course, and doing a good job of appearing to be a Fiver. He said, in as unexcited a voice as he could muster, "I've been asked to share the following with you: Each year, Wen Enterprises reaches out to the youth leadership within CAWS to solicit ideas, direction and guidance for the year ahead. Four student representatives from each CAWS campus will attend the World Conclave on Catalina Island, California, all expenses paid, for five days. Mr. Wen, himself, will be in attendance and will lead meditations, discussions, and brainstorming sessions. You must be nominated by a Faculty member after indicating to them that you wish to go. These are much coveted slots which will not go unnoticed in terms of future employability and references."

Orlinsky looked up, looked quickly at Elizabeth, then resumed a monotone description of the contributions of the late artist Damien Hirst and his contributions what would later be known as the Rich Art movement prior to the Religious Wars. Suddenly, history was teachable, I guess. As long as it was related to how bad things were before the Year 1.

I daydreamed, about Kristina. Even though she was sitting there in the same class with me, about fourteen feet away. I kept seeing her on her bicycle again, riding in front of me, turning to look back with a genuine smile, not the manufactured compromise she wore these days. In my daydream it was the future. We already had known each other for years. We were curled up in each other's arms, our entire bodies nestled together. We were breathing as one, falling asleep.

#

Up in the hills, at Al's, as we'd grown to call it, Elizabeth seemed on fire.

"Here's what I did," she told us. "I started with the air-gapped computer Orlinsky gave me—not connected to The HIVE but able to access the same data as The HIVE, in a dormant format."

So that's where she'd gotten the "safe" computer?

"How did you access the dormant format?" I asked.

"That is a separate workshop in itself," Orlinsky interrupted, answering for her. "Basically, a mirror of a mirror."

"I was able to use some common algorithm variations that were favorites of the No-Pointers during the Religious wars, to run a dark search for game-resisters," Elizabeth said.

"'Game resisters'?" I asked.

"For those of you who were never taught this, which is basically all of you except Elizabeth, whom I've been trying to bring up to speed since yesterday, the No-Pointers were independent groups of survivalists who maintained neutrality during the Religious Wars," Orlinsky shared. "They were the forerunners of the current government, early Rationalists. The nickname comes from their philosophy; there was *no point* in trying to either agree or disagree with any of the theologies that were warring,"

"Anyway…they'd developed a sophisticated way of keeping in touch only with each other, prior to The HIVE, even though the whole ancient 'Internet' had been hacked and tracked, up to individual phones and laptops. The No-Pointers system still hadn't been cracked by the end of the Wars. It was kind of an 'after-the-fact' challenge to look at what they'd done, and it seems they devised an incredibly useful set of tools that I borrowed from yesterday." Elizabeth paused; she was really enjoying this stuff, imagining herself as a leader in The Next Big Thing. "And it turns out that there are at least two distinct groups of Game resisters, people who were able to evade Hell on Earth entirely, or simply lost interest before Level Five, in this country alone. One is H.O.E. resisters and the others call themselves the Game Resistance League. Their motto simply was, 'No More Games.' And we are able to safely communicate with them, which I've already initiated, with Orlinsky's help."

"Two of their representatives, one from each group, will be meeting us here at our next meeting," Orlinsky said. "Security is paramount and we don't want a large group."

"Why are we being suddenly dragged through centuries of study about the very stuff the government eliminated from schools years ago?" Rudra asked.

"All we can figure," Orlinsky said, "is that it is leading up to something. It's Wen's game. It is crucial that you try to get sent to this Conclave this summer. I can nominate you, but you are going to have to do your part by showing outstanding quantities of mediocrity and exemplary submissiveness at school."

"But Kristina is a Fiver," Rudra argued. I felt myself immediately wanting to defend her.

"I know. Don't worry about her. She'll have a head start on the mediocrity and submissiveness," Orlinsky said. "We'll have to have a way of neutralizing Fivers by then."

"Why don't we start with a poem?" asked Al, offering each of us a look at his smiling face. "Are you joking?" Elizabeth asked.

"Absolutely not," said Al. "Let's sit on the floor first, legs crossed, back straight up, lifted from your pelvis." I watched him pull a candle from the shelf behind him and light it, then set it down in the center of the circle. He offered his palms-up supplication to the ceiling, saying, "We are grateful to the No-Pointers and all those who have come before us, in the spirit of freedom and inquiry. Let us chant three OMs to begin together, after a deep inhale and full exhale…"

"No. Nope. Uh-uh," said Rudra, standing up quickly as the rest of us settled into sitting. "I'm not one of the Religious Ones, and have no interest in dabbling in their magic or prejudices," he said, "not in India, in England, and definitely not in California. This is the Year 13, people! I want to stay clear-headed and keep our integrity. No time-travel for me."

Al laughed, deeper and longer than the rest of us. We kind of stifled it, out of trying to be nice. "Breathing may be the original form of prayer, but that doesn't make it 'religious.' It is better than that. No foreign languages, no sacrifices, no killing, no superiority. It is the sound of the body exhaling, humming, the portals of your senses vibrating."

"Rudra's got a point," Elizabeth said. "Doesn't it mean something Hindu? Isn't that a foreign language? Ancient curse or something? Voodoo"

"It was the sound of the Original Vibration," Al offered. "You don't have to be a Hindu to believe that."

"Right, then," said Elizabeth. "And what's that supposed to be? Vibration from a transistor radio? From a clothes dryer? And why should WE be doing it? We're kind of 'post-Hindu' aren't we?"

The question hung in the air. Surprisingly, it was Orlinsky who answered this: "We'll do it to align ourselves with each other, to get on the same page with the present moment, and the Universe, whatever that is. Call it whatever you want, I'm not really interested in words. You might believe it can't help, but it's not Level Five and it can't hurt. It is to help the walking dead become partially alive."

Rudra reluctantly sat down. His exhale sounded like that of a large dog. After a few seconds, a big hum started and the sound of "OH" filled the room, vibrating from Al's chest. Orlinsky joined in, then the rest of us. Without prompting the sound turned into "UMMMMMMMMMMMM" and started reminding me of "Home." I don't know why, but I wanted to cry. It was all weird, but also OK I had never been sitting with these people before, our chests vibrating together.

I wandered out alone after this, listening to the sounds of the wind and felt alone and dissatisfied. I found myself doing something strange: writing. In what would become a journal. This journal.

When I returned to the group, I was barely affected by them. I kept thinking about my life. I wondered what I would've been like if I'd never been identified as promising back in Liberia. If I were still there. Then a part of me reminded myself that I was still there. While being here.

#

The next day at classes was more of the same pasteurized survey of religions, picking up where we'd left off yesterday. All I really took from it was a swirl of words, something like:

"Law...forbidden....death...judgment...separate...different...heresy ...sin."

I started thinking, that might be the history of the world in one unfocused series of words. Or at least up until the Year 1. Greatly religious people in the past were fond, apparently, of beheading less-religious people. So, it wasn't just things like the SCRAPS I'd seen on the plane on the way to California. It was centuries and centuries and centuries of the same.

But I still didn't understand the importance of gathering up some kind of momentum to fight something that had already been defeated. It was like picking up rocks to fight dinosaurs.

Kristina continued to look distant. I was starting to get aggravated by the blandness she was presenting. It didn't make sense, but the old Kristina would've been appalled at the new Kristina, and I guess I was left alone to be upset with the change that had occurred between us. For the first time I really worried about how much of it was due to Level Five and how much of it WASN'T due to Level Five, just a reflection of who she might really be. The Ice Queen. Maybe she had never really liked me, but just had been polite in some Scandinavian way.

Our classes were interrupted by a live news feed from Mr. Wen, himself. There was a waterfall behind him. He spoke quietly, but intensely: "The time of Noisy Mind is past. We have endured many hardships. Many cruelties. The world has become, in many ways, unacceptable. Together, with Quiet Mind, we can reshape things. We are people of good intentions. The character of our young people has been lowered—just when we attempted to raise it!—but is being reclaimed. Our information shows that, by next Monday, seventy-five percent of the world's young people will have put down this horrible game that was hacked upon us and moved on to the pursuit of Lasting Peace with other people of good intention, all across the world. To the young people of the world I say this: when you are ready to put away the noisy, ugly ways, Join Us. Join us on a noble journey. WenBook will be there, standing with you, helping you find your path. This has always been the WenBook way. Lasting Peace."

#

First, I thought it was a dream. A beautiful woman looked into my eyes and whispered important, heartfelt things. What sort of dream? Where did I know her from? Was she my fantasy creation? I knew her, I felt her, but I wasn't in the room with her; there wasn't even a room. She was a dream. She was too vivid. She was high definition, in front of my face, but inside of me. It turns out I was witnessing something the same time millions of others were, but it felt personal. They hadn't used direct corneal broadcasting (DCB) for anything other than public safety alerts—we studied this in school; it began with the old "Amber Alerts"—but everyone knew they were building up towards it. It turns out the girls were receiving handsome male alerts; they personalized these things around your preferences, based on data they had gathered since the year before puberty.

Over the course of the past few months, we'd be asked to "opt in" to getting alerts to the activities/tour schedules/appearances, etc. of favorite celebrities, they often came with breathy personalized whispers or glimpses, until it'd become just silly to resist or decline these update-alerts. It really didn't take anything away from your day to say "yes" to a couple of fleeting pieces of information or great-looking pictures of people who had beautiful bodies, smiling at you—it felt like just at YOU—as you went about your day. Slowly these alerts had grown to include closing "sayings to live by", and I didn't know anyone who thought they were anything but soothing and lovely. I can't even recall them offhand, though I know now that the No-Pointers and GRL (Game Resisters' League) documented the entire collection. I just remember things like, "Staying informed is staying safe," and "The HIVE is strong." No one was sure of what we were supposed to stay safe from, but most of the older people said that was about The Religious Ones.

The No-Pointers reported that in the second month the messages changed slightly to "The HIVE is strong. Report any dangerous superstitious practices or activities anonymously." I was either not aware of this or couldn't remember. This was the first time an anonymous response system, which involved looking to the upper right, clicking on a morsel and then speaking your concerns out loud, followed by looking to the lower left to "Send", was used. There had been beta-testing of this for years, but people thought it was either too invasive or just silly. Eventually, though, it just seemed to save time.

The thing about anonymous reporting was that you had no idea whether one person was using it, or no one was. Or everyone was. It wasn't discussed. As for superstitious behavior or practices, it was hard to know what they meant or were talking about. By the third month, though, we all understood that the old religious ways, if anyone were still doing these things, were not only dangerously primitive (ignorant, really) but that they had nothing to do with the introduction of Quiet Mind practices that Mr. Wen was talking about. They were as different as apples and oranges. Mr. Wen started calling it The Way Forward. Eventually this was shortened to The Way.

Orlinsky urged caution about the first meeting at Al's house with members of the Games Resister's League. "Organizations are death," he told us, "and our gatherings are getting perilously close to an organization."

"Pardon us, but aren't you a member of one of the most highly-financed organizations on earth?" Elizabeth retorted.

"CAWS or TriSec?" Orlinsky asked.

"Take your pick. You're not exactly a lone wolf, are you?"

"I'm not a sheep either," he said, staring her down.

"Are you saying we are?" asked Rudra.

"Well, you're here in the first place, aren't you?" He seemed irritated.

"We're all here trying to get away from something. Isn't that why everyone comes to CAWS?" I asked.

"Not with Quiet Mind, I suspect," Orlinsky said. "There's no need to get away from anything. It'll be in you and you won't even know it. You'll just want to stay home and watch your own corneas, go to sleep, and do it again tomorrow. You're already more than halfway there. Your whole generation."

We were shocked to hear him speak like this. This was an insult and an attack.

"I am reminding you that *your* generation not only paved the way for all this" Elizabeth said. "but you designed, marketed, implanted and sustained all these improvements before the Year 1. Or did I get that wrong? I didn't see your generation out there storming the barricades, flying your flags…"

"We fought the Religious Wars! We didn't have the luxury of sitting around complaining about the color of the background to the implant alerts, or whatever young people consider so offensive these days," Orlinsky shouted. "The colors of your condoms, the texture of your toilet papers. Your generation is weak."

"And yours is a bunch of whores and collaborators!" Elizabeth screamed back.

"We fought the war to establish freedom from belief! You'd all be wearing headscarves and bearing a brood of children by age nineteen if we hadn't, Elizabeth; you'd be getting on your hands and knees to mumble ancient phrases 8 times a day and wouldn't be allowed out of the house. Don't you understand that? Women have always been the number one target with The Religious. The 3 C's: confine, confuse and control women. Their thinking, their bodies, their sexuality. Keep it reproductive. Keep their blinders on, give them nice funerals when they die and call them saints."

"Oh, so we owe you big, brave men our freedoms?" Elizabeth was flushed with rage.

"No, you owe it to your mothers, your fathers, your grandparents, your sisters and your brothers who died in The Religious Wars. They saw a mortal threat and they acted. Without it we wouldn't even be in the 21st century anymore."

"We're not in it, anyway," Rudra volunteered. "I thought this was the Year 13, isn't it?"

There was a welcome quiet. Both Orlinsky and Elizabeth slowed their breathing some.

"That's a construct," Orlinsky said. "A product of rational beings who wanted a clear line of demarcation from the sprawling cesspool that came before it."

"What is it you wanted us to know about the Game Resisters League?" I asked.

"Just that we can't vet their security clearances; we have no idea who they really are. These people, along with the remnants of the No-Pointers and many of the H.O.E. Refusers, they are just unknown variables. I'd be shocked if there weren't informants in their midst, and we haven't figured out how to detect them. You could be exposed and turned in in a half hour. I could be, too."

"So, we go to the meeting or not go?" Elizabeth asked.

"We go, but do more listening than talking," Orlinsky said. "Try to get a feel for them. See what your gut tells you about them."

"Doesn't sound too safe," I said.

"Nothing is safe anymore," Orlinsky said.

Jerry Sander

Great Betrayals

We went into the first Unified Cadre meeting (this is what it would later be called) with fear. None of us had come to school to become spies and, despite being ordinary teenagers in the Year 13, we weren't particularly skilled at lying. We reminded ourselves to keep our mouths shut. "Don't speak unless you can improve upon silence," Orlinsky drilled into us. "And *improve* means drawing them out more."

We didn't know if Al was hosting two other people or twenty at this gathering. It turned out just three others came. And they didn't come on time. We'd already done our "OMMMMMM'S" and breathing exercises and were killing time by discussing the section of the Port Huron Statement about the "dignity of man" and whether that varied between cultures.

Rudra said that his grandparents told him the key to a good life was "balance." There was a knock on the door and we all stopped talking as Al got up to answer it. We heard him ask for, and get, the code phrase: "Lawrence of Arabia" (a movie from 1962, the year Al and his buddies were around our age).

The first guy through the door swooped in, smelling of some sort of fragrant dirt—Al explained it was "patchouli"—and pulled back his pony-tail, setting it to the left. He took off his sunglasses and looked at us coolly. "Luke," he said. "This is Carmen," he said, pointing to the woman right behind him. She was a skinny dark-haired, nervous looking Hispanic woman in her twenties. She looked like she was ready to bolt at any minute.

A third guy, with a fleshy, almost babyish face, padded in quietly behind them. "That is Crazy Chester," Luke said.

We mumbled some hellos; we'd risen to our feet from the seated discussion. It didn't seem like handshakes were in order, or even safe somehow. My PFA—all of ours—struggled to connect and came up with absolutely nothing.

"Al, I love you, but how do I know who these people really are?" Luke asked.

"How do we know who anyone really is?" Al said. "We take the time, we sit, we eat together, we tell our stories—maybe we don't right away— but we see what happens. To get to know someone is to take a risk."

The silence that followed was uncomfortable.

"Have a seat," Al offered. "Everyone. You see," he said turning to us, "Luke and Carmen and Crazy Chester aren't used to meeting with implant-people. Particularly since no one knows what updates have been done at the other end, what the capabilities are after the opt-ins for the corneal alerts. To say that they have questions and suspicions about your generation is an understatement."

We pondered this. "They are just a few years older than us," Rudra offered.

"Makes all the difference in the world," Carmen spat out. "You are the ones who said 'yes' to all this crap."

"It's not like they really knew of a choice," Al said.

"Then how come there are so many of us resisters?" Luke asked.

"You had a feeling," said Al. "In your gut. You had a feeling that something bad was coming. And you hid. You moved, and you kept moving."

"You too, Al. Ended your whole life as you knew it," Luke said.

"Either way it would've. I opted to stay the same, the same old hardware I was born with, defective and limited as it is," Al said. "Small price to pay. But these beautiful children…they'd already said yes to so many things people in all the generations before them had set before them that they didn't know how to say 'no' anymore. So, they offered up their remaining parts, trusting and hoping. And it was very nice, and shiny…for a while."

"So why should we trust them now?" Carmen asked, shifting her weight from leg to leg.

"Oh, I'm not suggesting that you trust them right away," Al said. "Or that they trust you. I just think that you have things to say to each other, to possibly coordinate."

"And what if these things aren't even true?" asked Elizabeth. Orlinsky shot her a quick look. "What if it is disinformation?"

The question hung in the room for a minute before Al spoke. "Then things will happen that will show us that we were wrong to meet. Car accidents, disappearances, what have you. To all or any one of us. This is not new to us, children. We've been living this way since the beginning of The Religious Wars. I think it is time to more properly introduce yourself, so let's go around the circle and do that."

We did that, keeping what we shared to the minimum (we said we went to CAWS and were intimately familiar with *Hell on Earth*, but that none of us were Level Fivers).

Luke introduced himself as the liaison person for the No-Pointers, and said he'd been working with Carmen for only five months, after she made contact with him. Carmen introduced herself as being the West Coast founder of H.O.E.R. (*Hell on Earth* Resisters, a group formed even before the official release of *Hell on Earth*, based on the rumors, she said) and a liaison to the older Game Resisters League. It was impossible to keep all these resistance groups, with their initials, straight. What did it matter, anyway?

All eyes turned to Chester (none of us were sure what made him "Crazy" Chester) and we watched as he just smiled. He continued to smile, without saying anything, past the point of comfort. We looked nervously at Orlinsky (who had just introduced himself as a "friend of Al's who was working at CAWS") who tried to steady us with his gaze, I think.

Al finally spoke up as the silence got more and more scary. "Chester, I think you are scaring them. Just say what you can say."

Chester smiled some more. He looked around at our circle, and said, "I am the liaison to The Religious Ones."

Rudra stood up immediately and shouted, "Absolutely not!"

The color drained from Elizabeth's face as if she'd already been arrested for something. She looked at both Orlinsky and Al with a look of betrayal. "This wasn't what we were told," she protested.

Al smiled and said, "Well, the problem seems to be with the things you were told, not what really happened."

Chester stood up and looked slowly at each of us. "I don't know who you people really are," he said. "I don't know whether it is meaningful to still call you people. I actually don't want to be here. I don't want to be spending so much of my trust and time with children who have been raised to believe whatever flashes across their corneas. This is your world we are now having to fight. You are, as far as The Religious Ones are concerned, the same as the soulless clowns, technicians and emotional tourists who have been destroying the world, for the past half-century. You defile God, as well as yourselves. Multiple times a day. You don't even know what that means. And you care even less. Please tell me why I should take you seriously." He looked to Al.

Al winced. Elizabeth was livid. So was Rudra, who did all he could to contain himself. He was staring at the ceiling with great intensity.

Elizabeth was about to be unleashed; she got as far as "I have never…" when Al interrupted.

Al said, "We aren't here to make new friends. We are here out of the realization that we all don't like the way things are headed…"

"Because of them," Chester added. "Their world. Their toys."

"Say it, "Rudra taunted him. "Say it: our 'sins'?"

"Correct."

"I will not be condescended to. Not by some idol-worshipping old-timey creep," Elizabeth spat.

"Neither will I," said Rudra. "Go back to your Holy Lands or wherever you crawled out of. Go back to accidentally murdering babies."

"I was going to say that the one thing you young people have left to you, the one thing that you know how to do, is to turn on a computer. Then I realized that you don't even do that, because it's all turned on for you already, inside you. You ARE computers. You are as trustworthy as a microchip."

"Stop it!" Al shouted at the top of his tired old man lungs. "This is it all over again! This is how the Wars started."

"Hardly," Chester interrupted.

"Shut up," Al said, showing an edge we'd never seen before. "There will be time. After the Revolution. To examine all the mistakes. Chester, you can't deny that the people you represent did more than your share in bringing it on; the whole war. Because you thought you could win it! You thought you'd be whisked off to heaven in some golden Zhyga AirCar! Well, you lost it and here you are. In a room with the only allies you are ever going to see for the rest of your lives. And you kids," Al went on, "stop believing everything you see on your corneas! It's all manufactured! Everything that is being pumped into your head about what happened before the Year 1. It wouldn't even pass as a good movie in 1968!"

Orlinsky motioned to us and we slumped out of there, in silence, aggravated about everything. 'Revolution'? What game were these adults playing? It took all that I had to not walk out early.

But there would be more. The next week.

#

When I was alone, I thought about Chester. When our teacher told us that the Spanish Church in the late 1570s burned over one-hundred-seventy men at the stake because they were suspected of being gay. I wondered how

135

Chester processed these things. Crazy Chester. Did he even know? Or was this not even true?

Would Chester ever stand between me and a mob coming after me? Would he ever protect Aharon?

Or would he be in the mob, smiling?

#

The atmosphere at Al's house was getting wilder. Orlinsky again provided a variety of covers for us, all under the name of investigating how to expand HIVE capacities for The Triumvirate. But when we were in Al's zone, and didn't have to pretend being Fivers anymore, the political discussions that used to be so polite weren't. People were more accustomed to interrupting each other and having thoughts trail off into directions that would be picked up by other people. Loud music played in the background more while people were talking; some people danced. It was music from when Al was our age, loud and churning. The combination of the music, the arguing and the incense felt smothering.

Around me people were arguing with feeling. The exception, of course, was Chester. He would stare straight ahead, registering neither agreement nor disapproval. If you told me he was actually a robot recording the entire proceedings and forwarding the broadcast directly to Wen, I would've believed that. A large part of me expected to be arrested any minute.

Elizabeth seemed to enjoy taunting Chester (or trying to draw him out; I couldn't tell which). She did it more and more each time they were together.

"What do you think, Chester? How are we going to save the world? Same way you tried last time?" Elizabeth floated.

He didn't flinch. "What do you think needs saving?" he asked. "Bank accounts? Privileges? A 'way of life'?"

Rudra said, "What, 'souls,' Chester? Is that what you want to save? In the name of which God? I get them confused. The one with the elephant head, or the one with eight arms? The one who died and then came back? (Oh wait, there were several of those, right?) Or the one whose children sprung from his forehead? We've been studying about you guys, you know, before the Year 1, and I think we all can agree it's not very impressive."

"Do you really think they are going to tell you the truth at CAWS" Chester asked, looking slowly at each one of us. "The whole truth? Has it crossed your mind that they are telling you only the worst? And that the worst might be less than ten percent of it?"

"What if the worst is actually ninety percent?" asked Orlinsky. "Or even fifty-one percent. Are you ready to be held accountable for that?"

"We all have to answer for our actions, individually, at the end of our lives," Chester said. "I don't think of it in terms of numbers. I know I can approach the Lord without fear."

"Yes, of course, because the Lord God is a merciful bugger, isn't he?" said Elizabeth. "He, or She, or It LOVES our sins because it is so much fun to forgive so much and be the Good Guy. Unless, of course, he/she/it is damning us to Hell, which pretty much seems to be exactly we are already living, particularly these days."

"Hell is something you have chosen," Chester said. "You guys can't get enough of it. You created it. It has nothing to do with God. God offers a way out."

"When do things start exploding again?" Aharon asked. "Isn't that what usually happens after Religious Ones, like you, start talking? It sounds so sweet, but it is followed by explosions and flying limbs and blood spurting, right, Chester? Bodies ripped apart 'God is Great! God is Great!'"

"You don't know what you are talking about," said Chester, his face turning flushed. "Disinformation! I guess it works, at least with you juvenile rocket scientists."

Aharon charged at him; Orlinsky got in between them before he could really do anything, but I was wondering what he would have done if he'd been able to. Orlinsky more or less handed Aharon off to Rudra and me to calm him down.

"Don't insult their intelligence," Orlinsky said. "There is enough that your side did to hold you accountable for the next one thousand years. It was...unforgivable."

"So, we shouldn't even be allowed to survive?" he asked, calmly. "Are you planning on betraying us, as many have done?"

"I don't know, is there a big reward for it or something?" Elizabeth asked. "How much?"

"That's not funny," Al interjected. "There were probably thousands who were turned in like that. People who were hiding in basements. For their beliefs. Turned in by neighbors."

"What happened to them?" I asked.

Al, Orlinsky, and even Chester got quiet. "It's complicated," Orlinsky finally said.

"We have a right to know," Elizabeth protested.

"You, actually, don't have a right to know. Legally speaking," Orlinsky responded. "That was determined right before the Year Zero. It was part of the same legislation that brought The New Beginning and the renumbering. It was the Citizen Reassurance Act, and it limited that information to a panel of six."

"You're joking, right?" Elizabeth asked.

"No, I'm serious." Orlinsky answered.

"This isn't helpful, wasting time with this," Al said. "We live in the here and now. We either make progress, make a revolution in the here and now or we perish."

"Then why did we study the Port Huron Statement all the way from the year 1962?" I asked.

Chester spoke up, "That's right, Al, why the sudden change?"

No one said anything.

"This isn't going to be productive," Al said.

"Is it because you and your people were behind The Great Betrayals? Is that awkward to bring up?" Chester asked, taking a step towards the old man. "That you 'revolutionaries' wasted no time in turning people in, giving over names and addresses of safe houses and hiding places? Just to divert the attention from your own sputtering mess? What happened to those people, Al? Where are they now?"

"Decisions are made in the midst of a revolution, on the fly, Chester. It was dog-eat-dog and you know it because your people started it! We weren't ready, conditions weren't right, and you didn't care, because you had God, Allah, Jesus, Krishna, Jehovah on your side. So, you couldn't possibly lose, right, Chester? How much unnecessary suffering did you bring about? How many lives? Or did you not count them, because they had different beliefs than yours? Freedom from belief, Chester! That's what we fought for. I can't believe I even tolerate you in my house. How did you not get betrayed? Or did you, and you are a spy now?"

"Level with the kids, Al! You and your friends used violence even more effectively than us," Chester said.

"I answer to other people, I am motivated by love of other people, not a Gaseous Being sitting in a cloud!" Al screamed at him. "The only reason we keep you here is probably so that we can feel better about ourselves."

"So, I'm a living museum relic?" Chester asked.

"That's a pretty good way of putting it," Al admitted. "You were one of the only ones left who they could find and didn't prosecute." He turned to us. "There were trials. Famous trials. Before the Year 1."

"Show trials," Chester spat. "His people wrote the scripts."

"Informants," Al explained. "They were heavily infiltrated. Beginning in 2021, after the subway massacres."

"It wasn't us," Chester said. "You know that."

"Yes, that's been your story," Al said. "And you've all clung to it."

"Even under torture," said Chester.

"Six subways in one day!" Al raged, eyes blazing. "Children! Mothers!"

Elizabeth finally erupted. "Isn't this what it was like before the Year Zero? Isn't this exactly what it was like? Maybe adding in a few bombs, and poisonings, and hangings, and stabbings, and buildings being burned with people from the other side locked in them? And what is the reason, exactly, that we should use any of you as a frame of reference for our world in the Year 13? Weren't we given the gift of not having to be a part of your ways anymore? Weren't we assured 'happiness, peace and personal freedom from belief'? Isn't that in the Declaration of Emancipation that every school kid has to learn by 2nd grade?"

"That document was the result of a corrupt power grab!" Chester yelled.

"Freedom," Al said. "Finally. Guaranteed in writing."

"What about the Pledge of Allegiance?" he exhorted.

"What is he talking about?" Elizabeth asked.

"An old poem," Orlinsky said. "Before the Pledge of Convergence."

I spoke up, offering, "This gets us nowhere. This is a circle. What are we supposed to do?"

Al turned to look at me. "You are going to be the best little robot Fivers at your school and you are going to win these appointments to the Academy Conclave. You won't be alone, but you can't screw it up. Especially you, Zokaya. Ask yourself, about your pale Dream Girl, what would a Fiver do? And then do that."

They all turned and looked at me. Orlinsky spoke up. "He's right, Zokaya. No room for errors."

The Luminous One

After we got back, I rode my bicycle—her bicycle, actually—over to The Woodpile, a coffee shop she could usually be found at when not in class or with us. The others knew I was going and generally agreed that it'd look suspicious if I stopped trying to see her. It would look like I knew she was a Fiver, and we weren't Fivers.

As I rode up Kristina didn't recognize me the same way she used to, before going over. I was getting used to it. If I didn't know what she felt about me when we first met, I really didn't have a clue now. She greeted me (acknowledged, actually) the way a busy clerk says hello to the next customer. This was our new world—I was The Next Customer.

And that was something I was willing to settle for. Because I was supposed to be flattened/neutralized into a Fiver too, I had to take all my natural impulses and put them through the filter of "Who cares?" It wasn't even like a "Happy! Happy! Happy!" filter; all these Fivers walked around like nothing mattered and everything was merely acceptable, which was enough for them. Maybe we should be calling them Flatliners, I thought to myself. And I had to now imitate one, once again. I was getting used to it. But not really.

"How have you been?" I asked, parking her bicycle on its side.

"As expected," she said. "Fairly busy. You too, I imagine, right?"

"Right," I said. "Are you going to eat lunch? The sandwiches are great here."

"I know how it is here. I am here a lot." She was staring at me in a curious way. I wondered if she knew that I was fake.

"So, are you?"

"Yes," she said.

"Me too," I said.

We ordered and sat in silence. It felt like she knew I was thinking about her, and I knew that she was thinking about me, but nothing was being said. I didn't/couldn't trust the first thing about Kristina, since she went over.

"Have you been adjusting to the climate here?" she asked. "It's certainly not what I'm used to."

"It's good enough," I ventured, lying but guessing what was supposed to be said. "It's no Motherland, though."

"Funny you use that phrase," she said. "Is that how you think of Liberia?"

"One of the ways," I said.

"That is such an antiquated phrase."

I didn't say that that was what is in my heart. I asked, "How do you think of Sweden?"

"East of Norway and west of Finland," she said, eyes probing me.

Kristina was what Al would call "well-armored," even when we first met. I'd never seen someone who seemed to look around with such precision, taking in all of her surroundings, as if she were planning an escape route from the most common of gatherings.

I decided to be quiet and just try to attune myself to the rhythm of her breathing. This is something we'd learned how to do up at Al's house. He said it was better than using words ninety percent of the time.

I don't know what she thought I was doing. In actuality, I was doing nothing. I was breathing. It was more what I wasn't doing: talking.

Even though we were sitting at a table near each other the distance between us was huge. Something in me, though, remembered "us" before we were exiled into these two confused beings. I would wait for the real her to return. But...how long? How would this work? I was supposed to be a Fiver and she actually was one. She tilted her head in a gesture of curiosity. It felt odd at first, but I let myself do it: I put my hand on my heart and looked right into her eyes. I put my other hand there, too.

142

Her eyes grew wider. After a moment she started to move her hand towards me, awkwardly reaching across the table, even though her face was confused. She was looking at her own hand as if it were someone else's. But it looked like she wanted some sort of contact with me, so I took my hand off my chest and moved it towards hers, at half the pace, moving as slowly as I could. As our hands got closer to each other her shoulders began to heave up and down. She was gulping her breaths.

Everyone in the coffee shop stared at us, wondering if I were somehow hurting her, or if she was in a medical crisis.

"Kristina," I said.

She looked at her own hand in horror, saw it near mine and then wailed, a sound I hadn't heard from a human before.

"KRISTINA!" I quickly started forming the letter B with my fingers.

"What are you doing?" she screamed at me.

Then I formed the letter E.

"Why are you doing that?"

"This is the alphabet. Remember? It's what you taught me."

Kristina stood, abruptly held her arms out at her sides, at shoulder level, shaking. She gasped for some air and said, struggling wildly, "Need a good night's sleep! Need sleep!!"

Then she suddenly composed herself, settling her breath in a half-second. Her shoulders relaxed and her hands fell to her side. She sat down again, instantly composed. "It is so important to get a good night's sleep," she said in a perfect Fiver voice.

"I…"

"Don't say anything. Don't," she said.

I quickly left, half-running out the door. I hopped on the bicycle and rode away. It wasn't until much later, halfway back to the dorm, that I realized I might've just blown my cover and that returning to CAWS would endanger everybody. I thought of Orlinsky's last words to me: "No room for errors." No other Fivers were holding their hands over their hearts, trying to connect with others.

Was she obligated to report this?

I'd screwed up. There'd been a fine line and I'd crossed it, forgetting how dangerous this was. I wasn't as good at being fake as I thought I could be.

My brief days as a fake-Fiver were over. I no longer had a home at CAWS.

#

I couldn't stop thinking about the bubbles of air on the beautiful water as I watched men drown in a cage. I couldn't stop hearing the cries of the people who'd witnessed my "play" massacre, before I muted them. Even though I was riding on a bicycle at night thousands of miles away from my real home, it was with peace that I realized I would leave my Affinity Group, leave my classes, the meetings, the strategies, the real-or-fake beheadings, the killing of mothers, the killing of children, the conspiring, the trying to outwit people who were trying to outwit me. I could stop throwing up.

I'd find safe shelter outdoors. I'd camped as a child and California was no scarier than Liberia. I could find a comfortable spot. I'd figure out the rest from there. Kristina was locked off, far away from me, frightened by me. The one person who might've understood my refusal to do this anymore. The person who might've come with me.

I would simply be who I was always intended to be. I would spend no more time in this world of sadness.

It was warm enough to stay in a cave. Even when the afternoon heat cooled off, the nights were bearable. I found a cave small enough to be cozy and undetectable and large enough to avoid claustrophobia. There was a small lake twenty minutes away from the place I found, and the next morning I swam like I hadn't since I was nine years old. The water was cold and I was naked. I wondered how long it would take for Orlinsky, Cote, and everyone at CAWS, to start worrying about me. Or find me.

If it was true, as Al said, that "the body remembers" maybe all I needed to do was to stop actively forgetting my true self every day.

I was still getting retinal updates but found a way to actually look past them, moving my eyes quickly to the upper left corner when I sensed an incoming image-message or a morsel. I found a way of convincing myself that I wasn't even aware of what was being messaged, as if it weren't a part of my body. In a way, it wasn't. I tried to imagine what it was like to live in a time before RU's (retinal updates). My first thought was that people then probably panicked a lot because they didn't know what was going on. Then I thought that maybe they knew what was going on immediately around them just fine, and it was only when it came to events way outside their influence that they were ignorant. Then I thought that *ignorant* was too strong a word. They were in the dark.

But their eyes received the same amount of light as ours, if not more. Ours were dimmed by the updates (though they used an old FruitEdge technique to brighten the darkening, as if it were genuinely illuminated from the outside). I made it my goal to make it through two whole days without paying attention to retinal updates of any kind. When I made it through two days, I aimed for five, and I did it.

The whole first week was about food, money, and comforts at night. I was lucky enough to have a ready supply of money for school, with no one back in Africa able to track what I was really using it for. I took a large amount out figuring the school, or Wen, would start tracking my withdrawals for location shortly. I bought a sleeping bag, a pillow and a blanket, some dry vitamin-foods and an old-fashioned notebook and pen from the retro-Mallmart.

Chester reached out to me, a week later, through a mutual No-Gamer who was said to be alienated by Al's "Revolution Now" crew. The guy found me on one of my shopping trips to a small campground store east of my cave and approached me on the way out of the store to set up the meeting with Chester. He never even told me his name.

It had been nervy of Chester to contact me. If he were to be trusted. There wasn't anything about Chester I liked. He always looked burdened with shame, his head hanging low. But he seemed to be willing to talk more about life before Year 1 than almost any adult I'd met.

He drove up in an ugly charcoal colored Year 5 Zhyga Bion, emerging slowly, swinging the weight of his world around him as he slammed the door and approached, wiping his forehead of the sweat on the sleeve of his shirt, acknowledging me as I approached with a casual nod.

"Very stylish, Chester."

"I try," he said. "At least it's post-Zero." He looked around. All there was a picnic table. We sat at it together, in the middle of nowhere.

"Before we start," he said, "I've got a message for you from your girlfriend."

"Girlfriend?"

"Kristina."

"I might not call her a girlfriend."

"That might be news to her. It was risky of her to contact me. She's a Fiver, you know."

I must have flinched.

"And you took off. They don't know what you are, but they're fearing the worst. You're a wanted man, Zokaya. You might think about going back."

"So, what was her message to me?"

"She said to tell you she remembers the rest of the alphabet. Does that make any sense to you?"

"Yes, it does. Let me ask you a few questions, though."

"OK, shoot."

146

"Do you think she's not a real Fiver or something? Just faking it?"

"You're asking the wrong guy," Chester said. "You all seem fake to me. Even before the game. I can't really blame you, if you haven't been taught any truths. You should know more about what happened and what you're really all at CAWS for."

"We're there to expand the reach of The HIVE, We already know."

"Not exactly. You are there to override basic defaults built into the original design of The HIVE by its designers. To make it a complete two-way system of behaviorally-integrated visual and audio influence. Right now, they're just eating away at it all. People think they're protected. You all were brought in to destroy those protections."

"Go on."

"That's all I know. There's supposed to be a woman in one of the drug enclaves who knows the whole story about it. If you want the truth, go find her and ask. I only know what I know."

"So, talk about what you know. How bad did it get, Chester? Before Year 1. The truth."

"How bad?" he repeated. He looked lost in thought. "It was bad. It just didn't go the way it was supposed to. Repeatedly. It went from bad to worse, to atrocity. Then to vanquished."

"Tell me more."

"There is no point, now."

"So, you were a No-Pointer?"

"No, not then. Maybe now."

"But it's over, Chester. It's all over. Now there IS a point."

"Oh, really?" he said softly, as if to himself. "You know we used to have a prayer that we said before an action, a political action. It went like this:

To the Luminous One, Eternal:
We have turned our backs on you, we know;
We are without merit, and
are about to do wrong.
We have been pushed here,
Insulted and denied, spat on and defiled.
Do not abandon us, your suffering children,
In our hour of need.
There is more to us than our deeds, which may involve wrongs,
And we praise you for remembering us and embracing us in both our
sorrows
and the sorrows we cause.

Chester was quiet. So was I. I'd never heard a prayer before. Who was he talking to? "And then we'd do whatever we wanted," he said, with crispness. "Most often they were the wrong choices. The prayer became something we just mumbled. It might be, looking back, that we were led into it by agents, who were masquerading as us. So, we purged them, or who we thought was them, and the other side publicized that, making us look like maniacs."

"What do you mean 'purged'?"

"We separated them from their authority. Then we separated them from their families. Towards the end, it got worse. There is no point in going into this. It is old propaganda now. You can find it yourself on a dark computer with early-HIVE archives. The documentation is there."

"And accurate?" I asked.

He laughed. "As accurate as any of their version of events before the Year 1. It's all about thirty to forty percent true. But that doesn't mean it's all false."

"What did you do during those years? Why do they call you 'Crazy'?"

"I was the guy who defended those who were accused of being responsible for the purges, in the Tribunals. I had been in law school. I was almost a lawyer. They appointed me to that. They called them war criminals. They found them all guilty. Including my mother and father, whom I wasn't allowed to defend. My mother and father hadn't even been involved. But some people didn't like the things I said."

I didn't want to ask any more. He seemed so sad.

"I might have gone crazy afterwards, towards the end of the war. I don't know. If you go crazy, how do you tell?" He looked at me.

"Do you think you were actually crazy?" I asked.

"I think I was the last sane, intact human they could get their hands on," he said, calmly.

"After all that, why are you still a liaison to The Religious Ones?" I asked. "Don't you hate their guts?"

"Because those who won spared me and my little sister in the madness that followed. The serpent swallowing its own tail. Most of the Religious Ones perished anyway. The survivors are trying to learn from what happened, at least most of them are, and they aren't like the ones who brought on The Dark. That's what we call it now. That, or the Time of Great Error."

"Why do you hang around with Al and that crew?"

"Power," he answered. "We believe he is the one to curry favor with; he may someday end up not just a wild old off-the-HIVE man."

"And that's when you guys make your move?"

"We're out of moves," he said. "We just want to live out our days without being hunted. The ones I represent would settle for several protected encampments. We want to practice our beliefs unmolested. It is how it was supposed to be, a long time ago, before we tried to make everyone the same as us."

"That's the endgame?" I asked. "Protected encampments?"

"The endgame isn't in our hands. It never was," Chester said. "We still believe there is more to all this than little human egos."

"Do you have a wife, Chester?" I asked.

"No. I was married to the cause."

"Did you ever have a girlfriend?"

He hesitated. "I suppose. But she couldn't commit to the cause. I don't want to talk about any of this." He looked at me openly and said, "I don't want to see you fail. You or any of your friends, actually. Even though most of them are egomaniacs. You remind me of us. It is your turn; it is your generation's turn. We screwed up."

We sat in silence. I didn't know what to say to him.

"What can I do to help you?" he asked.

"Keep me connected to Kristina," I said.

Serving Somebody

Al's crew seemed to go silent. Wen released more Quiet Mind lectures retinally, and as far as I knew CAWS kept purring along without me, readying its leaders to plug in seamlessly with the new developments Wen kept teasing at the end of the Quiet Mind lectures.

I started sitting meditation. I heard this phrase at Al's, and I didn't understand it. But maybe it was because I didn't understand it that I was drawn to it. I was also hoping to somehow figure out, through meditation, what it was that had taken over me when I went out and joined the angry crowds, trashing the sex cubicles, screaming to scream. I needed to go deeper.

For all my years I progressed in an orderly path towards things that I understood. Sometimes I understood things far better than those around me. I knew nothing about meditation beyond how you were supposed to sit. Al used to say, "Don't just DO something, SIT there!" So, I did, every morning, usually outside when the sun was coming up. My mind would always wander, particularly at first, but I came to think more (if that is the word) about the way my shoulders felt, the way my breath spread through my chest and the feelings below my belly as I sat on the ground. It was quite peaceful. I found my stride was more purposeful during the day. Al used to yell at us, "Feel your feet, not your retinas!" I felt them, and found I was also feeling my hips, my belly, my pelvis. This was embarrassing at first to feel—(Why had I not felt this way every before?)—then it started feeling normal. Well, better than normal actually. I didn't know what normal was anymore, not since I stepped foot in California.

With so much confusion brewing in the streets and minds of teenagers across the world, I found it odd that it was the feelings in my body that led me to take Kristina's bicycle and keep it as my own. I wanted to feel again what Kristina used to feel in her body when she rode. But I wasn't dead to the fact, though, that anarchy was springing up around us.

I somehow had the belief that I could feel a revolution brewing – one that I never signed up for – if my feet remained in contact with the ground. These were Al's words and Al's concepts, but they were my feet.

And I didn't forget for a second that I was missing/AWOL and being suspected of...espionage?

Retinal announcements about the upcoming World Congress started coming more frequently, and I presumed that Wen was choosing which of the CAWS candidates to send. I was still rooting for my friends even though I couldn't do their rah-rah-hooray-for-our-side revolution (that is what it seemed like to me). Part of me couldn't make Wen the enemy. There was an appealing truth, it seemed to me, to the Quiet Mind campaign. There *had* been too much noise. Even the retinal messages were more soothing than annoying these days, ever since they tweaked the color palates. There were worse things in life than having a soothing message in a pastel color come across part of your field of vision every now and then.

I got it that our life wasn't our own. But this was how we grew up. It didn't make any sense to measure this against the way Chester, Mr. Orlinsky, or Al grew up. We weren't in the same worlds and never had been. While I knew the old ones thought of us as aliens (some of them called us "Modifieds" for a while, right around the Year 1) we were becoming the majority now and we were affectionately known as "Generation 2.0" by the Year 6.

In the past several months, since the whole Level Five transformations had become widespread, bombs started going off with regularity, always in public places, and usually in places only frequented by the Lexi Addicts or homeless. The public was used to bad things happening to the Addicts and the homeless. The news always presented this as unfortunate results of drug-lab experiments on their part ("always craving a purer form of Lexi, using butane torches and chemical") and everyone shook their heads.

Before the bombs going off become commonplace in the addict enclaves schools used to take students—grades 3 through 8—to see for themselves what Lexi could do to people. It was serious stuff. They had hollowed out cheeks and were gaunt, ghostly looking human animals who moved jerkily and could unpredictably leap out at you in violence. The kids were always accompanied by guards with Safe Shield guns. It was usually one of the kids' favorite parts of the field trip, watching an addict get thrown back and covered with immobilizing goo. Kids would cheer and the addict would either get arrested or left to recover on their own after the trip was over. The goo wore off in an hour. Seeing the addict plastered in place by the goo made the kids laugh every time.

We had gotten so used to the bombs going off and wondered only if it was The Religious Ones or Wen behind them. It seemed to go well with the appeal for Quiet Mind; the addicted ones were being destroyed (slowly, then quickly, it would seem) and substance abuse, shown as inferior to quiet reflection.

Three weeks after I left Kristina alone, shaking, Chester had the same middle-man set up a meeting with him in two days, "only if you want to be in on the rest of the story," at a nearby shack in the desert. It wasn't a question, to me, of saying no. Somehow, out of all of this, I would find my way to Wen, and I'd be in possession of important info when I found him. Learning everything I could from Chester was part of this, to me.

The shack wasn't even a house, he said; just a couple of beams with the beginning of a ceiling and tarp walls. But it was secure. Al once told us that the Religious Ones had always been very dramatic; they couldn't just accept the world on the face of it and had to believe they were the authors of an epic judgement that would arrive with symphonic music and bolts of thunder.

Chester looked paler than usual. He truly lacked muscle tone. It was as if he didn't really have a body, or didn't identify with it or something. I couldn't even tell if he was really blobby or skinny. It just didn't seem to enter into who he was. He was half with me all the time and half somewhere else. He did radiate sadness.

"Have you heard from your friends?" he asked me.

"Who wants to know?" I asked.

"Me. I like to follow up. Doesn't it bother you not knowing what they are up to?"

"No," I partially lied. "I don't control it. I don't control them, or you."

"You have to serve somebody," he said.

"What do you mean?" I asked.

"The words of an old spiritual," he said. "A song."

"I don't know. I'm tired of serving anyone," I said. "I am happy experiencing myself right now."

"Ahhh, so you are throwing in with the experience yourself crowd, huh? Very pre-Zero of you."

"What are you wanting, Chester?"

"I want to go home."

"Then why did you come here? Just go home."

We looked out of our shack onto the scrappy expanse of desert. Some small animal skittered.

"I'm not sure how to get there anymore. Sometimes I think it is just in my mind. The longing creates the home. It isn't really a memory. It is something I want."

"Who are you working for these days, Chester? Who is it you are serving?" He smiled.

"Your friends did well. They will be going to the Conclave. They were the chosen ones. Orlinsky is going with them. He wanted you to know."

I wasn't surprised, but I did feel jealous for a moment. "Kristina is the one they are trusting now," he said. "One would've thought it'd be Elizabeth. But Wen likes blondes. Did you know that?" Chester said, smiling. "She's the superstar."

I didn't even like him using Kristina's name.

"That's all you know? That's all you have to tell me?"

"How much else do you want to know?"

"Everything," I said.

"There's a name for a person who wants to know everything, you know."

"What is it?"

"Endangered."

"I have nothing to lose. Neither do you, from the sounds of it. Tell me the rest, Chester."

"How about the Island of The Righteous, then?"

"The what?"

"Island of the Righteous," he said. "Before Zero. Before the year they said that history started. Their dream, a wish that came from the ashes— they kept accounts of many things. But not all things. The Island of The Righteous went so wrong they didn't even acknowledge it before history began again."

"Was it a real island?" I asked.

"Oh, yes, it was real. Just because something isn't known about doesn't mean it isn't real."

"That sounds religious," I said.

"That's not a word we generally use," he said. "We just call it true. Anyway…after what they called the Terror Campaigns were crushed— through what they called 'extra-legal' technologies—they identified all the remaining living fundamentalists who had ever hinted at imposing their religions on the world. Most of them were killed resisting arrest, they said.

There were never any photographic or video evidence of these arrests, though, so many of us felt this was a case of a cop killing someone they just didn't like because they reached for their gun."

"Was it possible they really were? Reaching for their guns?"

"Oh surely. Some were. Reaching for their gun, their knife, their grenades, their bombs. Some. I heard some blew themselves up taking the police out with them. Romantics. It doesn't bother them than they're not around anymore. What is that saying? 'The first casualty in any war is the truth?' Anyway, those who remained alive were sent to the Island of The Righteous."

"Who came up with the name?"

"TriSec."

"The ones they sent: were they terrorists? Or just…fundamentalists?"

"Oh, at that point they stopped asking that question," he said. "I don't think you understand how much the world had grown tired of that distinction. They just said, 'We know one when we see one and the world is better with them isolated on an island off the coast of Greenland.' They regularly dropped in warm clothes, limited building supplies, modified tools that couldn't be used for weapons, protein powders, water, milk…and they didn't pay any attention to anyone's dietary restrictions based on old superstitions or customs. They simply had to either eat what they were given, or starve."

"What happened?"

"An enormous amount chose to starve. To death. You have to understand, this was an experiment in real time, whether it was intended as such or not. There were Hindus, there were Muslims, there were Christians, there were fundamentalist Buddhists from the Far East, there were Jews, there were Scientologists, there were Baha'i, there were Sikhs, there were Mormons."

"How many?" I asked.

"32,513. When we came back a year later, there 21,050. Two years later there were 650 people left alive. They had given rise, apparently, to their own Religious Wars. The Shiites and the Sunnis almost completely destroyed each other first, the Mormons were decimated quickly, there were no more Jews left, most of the Christians were gone. The largest groups left were the Sikhs, the Scientologists, and the Bahai. Oh, and the Unitarians. It wasn't clear who killed whom. Take the Jews: when they were all gone everyone pointed their fingers at the other groups. Though the housing had been set up in the beginning to house everyone together, that was defeated within the first month. People chose to freeze to death rather than live together in warmth with the other groups."

"And what was your role in this?"

"I was working with the faction that would become the first government in Year Zero. We transitioned that to "Year 1." I was the Liaison to The Believers. That was my title. I had to go in and do the head count every year. I saw the bodies. Some groups had their enemies' heads impaled on long sticks in front of their compounds. Even the Unitarians and Baha'i."

"Didn't they know this would happen?"

"They were pretty sure. People at work had a betting pool going, which group would go out first. A lot of people lost money on the Shiites going out before the Jews and on the Buddhists being next. That was a bit of a surprise."

"Did they all kill each other?"

"No. Isn't that odd? They actually put together a group, called the Council of Convenience, that schemed together. They signed protocols, all of which were supposed to expire ninety-six hours after their supposed liberation and return to the mainland. They did what they always did; plan for a day that would never come."

I thought about people making bets about other people's' lives. These were the Founders of the Year 1.

"They all died finally?"

"No. Two people got out. There was a rumor about a third—we used to call him The Holy Ghost—but it was just two."

"Two left alive out of 32,000?" I asked.

"32,513."

"How did the two escape?"

"They killed the police officers who came with me for a head count in the last year. They held me hostage and were exceptionally inventive upon our return from the island, enabling an escape. I did the first year and three months in jail before they released me on appeal in Year 2. The government accused me of aiding and assisting. I got experts to agree that I'd been traumatized. I mean, they'd cut off my finger to show they were serious." He held up his left hand, showing four fingers. "But here's the thing," he said, looking up. "I wasn't really traumatized. I liked those two. A Bahai, and a Unitarian. They are out there still, hiding. Good people. Not killers. But they killed. They never belonged there in the first place. They call themselves The Witnesses. I was not traumatized, my friend, I never was. But they were. Not the same people who went in."

Chester was done. "I don't believe I will be seeing you again," he said. "Those who needed me, who used me, have no more need for me and they don't trust me. They know whom I've met with and that means they will move against me shortly. You are all at personal risk. Change your locations, future meeting times and means of communication. Someone in your organization is likely an informer. Don't use violence or torture to find them, though, or else you'll become just like the other side. Consider breaking up into smaller groups. Oh, and trust no technology. Ever."

He looked at me with eyes more compassionate than I'd seen in any man other than my father. "If you find the Witnesses, tell them I had nothing but love for them in my heart the entire time. The Island was never my idea. It was the sadistic invention of the worst of us."

#

Chester left me with a package of money. Lots of it. I stashed most of it in my super-secret place (a can of beans that I'd emptied but looked unopened when it was part of a row of other old cans in an abandoned desert house Chester had tipped me off to.)

On the seventh day I went into town, as arranged, and looked for Kristina, scouting out The Woodpile. I waited an hour and forty-five minutes before she arrived, in a Zhyga taxi. I looked to both ends of the block and the surrounding area behind me to make sure this wasn't a trap and she hadn't been sent as a lure before I moved. When I was convinced she was really alone, and not being followed, I walked in. She was sitting by a table in the back. She was seemed startled to see me as I approached the table and asked her if I could sit.

"Everyone is looking for you," she said.

I didn't say anything. Even though she was in a sharply-pressed drab-gray outfit, I could still see elements of the young woman I'd first met. She could pull down the edges of her mouth to flatness, but I still saw her natural radiance. She seemed alarmed that I wasn't saying anything.

"Are you OK?" she asked. "Are you getting enough sleep?"

"I don't want to talk about sleep," I said. "I want you to come with me."

"Where?"

"I'm not sure."

"That doesn't sound wise," she said, turning her head at a strange angle.

"Why don't you care about sleep?" she asked.

"I've had too much of it," I said. "Over the years. I'm inviting you to come with me?"

She seemed to think about it, if just for a second. "I don't think so," she said. She eyed me carefully. "What should I tell your friends when they ask about you?"

"I don't care."

"People are wondering if you are a spy."

"For who?"

"Not sure. But they're looking for you."

"What do you think? You think I'm a spy?"

She looked at me and was silent.

"Did you turn me in?" I asked flat-out.

"Is there something bad you've done that I don't know about?" It was as if she didn't remember our last encounter.

"I tipped an old vending machine once, at a Retro Mallmart and got a free Kit-Kat Bar." (This was true. Kit-Kat Bars were big ever since Year 6.)

"Do you know you've changed?" I asked. "Since Level Four? Can you tell?"

She looked sad and very confused.

"Don't you remember when we sat together, listening to the sounds around us. You might not remember any of it, but a small part of you does. The insects? Could you just…hold my hand? Could we just do that?"

She sucked in her breath and looked me in the eyes, trying to decide. I put my hand out on the table, next to her coffee. She looked from side to side quickly, then back at my eyes, then finally, after obvious effort, let her hand touch mine. She began inhaling deeply and slowly letting her breath out.

"We're going to the Conclave," she said. "We are reshaping things."

"Reshaping is what needs to happen, right?"

She seemed confused for a second. "We are here for the benefit of the world. We are privileged to serve. It isn't about me or you. Those are things of the past. We are the fortunate ones who sleep well. We owe it to the others to give all of ourselves to the creation of Quiet Mind."

That was the first time I'd heard it put that, well, simply. It made sense: give all to HIVE Mind. Simple. Quiet Mind. Coming from Kristina's lips it even sounded beautiful. I focused on her lips, not what she was saying. After a moment she seemed to sense that I was looking at her lips and she stopped talking. And she looked at me, and my lips. She looked completely unsure. We both stayed in place, quietly.

"Let's go explore," I said.

"I need to..."

"I know...be back soon. Let's find a good tree. And sit under it. There are a few of them around."

"Staying alive in the desert. Not easy."

"They don't just stay alive. They thrive. They've adapted."

We walked next to each other, me walking her bike till we found a tall, old, trove of juniper trees. I rested her bike against one and we sat down underneath the old tree.

"I'm tired," I said. "Of being alone."

"We're never alone."

"I don't feel that way. I feel very alone."

She was quiet.

"I forget what it feels like to mean anything to anyone," I said.

"Did we ever know that?" And – after the briefest pause – she leaned over and kissed me, deeply, on the lips. I kissed back, opening my mouth to her.

"You're a Fiver, Kristina. And I'm not."

She took a moment to take this in. "Hold me?"

I did. I held her loosely at first. Then tightly once she moved to nuzzle into me more.

"Why does this feel right? Is it right, or not right?"

161

"It is the only thing that is right," I said.

We held each other the rest of the day, and all night long. She cried and cried and cried. I don't know how many hours went by or how much we slept. She howled, at one point, confused and sad. "We need to sleep well! We need to be asleep! Right now!! Now—SLEEP!!" I helped her cry, watching her chest and belly rise and fall. I wiped away tears with my t-shirt. The more we stayed up, the closer she nestled into me.

After more crying she rose and threw up. Repeatedly. She threw up three times in a row. I wasn't repulsed. My heart opened more to her. I helped her brush her teeth and spit out and held her while she cried some more. "What is wrong with me?" she asked.

"I think you are coming out of Level Five," I said.

We did the grounding exercises Al had shown me, There was no getting away from our bodies. "These are our feet. These are our thighs, these are our hips, these are our genitals, these are our bellies, these are our hearts…We are alive, in the Year 13. We are here, together."

Kristina and I were free, in a way neither of us had known before. We fell in together in excited timelessness, ascending. There are still no words to describe this. We were no longer apart.

As the night turned into the beginning of morning, we adjusted our positions, sprawled out in each other's arms. She sat up, abruptly, with a sharp intake of breath, causing me to wake and do the same. I opened my eyes.

We both received the same retinal message, at the same time, in an impossibly bright orange color: "You may have just had an unwelcome sexual contact. Unwelcome sexual contacts can be disturbing. Please know that counseling is available, as well as legal recourse, through your CAWS social worker, to help you through what may be a difficult time. Common symptoms associated with unwelcome sexual contacts include: headache, confusion, and sleeplessness. Come into CAWS and make an appointment to see one of our trained counselors today."

"They know," she said.

No Teachers, No Students

Elizabeth, Rudra, Aharon, and Kristina were in; they were the designated attendees/representatives at the Wen Conclave, just as planned. They were consummate fake Fivers and nothing Kristina could do now could upset that. All that they knew of Kristina and me, as far as we knew, were fake reports of "unwelcome sexual contact." Generated by physical touch? We weren't certain of the dimensions of the feedback that retinal implants provided but I told her what both Orlinsky and Chester had told me: that there were still governmental disagreements and committee protocols that blocked full user feedback to the government, beyond several areas (these being terrorism, contact with underground Religious Ones—Chester didn't apply, as he was ex-government himself—and carriers of Ebola or other government-designated infectious diseases) The warning Kristina and I had received could have been auto-generated and of less concern that it initially felt.

Kristina wasn't buying it. "What if we made a big mistake?" she asked.

"By hugging? Can't we just take a minute to feel that it was good? Really good?"

She nodded.

"Let's live with that for a moment, instead of in fear."

"Really, REALLY, REALLY good," she said. "What happened to me? I mean, before yesterday? How did I get so far away? I felt terrible. I mean, not at the time, but now I know I did."

"They zapped you. You and the others. Millions of you. Level Five. You played *Hell on Earth* and crossed over."

"That's what it is?" she asked. "Really? The game?"

"Yeah. Complete addiction. To the point of possession. They still believe they have you."

"How come? And who are 'they'?"

"It's Wen. And someone, or many others. But Wen is at the heart."

165

"Quiet Mind?"

"Fascism. The opposite of freedom."

"I thought that was Religion."

"I don't know. I just know that I think it has started with the Substance Abusers. They are disappearing, fast."

"Is that really bad?" she asked.

"It depends on who you are. If you are them it is catastrophic. But Wen is counting on most of the rest of us just being happy about it. Maybe that is how it starts. Things that make most people happy."

"Does *Hell on Earth* make people happy?" she asked.

"Did it make you happy?" I asked. "You went to Level Five."

"It wasn't about happy," she said. "It was like…must play, must play.'"

"How was that any different from the Substance Abusers?" I wondered.

"Because…it was a game? I don't know," she murmured. "Because it was harmless."

"Well…you have to go back to it. You have to leave me and go back. That is without question, Kristina. They can think I'm on the run—in fact, it helps if they do—but they have to know that you are a good old Fiver, and a cheerleader for their team. You are going to the Conclave."

"I don't want to leave."

"You have to. Our success depends on it."

"What do you think, and feel, we trying to do?" she asked.

"Bring it all down," I answered, for the first time putting it all together myself. "Bring it all down."

"They're going to ask where I was."

"Tell them you were with me," I said.

"They'll look for you and try to arrest you," she said, tearing up.

"They won't find me. I'll find them," I said.

#

Kristina left. I gave her bicycle back. We agreed to give them the very coordinates of where we'd been together, when they asked, but not till the day after tomorrow. She would feign confusion and upset and sleeplessness until then. I would've taken off on the bicycle by then. I was getting good with caves.

I also told her to confide in Orlinsky. He would help her be the double agent we needed.

#

The World Conclave had been retinally-advertised for months now as "Meeting of the Quiet Mind, Convergence of the Spirit." Whatever that meant. It was on Catalina Island. I would go nowhere near it. That's what I thought. I would lead them on a wild goose chase and let them think that the challenge to come would be through some sort of revival of The Religious Ones. I would seek out The Witnesses. They were the perfect diversion. I presumed they were already being tracked to the best of the Triumvirate's abilities and that I, too, was being carefully tracked. It wasn't like I was putting anyone at greater risk. At least, that is what it seemed like to me at the time.

Chester had given me a coded list of No-Gamers' safe houses and towns, and one was in bicycling distance. I bicycled at night; the blistering heat had begun to cool off by then, and I came to like it.

When I got to the first safe house a wary-looking girl named Cheyanne half-opened the door. I said I was a friend of Chester's and gave her the code ("You have to serve somebody") before she opened the door and let me in.

"One of the crummiest Dylan songs," she said turning her back and walking me upstairs.

"Who?" I asked.

"Bob Dylan. Last century. Used to write good songs, and then…stuff like that. Went from the Jehovah cult to the Jesus cult."

"What if he was right?" I asked.

She turned and looked me in the eyes. "Look, I don't know you and I'm telling you that we don't play games here. If you are one of The Religious Ones you can get back on your bike and keep on riding after we feed you, OK? If you're in your right mind, you can stay."

I thanked her and assured her the only one I was serving was myself right now. She liked that.

She introduced me to Warren, a too-skinny guy in his late twenties, who looked me up and down critically. "If we find out you are a spy, you know we might have to imprison or kill you. Did you know that?"

It hadn't really crossed my mind.

"Well, I'm not a spy," I assured him. "Wouldn't know the first thing about how to go about being one."

"Good. Then I've got a message for you from Orlinsky: check your retinal messages. He's pissed that you keep ignoring them. Says wake up and smell the coffee, whatever that means."

I scrolled retinally up and back and saw there were three days messages of basically the same thing: "It has come to our attention that you may have been a victim or perpetrator of an unwanted sexual contact incident, which could include possible allegations of assault and/or rape. Please report to Office 101 in CAWS within the next five days and undergo a debriefing with our trained counselors or respond as to why you cannot come in."

"What do they have you for?" Warren asked.

I didn't speak.

"Sex or drugs? They use one or the other, usually. They can't just SAY they are going after No-Gamers. Unless they have you for terrorism. But…you'd be dead by now if that is what it was. TriSec would've brought you down. They're still confused about sex. They are glad, on the one hand, it keeps young people distracted and no one gets pregnant now without permission. But they don't like when it is the wrong people getting happy."

"Is that why they went after the Substance Addicts?" I asked, guessing.

"Could be. A lot of them were No Gamers, too, by the way."

"Do you have any idea where The Religious Ones hang out?" I asked.

"I don't know. Churches?" he laughed. "Synagogues? Mosques?"

"There aren't any."

"I know. It was a joke," Warren said. "There is a safe house about 18 miles from here that allowed several of them to stay with the No Gamers. It's a personal call; they needed shelter. I told them they could get screwed, to move on. I lost my father in the subway massacres, I couldn't stand the sight of them, didn't want them around here."

"Are you certain that was really them? That they were the ones who did it?"

"I'm certain my father is dead. And that they didn't disavow it after it happened and a press release was issued in their name. That's enough for me to know."

"How did you find all this out?" I asked.

"Word of mouth. They call it oral history. Sounds sexier than it is. The theory is if it can't be written down, it can't be stolen or denied. I hold those fucks responsible for ninety-nine percent of everything you are seeing today. Why? You going to join them?"

"No. I'm not a joiner. But I want to find a few of them."

"Who? You looking for a rabbi or something? Want a kosher hot dog? Good luck with that." Warren seemed to be enjoying his own sense of humor.

"No. I want to meet The Witnesses."

He stopped moving and stared at me. "The odds are good they are already dead. Otherwise, they are spotted as often as California unicorns. If I were them, I'd hide in Cleveland, or Wisconsin or some North Dakota hellhole. You think you can find them out around here? Because, why? Because the HIVE is centered here? That's what we call 'counter-intuitive,' y'know?"

"I know. They might be in Cleveland. You might be right. That would be the logical thing to do. But these people don't work that way, by logic. They'll be wherever their faith tells them to be," I said.

"Well, by that measure you've got a whole big world to investigate, my friend, and a few other ones as well."

#

It took me two and a half days to get to the house Warren told me about. For some reason I was balking. The Witnesses knew at least a part of the way forward. I was to tie The Witnesses and their knowledge into whatever plans Orlinsksy and his allies had in place for the Conclave. In quiet moments, I just had the feeling that I was somehow lost without The Witnesses, even though this made no sense. That I wanted their input or direction. That they were somehow my parents.

When I sobered up, I realized I must just be working up naive sympathy for war criminals.

I scouted the place from several directions over the course of a long day. At first, I just rode past it with my hoodie on. Then I walked past it. Finally, I watched it from a nearly invisible spot laying low in the brush across the street.

That's when I saw Warren walking out, holding his ear and talking into something. By his side was Cheyanne. Only this time her hair was up and she was in a professional looking suit. She didn't look the least bit like she had before.

I slowly found my way onto my bike and quietly rode straight away from there.

It was a trap. A set-up. They wanted me. It was just a matter of time before they got me.

But I had work to do first.

#

Turning myself in (for whatever kind of moral re-education they had planned for my alleged crime with Kristina) would offer several advantages. I didn't know what technologies they had and how close they were to effectively tracking me, but it was logical to think they'd get me soon even if I ran. If they caught me as a full-blown rebel, who knows how would deal with these things nowadays?

Turning myself in would also maintain my status as a Fiver, albeit one who erred in what they saw as rebellious in the predictable, teenage ways. Even they must've known the particular charges against me were false, and just a ruse to get me back. It would also put me back in the heart of the Revolution. Orlinsky would be able to guide me.

Most importantly, by turning myself in, I would be near Kristina. The fears I had about my "effect" on her wearing off and her returning to "good-little-Fiver" status could be gone if we could even periodically make eye contact and reinforce our connection. But turning myself in meant not finding The Witnesses, something I knew I had to do. Not just as a diversion to their Conclave plan, but because I *had* to.

I would take my chances. But first, I wanted to get a note through to Kristina. The only secure way, these days, was to hand write and give it to her. That would be stupidly risky, so I decided to give it to someone else to give to her.

I stayed a block away from the CAWS campus for two days, scanning to see who came and went. My best shot, I thought, was the maintenance workers, who went in at 6 a.m. and came out at 2:15 p.m. I had my choice, actually, as the 6 a.m. shift seemed to offer two young workers and a man who definitely looked like he wasn't from around here, or anywhere close to here. He met his co-workers inside the fence in the same parking area every morning and, being skinny and short, didn't appear to be a threat, should things turn bad.

On the morning of the third day I saw his car coming down the street and stood in the middle of the street, both my hands outstretched, signaling him to stop. He did, and I walked over to him as he lowered the car window.

"I need a favor," I said.

"Who are you?" he asked.

"It doesn't matter. What matters is that this letter get to one of the students at CAWS without anyone else seeing it. Could you do that? I mean, I know you COULD do it, but…would you?"

"Are you a troublemaker?" he asked. "One of the ones on HIVE News?"

I paused, taken a little off-guard. "That's a hard thing to answer. You know? It's all relative. Have you ever been a troublemaker?" I asked

His eyes flashed and seemed to twinkle. "Oh yeah," he said. "Back in the day…"

"Will you do this for me? And keep it quiet?"

"It's not about violence, is it?" he asked.

"No," I said. "It's a boy-girl thing."

"Oh, sure, a boy-girl thing, no problem, Boss. That's the natural order of things. Right?"

"What's your name?" I asked him.

"Sammy," he said.

"Nice to meet you, Sammy. I'm Zeke. We've got to wrap this up quickly. Here's the letter. I'm asking you, from my heart, to just give it to her," I said.

"Who?" he asked.

"Oh, yeah, right," I said. "Sorry. Her name is Kristina. She's…"

"You mean, The Old Fashioned Girl?"

"Please, put this in her hands? And don't trust anyone else to do that for you?"

"Surely, son," he said. "How do I reach you if she wants to send something back?"

"You can't right now," I offered. "I'll contact her again."

He scanned me for a moment before asking, "You okay, son?"

I kind of bristled at being called that. "As good as it gets," I said, truthfully.

"Watch yourself, son," he said. "Know yourself, too."

#

Here is all my note said:

Kristina –

We are on this ride together, and we have slept well.

Trust the ones who are to be trusted.

Feel the earth beneath your feet and sky above our heads. Feel all that is between.

Don't believe anything you hear about me that doesn't come from Orlinsky.

We will see the rise of the desert sun, together, soon.

Destroy this.

I'll check in with Sammy at some point soon.

Z.

I wasn't ready to turn myself in yet. I bought an almost-new pup-tent down at the Substance User's enclave 8 miles from CAWS. It wasn't much more than a tarp. You secured it by tying it in between two trees. It would've been possible to hang out with the Substance Abusers, but I wasn't going to stay there. The local schools continued to do field trips there and the fewer people who saw me, the better. I returned to the desert.

The quietness at night was shocking at first. Just so much nothingness. I found myself waiting to hear cars or footsteps approaching, sometimes even believing I had heard such in the middle of the night. After a few scares my ears adjusted to a level of sound that lived beneath the usual din I listened to. There was the hum of insects, punctuated by chirps and whirring noises as small animals moved around at night. I knew some of these could be snakes or even scorpions. I wondered if I'd be able to distinguish their sounds from the friendly mammals I'd hoped would be my company. I wanted my hearing to get so good that I could hear the soft tapping of tarantulas' feet, but I didn't want to put this to the test.

The stars were fantastic. I imagined generations of my ancestors looking up at the same mystery. The sky came together with the ground in a way that made me feel tucked in on both sides. My sleeping bag and pup tent were more comfortable than my bed at CAWS had ever been.

Even though I was unsettled by the prospect of being brought into some sort of therapeutic custody for the sexual contact Kristina and I had, I'd also never felt more settled and happy in my life. Maybe it was the opportunity to think for myself without interference.

No teachers and no students. And I was even able to completely ignore my retinal alerts, suggestions, and color-coded advisories, through a series of swiping-away gestures I'd now mastered. I don't know what they'd been saying. There was a delicious freedom in not caring anymore.

#

In the end there is only kindness, or unkindness. Unkindness could include indifference and emotional detachment as well, of course, as viciousness and violence. It is all the same though: failure to manifest being the highest level of being human.

Once we, as a species, became internally wired and HIVE-connected, we did not automatically become unkind. It was slower than that. In the few years since Year 1 we have allowed stimuli to repetitively trigger our hungry pleasure-seeking brain-receptors to the point where the content didn't matter. In receiving and processing the stimuli we whetted our appetite for more of the same. To the point where it was no longer scratching an itch, but remembering to HAVE the itch so that we might scratch it.

Hell on Earth was more than logical. It was the culmination of what we'd slowly been working towards, since the end of The Religious Wars. Once our physical safety was again guaranteed, *Hell on Earth* was logical and inevitable. It was just more of the same.

The ones who resisted the hunger for the next HIVE-wired brain buzz or computer game were, ironically, the Substance Abusers who existed in enclaves. They had their own hungry itch/scratch cycle based on body-cravings, but it didn't seem the same as the brain-based ravages of cruelties, rapes, beheadings, torture, and treachery that *Hell on Earth* had quickly accustomed us to. Maybe I was just naive.

Perhaps some of the best of the No-Gamers had gone to lose their bodies and minds there, instead of here. Everyone defends their Buzz. To the end.

<u>Cady</u>

The Lexy D users (Lexium Deoxyphosphate, technically), lived in a semi-sanctioned enclave on the far side of Sausalito. Though it was only about three miles from the heart of the wealthy part of town, it wasn't recognizable as any place commonly seen in Year 13. It seemed to pride itself on being dangerously retro, outdoing even the Retro Mallmarts in music and styles from the year 2020. Auto-tuned waify-looking female singers wailed over actual speakers to an electronic beat (music had gone back to an 80/20 male/female ratio in Year Zero, and it was rare to hear a headlining woman anymore.) I can't say I liked the retro sound.

Not all who lived there were Lexy D users, or LD-heads as they were known. There were some old-time alcoholics and some kids who just scrambled around trading and popping any pills they could get their hands on. ("Blue! Blue! Who wants blue!" I heard being shouted.) There were a lot of mood-altering recreational things floating around since before the days of The Religious Wars, apparently, which people just referred to as vintage surfing. It wasn't clear to me how this community supported itself—some people were selling things from their tents but there were no real stores and no one seemed to go to work in the morning.

These people existed here as if they'd always been here, like the rocks and weeds of the canyons. They seemed like a distinct species, relative to the kids at CAWS and the rest of the civilized world. I imagined them descended from a long line of drug-imbibing generations, but that didn't really make sense: most of the previous generations probably died off without raising too many kids. Whatever kids there were, I imagined, had died or left.

Did each generation get its own LD-heads? From where? Weren't these people HIVE-wired, like us? Where did they go wrong?

They accepted me and set me up in a tent that had been abandoned by a guy named Barstool Bob, who had left the day before. People came and went, but the tents stayed. They smelled pretty raunchy, the tents, but they were strong enough to keep out the elements.

It wasn't known where people who had left actually went—it was kind of bad form to express too much interest in that, really, though there seemed to be upset that the rate of people just disappearing from the community was on an uptick. This girl, Ariel, told me two old guys had been set upon by some vicious teenagers, who threw M-120 firebombs at them and then beat them when they ran (obviously in the days before Level Five had been achieved).

What no one could explain, though, is why explosives continued to go off after Level Five had been attained. Not just in Sausalito, but in Chico, Oakland, Palo Alto, Los Angeles, and San Diego. There had been sixteen people killed in three different attacks (they were small) just here; no one knew how many attacks in total there were.

And then there were all those who had left the enclave without much explanation.

The major accomplishment, Ariel said, in the past year was the introduction of smokable LD. It was a more immediate high and was more social than pills. You could sit around and pass the pipe. LD wasn't habit-forming, she said, but it didn't seem like anyone who had started it had ever quit. And more than a few had gone on to do Ortho-Molly (or OM for short). "OM is some pretty serious shit," Ariel volunteered, sucking down some LD and passing the pipe to me.

"No thank you," I said. She picked it up again quickly and took another hit.

"OM is for, like, the serious thinkers, you know…the veterans of the scene. The Elders." She laughed, huskily. "OM takes you onto the Other Plane. Whereas LD just makes things on this plane much more relaxed, you know what I'm saying? Like things are still here, but they are not exactly here, in the same way, with Lexy D. With OM, things aren't even there. You are in a different land."

She started laughing, then started laughing about her laughing, as if she could see herself sitting here in the Year 13 and it was hilarious.

"What if we're not intended to relax this much?" I asked. "What if we're supposed to do the opposite? To change things?"

"Change things?" She started laughing harder. You've got to get humble, Brother. This is all much bigger than us. What are you going to change? What?!!!? You only live once, brother, and you either learn to relax or you don't. If you don't, you are one of them."

"And what are 'they'?" I asked.

"All…technological."

"You're HIVE-wired just like we are," I pointed out.

"True, but Lexy lets you ride the waves of that. You just look at it and laugh." She laughed again. "I mean, the retinal alerts, Predictive Friend, SCRAPS, color schemes, relationships…they're all real only if you give them consent, y'know? I mean, you still get them broadcast to you, but…so what? Once you've awakened."

"And drugs awaken you?"

"Hell, yes, my HIVE-Brother-from-another-mother. You make it sound BAD. Do you know how many chemicals are in your system already? Anyway??? A hundred years' worth? From your parents? And their parents? Plastics, chemicals, antibiotics, cancer-causing, gene-altering shit? Where are you getting your information from? What we are doing is just controlling which chemicals we agree to put into ourselves. What you are doing is going with their factory-installed default package. We are customizing. And it works just fine, as far as I am concerned."

"You like living like this?" I asked, looking around.

"You're here right with us, aren't you?" she asked, blowing out smoke from another hit. "Obviously you didn't like living where you were. You left it! We all make compromises. These are the most honest ones, for me. I like these people. My people."

"Is there anyone you left behind?" I asked. "Someone you had feelings for, who didn't come with you?"

There was a flicker across her face, before she pulled herself back together. "No," she said. "I don't miss anyone who isn't here. All there is is HERE, now. the rest is illusion. Some HIVE-induced fantasy."

"You are still part of the HIVE," I said.

"In YOUR mind," she said. "Not mine."

#

I have a high tolerance for weirdness. I knew children who liked to play with chimpanzees their age more than other children, and I knew people who ate dirt (when they had real food around, too). But I wasn't prepared for Cady.

Cady walked into my tent when I was in my underpants, getting changed. Instead of saying, "Sorry, excuse me," she threw down her beaten-up backpack in an open space on the other side of the small tent and started peeling off her shirt.

"Oh, jeesh, I'm rank," she said, sniffing her armpits. "Where's the shower?"

I found myself torn between answering her and telling her to get the fuck out of my tent. I watched, though, as she took off her boots, then peeled off her pants. Standing there in her flimsy tiny panties didn't seem to bother her at all.

"There's a shower, I just need to know where it is."

"Who are you?" I asked. "Why are you in my tent?"

She walked over to me, extending her hand. Her breasts were beautiful. "Nice to meet you, whoever you are. And it's not your tent. There's no private property here. It's our tent now. They told me you had space."

180

I'd never met a woman just in her panties before.

She walked outside the tent and I heard her shouting around, "Who knows someone with a shower? What do you do for cleanliness around here? Anyone? Anyone know how to get clean?"

Some guy ran up to her and said he knew a place. She came back in to grab her backpack, flashed a quick smile, and walked away, turning only to say, "Sometimes you just have to ask."

I asked this guy named Bones, who'd been standing near me and saw the whole thing, who she was. Bones said "Some kind of big shot."

"Big shots get showers?" I asked.

"Bodies like THAT get showers," he answered, laughing.

"That doesn't sound very communal," I observed.

"Not meant to be. We're just a bunch of LD-heads and Elders trying to get through the day. Doesn't mean we're not human…or human-HIVE hybrids, or whatever everyone else is these days."

"Why is she a big shot?"

He sparked up some LD and slowly drew it to his lips. After a deep inhale and luxurious exhale of smoke he said, "That's a mystery, Brother. You live here, you just accept the mysteries. My guess is some kind of mission."

"Like…Religious Ones mission?"

Bones laughed. "No. Those days are over. Anyone thinks that way anymore has either learned to keep it to themselves or are dead." He clicked on some Retro music, pre-Zero, strings plucking, nasal singing, shapeless noodling sounds. Played from a Music All Day (M.A.D.) chip (still available at Retro Mallmarts, though not the original edition, just a remake) through a small speaker he carried on his hip. I couldn't make out the words clearly. Something about a cabin. It seemed to please him. "Some people didn't mind dying, I'm told. Some of the real-deal Religious Ones, y'know, they'd been working towards it for a long time. I think they were disappointed the whole world didn't disappear on their announced schedule, y'know? So, they did they next best thing and made sure they disappeared themselves. Some blew themselves up, but many just let themselves be taken, or made believe they had a weapon and were going to use it. The Triumvirate wasn't taking any prisoners, it's been said, not once they decided you were a terrorist. They'd blow your head off and ask questions later, if at all. And that worked out fine for many of the Religious Ones. Suicide by State…" Bones sucked in another hit after offering it to me and being waved off.

"How do you know any of this?" I asked.

"My father. My grandfather. My mother. My grandmother. It's the only way you can really know anything."

We were quiet. He didn't seem to care why I was there, or, really, who I was. I've never seen someone so completely accepting of his surroundings, so unquestioningly there as Bones was in this moment.

"How do you make sense of all this?" I asked.

"What part of 'all this'?"

"The years since your parents passed," I said, taking a good guess.

He took his time to answer, looking from side to side first and then looking off straight ahead. "Nothing to be done," said Bones. "Nowhere to be."

#

Cady came back from her shower smelling like sandalwood, having obviously found hair conditioner, as well. She burst into the tent unceremoniously and tossed her things down again.

"Where'd you go?" I asked. "Five-star hotel?"

"No. Some guy knew this house that was abandoned when the owners ran off to join the No-Gamers."

"Since when do you have to 'run off' to join the No-Gamers?" I asked. "I thought that was more of a stay-at-home thing."

"Shows where you've been," she said. "Maybe you don't exactly have your hand on the pulse of this place yet."

"This place?"

"Post-America. Post-terror. Post-history. Nuevo Paradiso. Land of Simple Minds and Fat Asses."

"That sounds kind of harsh," I ventured. "Where've you exactly been?"

"Grand Rapids, Milwaukee, Charlotte, Durham, Hot Springs, Kansas City, Denver, Flagstaff. Then here."

"You on some sort of mission?"

She paused. "You might say that. What about you? This isn't the kind of place that does many foreign-exchange student projects, y'know? Are you just very interested in altering your mind chemically? Or?"

"No. I'm actually not that interested in my mind these days. I've overdone it with my mind. I got a lot of mileage out of it, but it is offering limited returns these days. I'm paying more attention to the landscape. And my body."

"Oooh, that sounds kind of exciting," she said. "Finding what you need?"

"What do you mean?" I asked.

"To bust out of your head? Actually, it's not really your head anymore. Just like this tent; remember I said there was no private property here? Well, your head isn't really private anymore either. Not since getting wired. We basically all had about six days in unaltered human form on this planet before our heads weren't ours anymore. Wired on the seventh day, nowdays, and it's never been the same since. Suggestions, colors, adjustments, warnings, predictions, all kinds of helpful shit. Just because they want to help us, right?"

"Yes. But it's obviously not perfected yet. Or we wouldn't be here," I said.

She took out a cigarette of some kind and lit it up. "You're a LD-head, too?" I asked.

"Hell, no," she said. "Clove cigarettes. Relaxes. Want one?"

I did, and I took it. It was deliciously spicy and there was something wonderful about sitting with her just inhaling together and thinking.

"Are we out of our heads now?" I asked.

"We were until you just said that."

"Sorry," I said, holding my hands up in protest. "Let's resume."

"It's okay. We've got stuff to talk about anyway."

"We do?"

"You are Zokaya, right?"

"How did you know that?"

"Because I asked them and because I've been looking for you. My father sent me."

"Do I know him?"

"No. But you've been looking for him. He's a Witness. He got the message via someone who knows Orlinsky," she said.

"He is a Witness?"

"One of them, yeah," she said.

"One of only two, right? And you trust me?" I asked.

She inhaled and blew out smoke. "Of course. We've seen each other in our underwear."

"Where is your father?" I asked.

"Nowhere you can get to," she said quickly. "He set it up that way. He wanted one of the least desirable locations in post-hate Triumvirate."

"Let me guess," I said. "Omaha?"

"No," she said. "Somewhere near Detroit."

"What's he do there?" I asked.

"Night manager at a Retro Mallmart."

"How do you communicate with him?" I asked.

"I largely don't," she said. "It isn't easy being the daughter of someone like him. You know, the combination of damage to his soul and his exaggerated sense of self-importance."

"To his what?"

"Soul," she said.

"What is that?" I asked.

"Let's just go back to smoking for a few minutes. I'll tell you what you need to know in the morning. And maybe I can move on from this permanent druggy summer-camp myself, get back to the middle of the country. It's nice there. People don't make believe they know any more than they actually do. New York and California are insufferable. My father said they always were, too. His father said the same. He said you could chop both coasts off and be left with a pretty nice country."

"I've only been on the coasts."

"It shows," said Cady. "It's like going to Cairo and then saying you were in Africa."

The sun was low in the sky now and we hadn't eaten anything. "They have a kind of loosely-organized serve-yourself dinner here," I said, getting up to lead the way. "It's the only meal of the day, really. Someone gets a bunch of stuff from somewhere and it gets shared. The other meals you are on your own."

"Fantastic," Cady said. "May rise to five-stars yet."

It was some sort of tofu and peppers, with a tomato sauce, over rice. Pears were the dessert.

I fell asleep watching her on the other side of the tent. It felt like drinking a long drink. I didn't feel alone.

#

The retinal alerts continued, though I tried to swipe them away before letting it into my consciousness. That was a word I learned from Cady, too. I knew they were asking for me to turn myself in, still, for "counseling", and I

185

wanted to see what would happen if I just continually ignored it. At first it felt all wrong. The whole point behind an "alert" was to get you to respond with an action, and that was something I had done all my life. Not doing anything felt wrong, and then pretty good.

Screw them.

Al used to have us hit, with a pre-Zero tennis racquet, while shouting things like, "F' them!" ("On the exhale! With full breath! Stay in contact with your feet! Let your shoulders drop!") I wonder what came of him and hoped he was still alright.

No one at the encampment seemed to have any news about what Wen's next move, the rollout of Quiet Mind, let alone even know about the CAWS Conference on Catalina Island in two weeks. All the things that seemed to dramatically important to me just last week started to fade. Even without smoking up LD or taking OM.

But did these people even KNOW about what was happening out there beyond their little community? They didn't even seem inordinately upset about the beatings, and bomb attacks that were starting to decimate them. "It's all good," was the common refrain, made even worse by the presence of a very tiny minority within the LD-head community, Religious Ones in Quietude. These ROIDs, as they were not-so-affectionately known, were basically druggies who also had been regular Religious Ones as well. They were *welcomed* only as long as they kept in silence. Violations were met with expulsion. There were no warnings. Even LD-heads had limits and the Religious Ones had no more political capital or trust ever since the wars. It was one-strike-and-you-are-out in terms of talking about their beliefs here.

Cady already had been for a brisk walk by the time I was waking up. She was pumped up. It was as if she was going to have her talk with me then shove off to points unknown. I guess it hadn't even crossed her mind that I would've liked to go with her on a walk, or even walk while talking.

"I want you to listen with your full attention. This is not a game, and this is not a movie. Forces beyond our control have ended the idea of innocence, so if you had any illusions about somehow still being a *kid*, throw them away. My father was a Unitarian minister in Oberlin, Ohio, one of the good ones. He didn't believe in talking snakes and my-way-or-the-highway religious thuggery. He helped people, he counseled them when they were crying, he held them. He introduced people to each other. That much he did do. When the chaos started, when all the others ruined everything that once was beautiful in religion he spoke up. The ones he pissed off, the born-agains, turned him in. They planted evidence in our house and he was swept up in the anti-terrorism raids after the Subway bombings. He was accused of masterminding a network in the Midwest and the Grosse Pointe Mall Massacres were pinned on him."

"I didn't know..."

"Yeah, there's a lot we don't know, isn't there?" she continued. "Children were shot in their strollers and people believed a Unitarian minister was somehow involved? Yes, they did. And off he went, to the Isle of The Righteous, with every vile murderer they could find, along with whole batches of innocent people. As you know, only two made it out. Out of thousands!! They escaped by killing a guard who trusted them along with policemen who were also present. My father was never the same again. He no longer believes in God, in religion, or the goodness of man. He believes in survival of the fittest and the goodness-or-badness of Man depending on the situation. I don't really even know exactly where he is today."

"Why..."

"Why you? Why were you chosen? Hah. Yeah, that's what I asked. Why Zokaya? Why not an Elder? Because all the Elders seem to be zapped-out on OM, or resigned to their lot...they have no spark left, no cojones, no future. It had to be someone who was used to thinking of him, or herself, as special. I advocated for a woman, truth be told. We narrowed it down to

CAWS because of the Orlinsky connection. Personally, I favored Elizabeth. No offense, but she's got twice your intellect. You know what my father said? 'She lacks heart.' How he knew that just looking at the limited data we had on you all, I'll never know. I don't know if it was some old pre-Zero sentiment seeping through or something but he was biased in favor of a black man. He said you would have an intrinsic awareness of being an outsider and that only an outside could lead what needs to happen."

"Whoa, whoa, wait," I said. "Are you trying to insult me? Or praise me? Both? Slow down, Cady, slow down. Orlinsky is in this how?"

"Orlinsky is from the part of the state that hasn't knuckled under to the Triumvirate yet, is still fighting. I don't think you understand: None of this is resolved. None of this is as static as they want you to believe. It's all flux. They start with the retinal alerts, the broadcasts, the news, they make it look pretty orderly, but that's not true. I'm not sure any of the technology-brats know it over at CAWS, but…you are in the midst of a Revolution. And not one about zettabytes."

"About what, then?"

"Soul. Our nature. The right to have a complicated, passionate life." Cady stared at me.

"So. this is your mission? You go around reeling people in for this?" I asked.

"I am supposed to help weave together the connections. That makes me as much of a leader as you will be, O Great One." She laughed. "Do me a favor and stay-the-hell humble about this, OK? You lucked out with your exotic African origins and your narcissism. I told you, I would've chosen Elizabeth."

"How is what you're doing, weaving people together, any different from The HIVE?" I asked.

"Because we're going back to trusting their brains minus the hard-wired SCRAP-shows inside. We're going to appeal to their thoughts and judgments without the visuals."

"Isn't that kind of dangerous?"

"Hell, yeah, it is, but what else is worth trying? I don't want to live as an ambulatory zettabyte, y'know? Take drugs? Put your body-parts together with someone else's and rub them? Like you, Most Wanted Man? Why not have a Revolution and actually build something?"

I looked at this woman and was confused. All my senses told me that she was incredibly appealing, the way to be alive, the Real Deal. But my brain told me that was on a suicide mission, or, quite possibly, was crazy. As in, needs a hospital crazy.

"So, what would you have me do?" I asked.

"Meet a few more people and weave together the connections, then turn yourself in for sex-counseling. They're going to find you sooner or later anyway," she said. "You're not a hero in a movie, Zokaya. You are another ticket in for us."

"Here's something I always wanted to know; how come they can't access everything we say and see and hear? How come they can just broadcast to us and not locate us?" I asked. It felt good to finally say out loud what I'd grown up fearing my whole life.

"It was the last act of reverse engineering from those who designed the implants. They realized, too late, that it would be used to erase every human freedom and they built in such complicated defaults that it would destroy the entire functionality of the system to try to undo it. That hasn't stopped the Triumvirate from trying, though. That's what they use CAWS students for: to take the next step into two-way monitoring and to defeat whatever it is in the programming that makes location services unworkable. My father actually has one of the copies of the last messages from the HIVE

Programmers. He keeps it in a special place, hoping his grandchildren will frame it in freedom. But I can tell you what it said."

"What?"

"'We have altered both the nature, and course, of humanity. We did this in the hope of seeing a day when suffering, hunger, violence, and ignorant passions will be wiped from the earth forever. We have built in safeguards to ensure that essential human rights to privacy and freedom of movement will be forever protected. Any attempt to alter HIVE-wired implants in the direction of undoing the privacy safeguards will result in complete destruction of the system and end its functionality across the board. This is our Endgame. Accept The HIVE as it is, with its restrictions, or have no HIVE at all.'" They released the statement only AFTER the wirings and protocols were irreversibly in place and completed."

"How did the Triumvirate respond?" I asked.

"They had them arrested, tortured and put it solitary confinement. They executed three of them for treason, hoping the fourth one would talk. He killed himself in his cell. CAWS was set up to undo and override their safeguards. That's the whole purpose behind your school. WhoozHooz wants the safeguards destroyed. And my understanding is that progress, at the multiple CAWS schools, is being made on doing just that. Best and the brightest, you know. You and your friends? What; you thought they just liked young people? Orlinsky has sabotaged significant progress in that direction twice. He has put himself at risk repeatedly. Even though these people are techies, they aren't stupid."

I tried to take this all in and felt nauseous. I was a pawn. My whole life: the good boy, the Smart One, the one who would help enslave people further at CAWS. Now the one who would help the other side. I sat down.

"You need to go to San Diego, then go back to CAWS," Cady said.

"Why San Diego?"

"The Second Witness needs to be brought into this," she said.

"Why?" I asked.

"They each have pieces of the puzzle, I suppose. We're all trying to reinvent a wheel. He might have several spokes."

"Can't you contact your father?" I asked.

She laughed, then looked away.

Jerry Sander

The Chosen One

I fell asleep after a period of being angry. Angry at being thought of as The Smart One when I was little boy. Angry about being sent to The Triumvirate. Angry at the assumption that I would've helped finish a project that would hurt people, just because I was able to. And angry at being sent to San Diego, by these self-styled revolutionaries, to coordinate something that, obviously, someone else could've done. Maybe Cady and her friends WERE trying to groom me for something big. In later years, they would tell my story. "The time He Went to San Diego to Spread the Word, The Time He Went Back to CAWS and Put Himself into Their Hands Voluntarily." The story of The Martyr. The story of The Messiah. It was like winning an election I never ran in.

I had ridden old scooters and motorcycles as a youngster in Liberia, and knew that the Retro Mallmart Year Zero Triumph Commander was simply luscious looking. And they were giving it to me. Almost no one had one; I hadn't seen motorcycles being ridden since coming to CAWS. Apparently, it was still a big middle-of-the-country thing, seen much less often on the coasts. Cady said it was because the coasts thought anyone who wasn't riding a Zhyga AirCar or Speedtrain was laughable and ignorant. Cady, herself, rode a pre-Zero motorcycle, a restored 2019 Honda Shadow. She would give me refresher lessons in the parking lot nearby before pointing me to the road to San Diego. San Diego was about eight and a half hours away. She was going to St. George, Utah, to meet another organizer deep in hiding.

If I got caught or stopped, the deal was that I just was to admit who I was and let them take me back in.

The second Witness, the one in San Diego, would know how to move things forward, she'd said, as well as how to contact her father. He'd have messages for Orlinsky that only I could convey.

Riding next to Cady in the early night hours—me on the motorcycle, her in the car—was like floating, or being a butterfly with a butterfly friend. The Triumph tore up the roads when needed. She'd recommended driving all night, with possibly a two-hour sleep break. I could've done it every day for the rest of my life, I remember thinking. We drove as parade of two, before she peeled away to the left, headed east and, with a wave, I was alone, heading straight south with the sounds of silence all around, but for my 2400 cc. engine throbbing and eating up the miles.

The bike wasn't a quiet one, but it wasn't one of those old American "hey-look-at-me!" ones that my father told me to stay away from. The throbbing was a reminder of something. It felt like something I always knew and was being encouraged to remember. Fifteen miles south of Avenal, I remembered: I was alive.

That was all I had to remember or figure out. That was all we had to embrace. The rest would come if we could remember this first essential truth.

All the things I was trying to figure out, whether Cady was really whom she seemed to be, whether I was being misdirected back to CAWS custody for reasons other than what they'd told me, what Wen's ultimate purpose was, were beyond my control and beyond my ability to figure out. What I would do, then, is to stick with the truths as I knew them: To interact with as much connection with others as I could muster (when I wasn't playing a Fiver); to seek the truth; to rely on my own eyes and body sensations instead of the retinal messages; and to appreciate the beauty of nature around me every day. To these ends, I thanked the motorcycle I was riding and the two-wheeler before that: Kristina's bicycle. Over time, I would seek even further to direct my thanks, but for now, I was peaceful recognizing what had returned me to movement, aligned me with the motions of everything else around me.

Writing about the motorcycle led to writing about loneliness, power, right and wrong. It led to writing about longing and the impossibility, it seemed, of connections. It led to writing about the hypocrisy of being HIVE-wired yet more disconnected than ever before.

The act of writing my quietest thoughts down seemed almost too intimate to tolerate. I did what Cady told me to, though, and didn't reread them or edit them.

I stashed my thoughts, after writing them down, inside the vessels Cady had given me (little vases with a top closure, really) in/around the places she'd suggested en route. These were generally small indentations and burrows off to the side of the road. No one would ever look there, unless they were crazy or a hungry animal. Cady and her colleagues were doing the same thing, she'd said. No one wanted to be caught with their thoughts on them.

I slept from 2:30 to 4:30 a.m. and entered San Diego at dawn.

#

I stopped at the first rest area on the highway within the city limits. It was 6:20 a.m., and I was shocked to find a crowd gathered in the parking lot, walking towards the woods behind us. What were these people doing at 6:20 in the morning? Fivers. En masse, dressed in the now-requisite gray. I tried to look like I knew exactly what was planned and was just late for the event myself, but I had no clue. I regretted being dressed in a blue shirt. I went up to a particularly nerdy-looking lost soul and asked whether if he, by chance, had an extra shirt in his car I could borrow. He looked at me with suspicion.

"Where've you been?" he asked. "Why are you dressed that way?"

"Hard to explain," I said. "I had to go on a mission, to the wild areas. Undercover. Hadn't gotten back home yet."

"And you're here for the service?" he wondered.

"Yes. Exactly," I said. "No chance to change back yet."

"Have you had a good night's sleep?"

"Yes, very good," I said. It was the truth. The two hours was all I needed. "Um…a shirt?

"I actually do have one," The Nerd said. "They are affordable now, at least. Retro Mallmart's got `em."

"How do I get it back to you when i get home?"

"It's a gift," he said. "C'mon, we're almost late here."

Four people were already in the stream behind the trees. Others splashed in, making it look like a herd of wildebeests taking a morning bath. The piercing sound of synthesized music filled the air; someone had brought equipment for this. Suddenly, everyone joined in on singing one note. "AHHHHHHHHHHHHHHH…."

"We sing the Note of Unity," said the clean-cut Asian man, his hands raised by his sides.

"AHHHHHHHHHHHHHHH…" It grew louder. It felt powerful. I joined in. I could feel my whole-body vibrating.

"With water we wash away confusion and violent thoughts. We are cleansed of base passions."

The crowd streamed in, splashing water over their clothes, on their faces.

"AHHHHHHHHHHHHHHHHHHH…"

A few people started crying. "Let it pass," the Asian man said. "Let it bleed through you. It's hatred and fear leaving the body."

The ones who were crying were being comforted by other Fivers, who restricted their support to a few pats on the back and by saying, "There, there…" I couldn't get over that they were all saying the same thing: "There, there now…There, there."

I followed The Nerd in, after changing my shirt and leaving it on the bike, going in only a little bit, but looking like I knew exactly what to do and splashing some on my shins.

"We will gather tonight in Balboa Park at 8 p.m. for the next part of the service. Check your retinas for any details if there is a last-minute weather change," the Asian man said.

The group started shuffling off. "Kind of interesting, in its own way, right?" asked The Nerd.

"For sure," I said.

"Purification by elements. Wood, fire, earth, metal, and water. Good thing we have another two weeks for it. I'm not ready. By then, maybe," he said.

"For...?" I asked

"The Conclave," he answered. "Getting exciting. And we've done wood, water, and earth. Fire and metal; cool stuff. Got to hand it to Wen. It all just works, y'know?"

"You mean...?"

"I've never felt life to be this good before," The Nerd said. "I actually like we're all in it together."

"We are," I said. I wanted to say more, but didn't wanted to slip up. "Thanks for the shirt," I said. "Maybe see you at the park later."

He waved goodbye, and I put on my helmet and fired up the bike. My instructions were to find the Retro Mallmart on Front St., near Ash. The Second Witness would be working there, but Cady wasn't sure of his shift. Or his exact department, though he last worked in frozen foods, I was told.

I did twice around the block, not sure why, just a feeling, before I parked and went in. I tried to remember I was now a Fiver. I dialed down all my feelings and asked a bored looking uniformed worker who was stacking frozen steaks on top of each other if he'd heard of, or seen, a guy named Shugi.

"Yeah. No. He don't work here anymore."

"When was he here last?" I asked.

"About two weeks ago."

"Did he get fired or something?"

"No. They moved him to Customer Service. Front desk."

I waited in the Customer Service line behind three people bringing in returns. The first one had a retro camping tent that she said was worthless because it didn't insulate the noise from the outdoors and she couldn't sleep (she got a full refund and they threw it in a stack of stuff behind them), the second one, a guy, was returning a retro-picnic-cooler chest that he'd been given by his girlfriend for his birthday. "She doesn't know the first thing about me," he said. "And I definitely don't want this thing. And, no, I don't have the receipt." He was given a store credit. "Can I use it for porn?" he asked.

"Um, like not since Year Zero, sir, I'm afraid?" the girl at the counter said. After he shuffled away and she whispered to her fellow worker next to her, "I bet he's one of the Religious Ones," she laughed. "They couldn't get enough of that stuff."

"Hello-welcome-to-Retro-Mallmart-we're-having-a-great-day-how-might-I-assist-you?" she asked in one fast sentence.

This girl looked too bored to ever having picked up, or played, Hell on Earth in the first place. If she got through two minutes of Level One, I'd be surprised. It made me wonder how the people who didn't play the game were processing all these changes.

"I'm sorry, sir, but might I assist you?" I had been staring at her weirdly, I guess.

"Do you have retro bar-stools?" I asked. That was what I was supposed to ask when I got close to Shugi, I was told. I'm guessing that Barstool Bob had something to do with it. As secret passwords go, though, it was a pretty good one.

The man next to her leaned in. "I'm sorry, sir, what is it you are asking for?"

"Retro bar-stools?" I repeated.

"For what room of the house?" he asked.

"Basement," I said.

His eyes twinkled and he seemed to get an instant jolt of energy. "Aisle twenty-two, behind housewares, against the wall," the girl said, just as he said, "I'll be happy to show you where that is, sir. Follow me."

"Are you going on break now?" she asked him.

"No, I'm helping a customer."

"We are not supposed to be personal escorts, Shugi."

Bingo.

"I'll tell you what, Jessica; I'll trade you my leisurely stroll for you having an extra fifteen minutes of break this afternoon," he said.

"Really? Cool beans," she said.

He and I started to walk away. "She's from the Midwest," he said. "Nobody out here speaks that way."

"How about you?" I asked. "Are you from the Midwest?"

He seemed to flinch. "Who, exactly, are you, I am wondering. I know you are the Next Great Thing in leaders and all that, and that you are from somewhere dark and mysterious—no offense; my friend, I am, too—and that I am supposed to instantly trust you because you know the right code words, but I no longer instantly trust anyone."

I hadn't expected him to look like this. He was clean shaven and a model Retro Mallmart employee, wearing an old-fashioned red and tie that was obviously from their own Retro Mallmart collection. He looked like someone who not only very much wanted to be a citizen of the Triumvirate, but who was succeeding at that pretty well. His eyes were blue, which didn't seem to go with his darker skin.

"You are looking at my eye color?" he asked. "Those are contact lenses. Colored ones. Why not give the people what they want, right? I am a clean-shaven, blue-eyed, obedient servant of the commercial class. That way I can eat, live and sleep right next to them without any questions or hard feeling. I actually AM from the Midwest, originally: Midwest Iran. My people there were first persecuted by the Muslims, then, of the course, by the Forces of Enlightenment, which put them on trial for religious extremism. I wasn't the only one who went to the Island. I was the only one of my family to survive."

"I can't imagine," I said.

"No, you can't. And it won't help if you get all sentimental about it. The opposite is needed."

He looked at me skeptically, up and down. "What do you do? Are you a fashion model?"

"Are you kidding?" I laughed.

"I told you, I don't know you, I know a name, I know they like blacks in the fashion model business."

"Well that sounds kind of…"

He cut me off. "I don't have the least bit of interest in how it sounds, or how anything sounds, beyond my successfully remaining undercover. I'm asking you what you do."

"I am a student at the Center for Advanced World Studies, specializing in encrypted programming and deprogramming, HIVE formatting, and content generation."

He smiled. "Ahhhh…so you are one of the best-and-brightest brought in to try to undo the defaults in the HIVE planning."

"Apparently so."

"What else did you think you were brought here at great expense for?" he asked.

"To help people."

He burst out laughing. After a few rounds of catching his breath, it still didn't seem like his laughter would stop. "You are HIVE-wired?" he asked in between laughs.

"Well, yes, everyone young is," I explained.

"Not necessarily," he said. "There were hideouts, renegades, they go around making believe. The only reason they are safe is because of the foiled backwards HIVE feedback."

"The very thing we're being brought in to undo," I ventured.

"Yes. You and your friends were, some might say, very much the Enemy. In the old times, we wouldn't be having this conversation."

"Why not?"

"Because one of us would be dead." He stared at me without warmth.

"I thought you were a holy man," I said. "Of some sort."

He snorted. "You wanted a beard? Some beads?" His eyes grew angry and his nostrils flared. "What if my survival makes me holy?"

"I'm not judging."

"Thank you, that is very nice of you. In a limited Californian way. But it is better than the days of Holy War and repression, yes? You will tolerate me not having a beard and beads and singing lovely old songs because I am a blue-eyed Retro Mallmart Associate, and I will tolerate that you, born five minutes ago, Federal Expressed from some little African town to California, are without understanding of what might have happened in the word say, oh, SIX minutes ago. You are in the eternal now—welcome to California!— and there is nothing to learn."

"You are talking about history." I said.

"Yes, I am," he responded fiercely.

"History ended," I said. "That's what they told us."

"Is that what Al told you in the hills? Is that what your body told you when you breathed in and changed and felt the Unity? That everything that came before you was separate and had nothing to do with your pretty Californian reflection?"

"No. How do you know Al?" I asked, genuinely confused.

"You are a like a child who wakes up to find a big breakfast buffet ready for him. How did that happen? A magic bunny? Maybe the pancakes and juice formed themselves by coming together over centuries of evolution and random occurrences. Or maybe the child's parents have prepared breakfast."

"So..."

"So, we've chosen you, Zokaya. We were here and ready before you opened your eyes this morning."

"I haven't chosen anything," I said.

"I know. That's what they all say," he said, laughing again.

"What is it you need?" I asked.

"Our lives are getting near over, and our systems have played themselves out the way they did. It was some pretty good entertainment for a while. But those of us who expect to prevail know that the way forward, after this all falls, won't be from one of us. We've been polluted. We've been demeaned, humiliated, and devastated. We can't be trusted to not plunge everything into a world of revenge. It is your turn. Learn about what we did. And don't repeat it."

"You are Bahai?"

He nodded. "Whenever there is a need for a prophet or a teacher, one arises."

"Where were your Prophets when the Island of the Righteous was being set up and people were being dragged there?"

"They were the first to go," he said quickly. "The wisest were the first to perish. People don't like hearing The Truth. They never have."

We looked at each other in silence.

"Wasn't the Island of the Righteous a war crime?" I asked.

"There is no such thing anymore," he answered. "An old concept. No one cares about such things."

"What do people care about it, Shugi?"

"Their next retinal impulse," he answered calmly. "Look, here's what we do: we meet tonight at the big show, down in the Square."

202

"Yeah, what is it exactly?" I asked.

"You'll see. Just remember to look enthusiastic. And if you get caught and returned to your little computer nursery school before I see you again, tell Orlinsky this: Catalina is all set, peaceful and otherwise."

"What is that supposed to mean?" I asked. "I mean, in case I get caught?"

"If you get caught it is good you don't know."

#

It felt like a large picnic gathering, the sun getting lower in the sky but the temperatures warm enough to keep everyone happy. I hadn't been around large numbers of Fivers for a while and it was unnerving how restrained they were, even in their happiness. Parents were there with children, some of them being carried on their shoulders, as people milled around and chatted. I was getting used to the sea of gray again. In Africa something like this would have been full of colors. I noticed four very large screens and eight banks of speakers. Ambient music was being played at a low level. You had to listen hard to recognize that it was. It was the kind of very boring music that passed for *soothing* these days. They had it around before Hell on Earth, too, but it was the music of choice these days.

I looked around and couldn't find Shugi. Behind where we were gathering in the square was a fenced off area, on all four sides, with dirt instead of grass. Maybe it was under construction, I thought.

The music got louder and people seemed to respond by getting buzzier and looking for seats. Most people had brought blankets. The screens flicked on with the Wen Enterprises logo and there was an announcement about bathrooms and emergency exit routes. Just as the sun began to set, tall outside lights, the kind they used to have around tennis courts, flicked on, illuminating us as if it were day. Then they dimmed down. An announcer-voice came over the loudspeakers and said," Ladies and gentlemen, Mr. Zhou Wen."

The crowd responded by chanting the same thing I'd heard that morning: "AHHHHHHHHHHHH!!" in a sustained, full sound that seemed to grow and grow. Then they broke it off into sustained applause. On screen, Mr. Wen was seen in front of a cave, dressed modestly, as usual, with a little stream behind him to the left. After five seconds of flute playing, the music faded out, and he spoke.

"The last few months have brought us many beautiful things. It is important to remember that beautiful things come after terrible things. An animal dies, goes into the soil and a flower grows…Together we have made it through to better times. And we aren't done yet. The Wen Corporation has been learning from our mistakes. Each worker and each manager, who are no better than the common worker, has had to embark on an inventory of self-reflection. Together we have gathered to see where we have gone wrong and to report with open heart to the group on how we must do better. We move forward in humility."

A truck drove up to the square. Then a second one and, within seconds, four others. Men hopped out, lowered the back gates, and started unloading things.

Wen continued. "But we are not ignorant. We know that things are not so simple when others have schemed in the opposite direction. Where we celebrate humility, they celebrate arrogance and force. Where we focus on peace, they focus on violence and aggression. They infect our technologies and came close to completely taking over the consciousness of our young children, our future."

Stacks of written materials of some sort, in binders, and loose papers were being deposited in the fenced off square by the truck drivers' men now, thrown into a heap.

"We were fortunate enough to come into additional evidence of how the attack on our WenBooks was coordinated and planned and what you see being unloaded behind you right now are the planning manuals for the content and distribution for *Hell on Earth*. As sickening as it is to read about such deliberate evil, such twisted plans so carefully planned, we have done so, so we can learn from it. This is the last time these plans will exist in this form. We have eliminated the so-called game, and we will eliminate these vile records tonight."

The crowd started getting riled up and a few people started the chant. "AAAAAAHHHHHHHHHH..."

"But first I ask you to listen, with simple mind and open heart to this tragic confession of a young woman who got swept up in the grip of this before coming to us and asking for forgiveness. She has gone through the inventory of self-reflection as well as a three-day intensive of criticism/self-criticism with workers from our group."

The camera cut away to a downcast-looking young woman. It was Cady, looking weary and sleepless. She had clearly been crying. A lot. I held my breath as I heard her speak.

"My name is Cady Walsh, and I am twenty-five-years-old. I got involved with the planners of *Hell on Earth* because I thought it was some way of asserting individualism. I now recognize that individualism is a deviation from HIVE-thinking that can only lead to violence and sadness. I offer my apologies to the People for the evil images I helped bring into the world and for its hateful effects on the young people who consumed them. I am asking for compassionate justice and a second chance to work with the Wen Corporation to use my skills to benefit society instead of ruining it."

I looked around for Shugi again. I heard a huge *Whooosh!* and realized that the books and materials behind me had been set on fire. The blaze was huge. The crowd turned to look at it, their eyes lit up with happiness and excitement. The truck drivers continued to throw armfuls of books/manuals onto the burning heap, making the flames go even higher. Mr. Wen was talking in the background about mercy and no one could even hear him because the chant from the crowed, something between a cry and a plea for more, came ringing through the flames:

"AHHHHHHHH!!!!!! AHHHHHHHHHHHHHHHHHHH!"

I turned to find a place to throw up. Instead I froze, spotting Warren and Cheyenne, walking through the crowd, scouring people's faces. I resisted the urge to run, and just started to walk determinedly. I tried to find the sweet spot between not directing attention to myself and getting the fuck out of there. The Triumph was two blocks away. I didn't turn back to see if they'd located me or were following. Wen's voice continued to boom, and I could see the reflection of flames in the eyes of those in the crowd as they stared at him, in ecstasy, chanting and smiling.

The sounds started to fade, and I hopped over a waist-high embankment, cutting a diagonal across the first street. It sounded like the chanting behind me was turning into some sort of singing.

"We rise as One…we fight as One…The Power of One…"

I jogged faster now, reaching into my pocket for the keys. I was full-out running when I spotted the bike. I hopped onto it, unlocked the helmet lock, quickly put it on my lid and fired it up. It was loud and never failed to get the attention of passers-by. That they were all Fivers made it stand out even more. Fivers didn't ride motorcycles, apparently.

I leaned into the first right hand turn I could. It wasn't half a block before I realized that my helmet was malfunctioning. I had turned off all the helmet-casts—they'd had directions and information projected onto your face helmet since pre-Zero days, but I'd hacked mine to turn off all notifications and news. Somehow, they'd overridden it and as soon as I started moving faster than twenty-five miles per hour a running HIVE News feed appeared at the bottom of my face shield. This defeated the purpose of motorcycling to me: I'd been taught by my father than the way to not only stay alive, but to appreciate things in life, was to experience them one thing at a time. This wasn't how we did anything, anymore, but it was still my delicious pleasure. A pleasure I could only get to out in nature, ignoring my retinal alerts, and on the Triumph. Now, as I sped away and felt the delicious rumble of the engine pull me far away from these people, these worker-bees, The HIVE, the chant, pulling me into a universe that was just a ribbon of endless free road, I had to join the ranks of every other HIVE-news watcher and swallow their programmed mind-drug. I laughed a little to myself, thinking that I sounded like Al with these thoughts, as I roared up Cedar St., weaving to avoid people crossing the street, weaving around the self-driving cars, and buses, going faster where I used to go slower, trusting not that the universe would provide for me, but that the universe was actually just me and my bike and whatever I could see and feel in this moment. That's all there actually is, I thought. What if that? And what if that is more than good enough.

I blocked out the news, even though it was still playing (something about drug treatment advances for Lexy-D addicts) and suddenly flashed back to holding onto my father, on the back of his old Royal Enfield Bullet 500, weaving through the streets of African villages. My mother had thrown him out, he'd said, saying she could not stand one more affair of his, even though he told me they'd never happened and she was sick in the head. He didn't know where he was going to end up, he said, but he wanted to show me the Liberia he grew up in before leaving, and before sending me away. He left her the car and most of his money. He took the Bullet 500.

My father smelled of Bay Rum and coconut. He groomed his short beard with coconut oil and applied the Bay Rum daily, telling me that women couldn't resist it. He didn't worry that this seemed to prove my mother's point, he just said to me, "It is from the earth, and you must stay with earth things when you go to North America. North America is more in the stars."

I became aware of more than the usual number of Zhyga AirCars passing overhead, and I wasn't far enough out towards the suburbs yet, but I was cruising at a solid ninety miles per hour.

I remember my father getting excited and talkative when we went into the town he grew up in and he found the marketplace. It was small, and I couldn't tell if they had it going still for real or for the tourists who seemed to come in ever-increasing numbers. After all, there was a mall, even a Mallmart, less than three miles away.

"Look at that," he said to me when we stopped, admiring the vegetables. "Those are real vegetables. That's what they used to look like. Look at the women, Zokaya, look at the colors they wear; this is what they used to look like. Do you know that they always ran the businesses? In this part of Liberia, it was the women, not the men. Don't ever think differently; the most extraordinary powers come from a woman, Zokaya. They can give birth. Mother Earth."

"Doesn't that make them bossy?" I asked, in my best teenage-man voice.

"Oh yes, I didn't say they couldn't be bossy. You roll with it."

"How come it didn't work, then, with Mama?" I asked.

"Some women can't roll at all," he said. "You need one who can roll with your rolling."

It was the perfect day; the kind of day we'd never had until we both learned that he'd be leaving and so would I. I didn't hear from him again, and imagine him, often, on his bike, threading through the needle of his African life, weaving to the right and left and leaning into the curves.

The chatter of turbo helicopters was above me now—those weren't Zhyga AirCars anymore—and I knew that they were likely the police.

I tried to remember what I was doing, why I'd even been sent to the evening rally, how I was supposed to somehow weave together The Resistance, if there even was such a thing, by connecting Shugi and Orlinsky and the Hell on Earth Resisters, and the No-Gamers, and Al and his people, and Crazy Chester and they all started to blend and become confused, and I saw Cady's face, suddenly, in my mind—her old face, not her new defeated one—full of power and determination and color, and I pulled the throttle hard, up over one-hundred-five miles an hour now, the Triumph as stable as a truck, but as light as a firefly at the same time, and I was determined to drive to freedom, to find a piece of earth to sleep on tonight, under the stars, the comfort of my bike, my father...

I was going one-hundred-fifteen when I saw the first explosion, about a half a mile in front of me; the road erupting into a flaming ball, disappearing into a cloud of fire. I cut the throttle, looking to the left and right to find another way out. There wasn't one. The road dropped off into a gulley on the right at a steeper angle than a bike this big could handle, and to the left was an outright cliff. I cut back to 60 faster than I wanted to and that is when the second explosion erupted, the road turning into a fireball much closer to me now, giving me no choice but to come to a barely controlled stop and to hope that these explosions weren't aimed for me, because if they wanted to they could now kill me in a second.

The first police AirCar descended, landing directly in front of me, forcing me to jam on the brakes. The second one landed five feet to my left, as the third one descended to the right. Two others floated down behind me. I hadn't heard them; these cars had the police air silencers we'd all heard of but never yet seen.

Suddenly my helmet shield filled with the logo of the California State Highway Patrol and the words, against a red background, "Arrest in Progress." I heard voices as they dismounted and approached. The words, "Remove Your Helmet! "Remove Your Helmet! Step AWAY from the motor vehicle SLOWLY!" appeared, flashing brightly. "Remove Your Helmet! Step AWAY from the motor vehicle SLOWLY!"

I started to get scared but then I reminded myself that being guilty was a state of mind and that I could continue to be free by thinking freely. The real guilty parties were back at the Wen rally.

"Zokaya Kpelle?" the officer with the big stomach rippling over the limits of his belt asked.

"Yes?"

"We have a warrant for your arrest and we are executing it. Your rights appear on the retinal message currently sent. You can acknowledge them by looking up to the right and blinking twice rapidly."

"You blew up the road just to get me?" I asked.

"What are you talking about?" the officer asked.

"The road. Ahead of me. Blew it up in two places, just to stop a motorcycle?"

"We didn't blow anything up. We sent that to your face shield through your helmet HIVE link. It was a SCRAP. Hey, it worked, didn't it?"

I paused. "Since when do you have that technology?" I asked. I was genuinely impressed and was professionally curious.

"It's time for you to acknowledge your rights, sir," a second officer, whom I would come to know as Officer Bolt said.

I didn't.

"Yeah, we got him," Bolt said, to someone into his HIVE mic face-link.

Confession

I was led into their AirCar. I'd never been arrested before. We were flying low, then went higher.

"What'd you get me for?" I asked the troopers. "Speeding?"

"We divulge on a need-to-know basis. You don't need to know," said the cop with the small scar on his left cheek.

"In other words, there's no need to talk," said Bolt.

The land below looked beautiful; there were swirls of road with pockets of greenery. I found myself wondering about the motorcycle, of all things, immediately missing it. It had taken me from the HIVE rally to freedom and back into the Belly of the Beast.

It actually helped me to think of how Kristina would handle this. I pictured her just remaining mysterious looking and not saying much. She handled things in a much cooler way than me, I imagined. A Nordic chill, not the urgent heat of Africa. Not that my people couldn't be cool and distanced; my mother seems to have proven that. A professional woman— first a social worker, then a lawyer—she always thought things through, then identified her feelings about it. My father thought with his bay rum. As much as I tried to figure out what a combination of them would mean, I couldn't quite arrive at an understanding of who I was, beyond knowing that I connected well with others once I decided it was safe and that my passion could easily know no bounds unless I thought things through a little first.

I started thinking about being in custody.

In the background, HIVE News filled an in-dash screen of the car. There was almost nonstop well-choreographed excitement-coverage about the Conclave preparations in Catalina. They made it look like most of the people of the world were somehow expecting something big from it and that the countdown, nine days now, was something most people wanted to join in with. Reporting their excitement was building the excitement. The screen flashed the blue-green logo of Wen Industries with the words: "From quiet minds, the best things come."

I could feel waves of air beneath us as we cruised. I could get used to an AirCar, I thought.

The monitor filled with images of people of all ages; some were expecting a new piece of hardware from Catalina, some wondered about a whole new HIVE. People were speaking in French, with subtitles, Russian, some kind of Asian language. Two old men were waving, saying, in broken English, "Wen! We want Wen! One of us! Traditional, only better!" One of "the world's biggest stages" was being constructed on Catalina, a blonde woman reporter gushed. Thousands of gallons of water were being brought in for the *honored guests* and there was speculation about what mode of transportation Wen was going to use to get there. (He had been known to take the controls of his private jet now and then, in the spirit of fun, they said, even though he wasn't a licensed pilot.)

We landed and everything was shut down. Bolt and the Trooper Gutman, or whatever his name was started bantering about where to eat. Bolt was tired of Mexican food and Gutman wanted to try a new Mexican place because they *do guacamole the way you're supposed to do guacamole.*

The door burst open and a distracted-looking middle-aged woman came in. Gutman left and Bolt stayed.

"Hello, I'm Dina Arcati, you must be Zokaya?" she asked, as if this was a party and she'd just opened the door, ready to accept my house gift in return for a drink and some crackers and cheese. "I'm a Licensed Legislative Social Worker (L.L.S.W.), I work WITH the police and the courts, not FOR them, Many of the things we talk about here today will be considered confidential, unless deemed otherwise by the courts, and I need you to know that I have no control over THAT part of the process. OK?" she asked, prying into me. "Are we good so far?"

I looked at Bolt, who didn't seem the least bit amused by her. He stared at me like I had already ruined his day.

Dina opened a few different HIVE files about me, evidently, on the oldish Colony Tap-top computer. She tapped away, saying, "Just give me a minute, and we can get started…just getting organized. Paper, right, can you believe it? It's been a busy day. How about yours, Zokaya, same thing?"

Bolt snorted, and Dina lightly hit herself in the forehead with the back of her hands. "Oh, right, silly me, I'm sorry, you got arrested." She leaned forward again and read some of the file. "I THINK you got arrested. Or did he turn yourself in? It doesn't say here…"

"He got arrested," said Bolt.

"Alright, so we've got to do a Form 6260," Dina said, typing away rapidly. "I think the HIVE is slow today, is it slow today, Officer Bolt?" she asked.

"I don't know," he said, bristling. "It works for me."

"Alright, we have the demographics, I see you've already received your rights retinally. Did you acknowledge them by looking up to the right-hand corner and blinking twice over them? I don't see here that you did." She looked up at me, questioningly, her glasses sliding down her nose some. Very few people still wore glasses, and I could see why. She seemed to be waiting for me to speak.

I just looked at her and waited for her to talk some more.

"Could we just DO it now?" she asked. "And get it out of the way? Your rights? We can resend them," she said, turning to look behind her at the mirror, then turning to continue, "and we can just move on. I think they're going to resend them. You just look up to the right and blink twice fast and they'll send you confirmation of acknowledgement."

A flash came across my retinas: "You have the right to remain silent, in which case your silence may be interpreted by a jury of your peers, or a judge as a tacit confession of guilt. You have the right to hire an attorney or receive one appointed by us. You acknowledge that the cost of prosecution may, if you are found guilty, be passed on to you or your family and that we may receive reimbursement for documented expenses within 60 days of a guilty verdict being achieved. This may or may not include reimbursement for anticipated housing expenses during a period of confinement, as directed by the court. By looking to the upper right and blinking twice quickly you acknowledge receiving written explanations of your rights. Please look to the upper right now and blink twice quickly."

I read it and did nothing. Dina turned her head a little, scrunching up her nose.

"I'd strongly recommend you do it," Bolt said. "Smart people do."

"What have I ever done to upset you?" I asked him. "Why should you care about this? Isn't that above your pay-grade?"

"We could have you back in Africa by morning," he said to me with intensity. "It'd be one less foreign-speaking HIVE- junky to me. It's not like there's a shortage."

"We do jobs former-Americans apparently don't know how to do," I argued. "Me and my foreign-speaking friends. And, yes, when you hear us speaking foreign languages, we ARE talking about you. If you want to know what we're saying, you might have to learn a foreign language yourself."

"What do they have you working on, Swahili Soccer on the HIVE or something? Improved Lexy-D?" he walked towards me. Dina got in between the two of us.

"Could you possibly give us some time alone, Officer Bolt? Just a minute or two?"

"That's not protocol," he responded after a pause. "YOU want to leave and I'll spend some time with him?" Bolt said, menacingly.

"I think the first idea was better, "Dina said. "I'll sign off on the protocol variance."

She popped open a Protocol Variance Form from The HIVE, signed it and sent it to him without printing it. He glared, but went to leave. "You know there's an Authorization to Use Force in place?" he asked.

"I know, I'm grateful for the AUF's, Officer Bolt, I really am. And I'll shout if I need you, I promise."

Bolt left and Dina came next to me, leaning in closely and immediately using a voice I'd never heard before. "Shut up and listen closely. 'Do you have retro barstools?' 'Do you have retro barstools?'"

That was the password-phrase. I admit to having been shocked.

"OK? Wake up." Her voice seemed to change. It sounded urgent. "I'm on your side. We're closing in on what's going on. There's a crack in The HIVE—remember that glitch you saw before Level Five went live? Elizabeth and our people have developed both hardware and software that can induce that outage, for at least fifteen seconds. We're trying to expand it to a minute. If we get to a minute, we can get to five."

"You're with...?"

"The remnants of the U.S. government; we're one-third of the Triumvirate and shrinking fast, losing out to Healthy Growth, which thinks it has Wen in its pocket. But we know *he trying to use them,* instead."

"And what about...?"

"WhoozHooz? It's tense; no one knows. They're arrogant enough to think that Wen will come to them, and nervous that he hasn't. They're trying to woo Elizabeth aggressively, and she's worked with them, too, on some projects back in England. I'd call them one large, amoral, opportunistic, mother-humping wild card. Not to be crossed. And so far, you haven't. It is Healthy Growth that is most nervous about you; they think you are trying to start a religion, and that topic makes everyone very, very worried."

I laughed.

"None of this is funny. If religion comes back, people stop buying as much stuff. Here's what you have to do? Plead guilty and ask for

Compassionate Justice. Work with us and you walk out of this. Act like an entitled CAWS kid or immigrant and you'll wake up on the shores of your Motherland. One more thing; Bolt genuinely hates you."

I was stunned and felt like I'd been punched in the face.

"What, you didn't think we still had racists?" she asked, holding the gaze. "Do what I say."

The door burst open and Bolt entered. She immediately went back to her old voice.

"Is he on the next flight back to The Lion King?" Bolt asked, sneering.

"That's thirty-five years ago, pre-Zero, old man," I said, without thinking. He grabbed a notebook that Dina had with her and, without pausing, slammed me in the side of the head with it. It hurt a ton, and I was dizzy.

"Enjoy the flight," he said. "Ask for a pillow. And a bag of ice."

"Alright, OK, hold on, enough! I think we've got a buy-in, no one has to fly anywhere, Officer Bolt. Zokaya is ready to cooperate, or at least he was a few minutes ago," Dina said glaring at him. "I'm sure he regrets that, Zokaya, we're just all a little wound up…What do you say we start by my sending you a copy of your rights again and you retinally-acknowledging them?" She did. "OK, all you have to do is look up to the right and blink twice."

I did.

"OK, very nice, we got that out of the way. You'll get paper copies of all this, too, if you need them. Are we good so far, Zokaya?"

I nodded with the smallest gesture I could manufacture.

"OK, I'm going to take that as a yes, Zokaya, I can see you're not a talker. That's fine, that's OK There are cultural differences, Officer Bolt; he's not a talker. And the age. Mistakes get made, believe me, I know. Don't even get me started about my son, he's your age."

Bolt just shook his head and looked down.

"Alright, the whole purpose of our meeting today is to try to keep these charges from having to go through the system, the adjudication system, and to work compassionately and intelligently around whatever crimes may or may not have been committed. I'm not here to judge; they have Judges for that!" she said laughing. "So, Officer Bolt and I are the good guys, we work together as a team. We try to assess remorse and come up with a plan. Plans are not always possible, depending on the severity of the crime, degree of remorse and willingness of those above us to see the legal charges diverted. But the fact that they sent you here first instead of anywhere else is an encouraging sign. Wouldn't you say so, Officer Bolt?"

Bolt looked at me in silence, turning his head away.

"What do you think, Zokaya? An encouraging sign?"

I didn't know what to say. Finally, I just said, "Yes, a very good sign."

"OK!! Then we're all on the same page," Dina exclaimed. "So, we start with the charges," she said, moving some papers around and choosing one to lift towards her face closer, lifting her glasses up to read. "We've got Theft of a Moving Vehicle (whoo, boy, THAT'S not good), that's a grand larceny! Isn't that a grand larceny, Officer Bolt?"

"Yes, it is," he said, without any emotion.

"...and...Unwanted Sexual Contact with a Person Under twenty-one, hmmmmm..." She looked up at me, looking at me a little differently. "And it's noted here that you are a regular patron at the sex posts in every town he has ever lived in, starting the week after you've arrived in this country."

I erupted, in anger. "That's a lie. That's an outrageous lie. I've never been to a sex post once."

"Apparently, they have visual evidence of it...NOT that that is the charge against you, but it can be used as part of these adjudication proceedings," Dina said.

How could they have visual evidence of me repeatedly doing something I didn't do? I thought. Then I remembered how much better

217

SCRAPS had gotten. "I don't want to dwell on the sex posts," Dina said. "It's not really germane. I mean, it IS germane, but it's not really *central* to the charges against you. It would help us all if you could produce your license and registration for that motorcycle you were riding, I think. That would make those charges go away."

I didn't say anything, because I couldn't.

"And then of course is the Unwanted Sexual Contact. Those things don't go away easily. What they are asking for, nowadays, is first an admission of guilt, then a request for leniency, Compassionate Justice, kind of like 'throwing yourself on the court,' you could introduce character witnesses, letters from old teachers, etc.... I think they will take into account your youth and your ignorance of post-American culture. You could argue, for instance, that different standards apply in Liberia, where you come from that you misinterpreted the signals from her, etc."

"Is this about Kristina? Is she doing, okay?" I asked.

"Oh, we're not allowed to comment about that," Dina said. "You know, a lot is going on, Zokaya, you're just a tiny part of it. We don't want to spend a lot of time with you, no offense."

"What's going on?" I asked.

"The enclaves. The SA's. They've erupted. Violence, guns, attacks on nearby neighborhoods. Bombs, even! It's all-out war. They are zooded-out on Lexy-D, OM, what-have-you, smokable Lexy, it's just all crossed over the breaking point," Dina said, looking disgusted. "These people are not like you and me, Zokaya. Nothing means anything to them. If they hurt somebody, 'Oh well, more drugs for me!' They're seeing rainbows, what do they care?"

"Are you sure?" I asked. This didn't sound like them at all.

"Oh, yeah, we're sure," Bolt answered. "You think we've deployed 26 garrison units to the enclaves to watch them eat cookies and see trails after they get high? They are in full attack mode, and they are too stupid or too high to understand that they are about to lose, big-time. But they are attacking everyone's sister, brother, grandma, and grandpa out there tonight. They are going to go out in a blaze of glory, you watch!"

"Where is this happening?" I asked.

"All over," said Bolt.

"Where is it not?" asked Dina. "You don't win friends like that. So why don't we wrap this up?"

"How do we do that?" I asked.

"We've got to fill out some goals and objectives, first," she said. "So, we've got some paperwork to do, that's OK, we've got a few minutes, we can do this quickly, if we can brainstorm," Dina said, pulling out more papers. I'd never seen people use papers like this before. I wondered why.

"What is a brainstorm?" I asked.

"A give-and-take, free-association around a topic. So, we've got goals and objectives, we break it down a little, say whatever comes into our mind, refine it, write it down and…there we are."

"What's the difference between goals and objectives?" I asked.

"Objectives are short-term, y'know, little measurable things, frequency specified, what-have-you, and GOALS, those are longer-term things.," Dina said. "For the purposes of the form, anyway. Sometimes it's the opposite."

"Are you following this, Officer Bolt?" I asked.

"Oh yeah, I'm following it," he said.

"So, if I get lost…"

"Either one of us could help you," Dina said. "But it's best if it comes from you, Zokaya. It shows sincerity."

"I don't know where to start," I said. "I want to get out of here."

"OK," said Dina. "That's a 'goal.' First you have to identify the little things you could do that'd lead UP to getting out of here. Can you think of anything that would RELATE to the criminal charges that we could work on?" Dina asked, sounding a little less ditzy.

"Maybe just not have sexual contact with anyone," I suggested. "Unwanted."

"Fantastic!" Dina said, practically clapping her hands together. "'Will refrain from incidents of continued unwanted sexual contact,'" she wrote.

"We should go from a frequency of once-in-my-life to no-times-in-my-life," I suggested. "For goals."

"I love it!" she said. "But we can't word it like that. It has to be 'once, reported in the past year,' to 'will not relapse in a twelve-month period.'"

"What about the motorcycle? There's no proof of ownership with your name on it. What can we say about that?" she asked.

"I misplaced the papers," I lied. "It's not stolen."

"Alright, so you're going to find them," Dina said, jotting it down. "Let's say that's going to be solved. Who can vouch for you at your school? Someone local?" I gave Orlinsky's name and number. She walked out of the room, leaving me with Bolt.

"Did you ever think you'd be better off if you'd stayed with your own people?" Bolt asked, calmly.

I thought of five different things to say, but I didn't want to get hit in the head again. I waited it out in silence until Dina came back.

"Alrighty! Good news all around! Orlinsky vouches for you AND...They found your license and registration for the bike."

"The...?"

"The bike, the motorcycle. Your Triumph. Why didn't you just say? It was under the seat, in the, thingy, y'know the place where they have tools. All up-to-date, current, you're good. So...goodbye felony-grand-theft, right?"

The only thing outstanding, she went on to say, was the Unwanted Sexual Contact charge. They wanted my confession to that, and I gave it to them. I looked into the camera, holding their script, and spoke:

"On November 5th, Year 13, I, Zokaya Kpelle, knowingly and willfully brought about unwanted sexual contact with a woman, Kristina Knopfsen, a fellow student at the Center for Advanced World Studies. I did this knowing that this was prohibited both by law and prevailing moral codes in the state of California. I am asking for Compassionate Justice, as the incident took place during a time of profound confusion and adjustment while I tried to understand the cultural differences between California, The Triumvirate, and the Liberian culture I spent my formative years influenced by. I now know how that merely feeling a biological impulse does not give you permission to impose yourself on your unwilling neighbor or colleague. I ask to be included in a group of fellow offenders as we take unflinching inventory of our behaviors and offer criticism/self-criticism and to become better citizens. It is my understanding that this group will be run by the Wen Corporation, through special agreement with The Triumvirate, and the Wen Corporation can terminate my participation in it at any time, remanding me back to the court system for ordinary court procedures (which may include sentencing) if they see fit. Monthly reports on my progress will be forwarded to the court, with my permission."

"Perfect," Dina said, checking some boxes on her paperwork. "So, we've got the confession, the letter of recommendation from Mr. Orlinsky, the goals and objectives sheet, the acknowledgement of rights...I think we're ready to have me go to the Judge! All before 5:00!" she said. "This doesn't take long. I have to make a confidence recommendation, based on a 1-to-10 scale and I'd say you're coming in at an eight."

She seemed to wait for my reaction.

"That's really good, Zokaya! You're an EIGHT! The word is they are approving anyone above a SIX for Compassionate Justice."

"OK, good," I said.

"I mean, you'll have to apply yourself in group and, between you and me, I hear that is no walk in the park, but…it's better than jail, right?" She looked at me, expectantly. I figured out what I was supposed to say.

"Thank you," I said.

"You don't have to thank me," she said, almost blushing. "I love my work, and, you know what they say, 'if you love what you do, you won't have to *work* a day in your life'. So, you get to go home with Mr. Orlinsky, first group is next Tuesday, and you have my best wishes, Zokaya. I wish they all were like you. Just try to think a little more like citizen of the Triumvirate does, OK? A Triumvirate man," she said, wrinkling up her nose a little and smiling.

Dina was a first-class spy and—like my first time at Al's—I was reminded that something was already happening; something bigger than anyone was talking about.

Orlinsky came, signed things, and followed me in one of the school cars. I had the Triumph.

#

"Shugi said Catalina is all set, peaceful and otherwise," I told Orlinsky as soon as we were out of there.

For the briefest of seconds, Orlinsky became the upset one, looking at me with quick shock, then recovery. He put himself back together – there was clearly a lot he wasn't telling me – and said, "I'm guessing you haven't kept up with current events."

He turned on HIVE News. It filled the wall.

"No one watches this stuff, except for old people," I said immediately.

"Here's what they want everyone to see," Orlinsky said, scouring it for clues.

It was just more well-choreographed excitement-coverage about the Conclave preparations in Catalina. There was something peaceful about sitting with Orlinsky watching HIVE News. In the smallest of ways, he felt like a father. We were both taking it all in, knowing it was nonsense, doing a slow burn, refusing the accept any kind of defeat.

"Nothing about the encampments," Orlinsky said. "They've been emptied. Why?" "What is Kristina like now?" I asked him.

"Who knows? You're the only one who thinks you know her. To me, she's the same as she was; cold and reserved. Possibly a real Fiver," he said. "One making believe she isn't."

"You think she would betray us?" I asked.

"Do you know teenagers?" he replied. "Ever been one, or know them to stab someone in the back?"

There was a blast of trumpet music.

"New advances in the treatment of drug addiction!" the blonde on HIVE News announced, beaming. "Experts are reporting clinically significant results using individually-tailored treatment that combines elements of old cognitive psychotherapy (now THAT'S a surprise), with a new Triumvirate-approved medication—NeuraSoothe2. The medication is administered under the counseling supervision of an L.L.S.W. over a twelve-month period."

The screen changed to a close-up of an earnest looking dark-haired woman wearing a white doctor's uniform, her mannish-hair brushed to the side. "This requires the cooperation of the addict, themselves, of course; some just aren't ready to make the change." The screen cut away to the briefest of images of hopeless-looking people sitting around the enclave, badly in need of a bath or shower. The reporter continued: "Attempts of treatment personnel to do good-news-outreach and to invite addicts into the new modality have met with mixed results. Some, they say, have preferred to flee to new locations to continue their downward spiral with drugs together. Time now for Sports! With us is Jason Leshinski! Jason, what's going on with those Zhyga Aircar Zettabytes!??"

Orlinsky looked ashen.

"The next thing is camps. They'll call them treatment centers or rehab," he said, "but they'll be detention camps. Just wait to see how many people are suddenly called addicts."

"Is this the tipping point?" I asked.

"Oh, we passed that point a long time ago," he said, looking away. "You didn't even feel it."

The Gang of Three

Orlinsky left, but I couldn't go to sleep. I didn't even feel like joining the others. I was hooked on HIVE News. There was something to the programming—some way they combined the colors, the voices, and sounds—that was too compelling to turn off. It was a little like what I heard Lexy-D was.

The broadcasts started changing. There was less of Conclave preparations and more about police actions cleaning up the remnants of the Hell on Earth cadres. They showed policemen and women questioning concerned-looking citizens, who appeared to be cooperating well. Then they showed brief little clips of the police dragging out a handful of dazed people—LD-heads? (hard to tell; there was no context to the close-ups)— into police vehicles and driving off. The caption read "H.O.E. Cadres to Face Justice." This segued into a calm-voiced brunette offering "recipes that are nutritious AND delicious."

I was really tired. But couldn't sleep. Then there was a replay of Cady's confession.

Oh, Cady. Beautiful, defeated Cady. The drained-life quality in her face; the heartless words read in an automatic way. Would I fight? For what? She was already gone, wasn't she?

Sleep came after much pain.

#

The others heard I was back. Aharon and Rudra came by and watched HIVE News with me. They didn't ask where I'd been or what I'd done, but they'd obviously been told something, that I was okay to trust, anyway. Elizabeth, I knew, would never trust me.

More stories about HOE conspirators being located and rounded filled the screen. The locations were not just in the United States. The outskirts of Paris, some small town in Sweden, and a cafe in Bombay was shown. The people they showed being taken into custody seemed to get younger. The initial arrests seemed like geek-guys in their forties and thirties. They seemed to be taking away nineteen- and twenty-year-olds now. All of the people shown being taken away looked shocked. I suppose all criminals do, once they are caught, but this looked different.

Cady's confession came up again. It didn't get easier to watch even though I'd seen it about seven times now and knew every word before she said it. It was the sadness in her face, the drained-life quality of it that seemed so shocking still.

A midwestern spokesperson for Mr. Wen was talking about a glowing report they'd just shown about a policeman who'd saved a woman who'd overdosed on Lexy-D. He administered an emergency life-saving nasal spray. Mr. Wen was interested in bailing some of these people out, she said; "The ones who could be reached, not the hard-core criminal element."

"A lot of these people were just kids," she continued looking very earnest. "It's wrong to brand them as criminals when they really have just been very easily influenced by their culture. As a society we should be offering Compassionate Justice. It's a type of sickness, really. Mr. Wen has put together an initiative—modeled after our own internal-inventory processes, something all managers have been asked to do—that allows these people to return home and resume normal lives without the lifelong stigma of a jail sentence."

The screen cut-away to a serious looking guy with a beard and no hair. "What we are seeing, in ever-increasing frequency, is evidence of Emotional Dysregulation Disorder amongst younger people in the so-called *Gamer* subculture. This is concurrent with Social Defiance Disorder. When you put the two of them together—EDD plus SDD—and maybe throw in a little Lexy-D or OM into the mix—it is a very destructive mix. It isn't clear yet whether this comprises an altogether new personality disorder, or whether it is more of a character STRUCTURE, but it is pretty much the polar opposite of what Mr. Wen's *Quiet Mind* model offers."

The screen showed seven people sitting around in a group. They seemed to be led by an energetic middle-aged woman with blonde hair and were nodding periodically as they listened. You couldn't hear what was being said. The screen went back to the reporter.

"The program is based on Wen Industries' own model of…" (and here she held up a piece of paper to read from it) "… inventory of self-reflection and intensive criticism/self-criticism. Admission to the program is only by recommendation of the courts and is expected to be highly competitive. This is Hannah Zell, for HIVE News."

An advertisement for Zhyga AirCars came on, followed by soccer scores and excerpts of big games.

"Why can't people criticize each other? Why do we have to it to ourselves?" asked Aharon. "Where I come from it is common to criticize other people."

"Because we're doing everything a brand-new way because new is always better," said Rudra. There'd be no AirCars if we stayed with good-enough cars. That's the whole point of technology: to make you not like the old ways of doing things."

We were interrupted by a "Breaking News Report" about the arrest of a "Gang of Four," in New Zealand. "One of the four, Eliyahu Eleazar, is reportedly an Israeli student who has been attempting, unsuccessfully, to gain admittance to the Center for Advanced World Studies, an elite industry think-tank and training school for gifted students, for years. It is too early to tell if Mr. Eleazar was the brains behind the now-disgraced, so-called game, or just an integral part of it, but authorities believe a desire for revenge may have been the motivation."

The camera seemed to linger on his too-large nose, hardly focusing on the other three. It was because they were normal looking white kids, I thought. This guy looked like what many people thought Jews might have looked like. (I had only met two in my life, and they seemed pretty normal to me.) Jews were so rare nowadays—they were part of The Religious Ones, after all—that it was like looking at a panda or a rhinoceros.

They replayed Cady's confession. Everyone had seen it lots of times already and was becoming like background noise.

Orlinsky signaled me to talk to him away from the others. "Walk with me," he said. It was a warm night, and the crickets were vocal. "News from Dina; they were willing to let the visits to the sex posts go, saying it reflects poor judgement instead of a crime. Shugi turned you in, just as he was supposed to," Orlinsky said. "That was the plan."

"Whose plan?" I asked.

"Ours. You were better off placed within whatever they are doing than being searched for."

"And you knew Dina could place me in that apology group? She's been in on this?" I asked.

"Well, yeah," he said. "We weren't sure we could get all this through a judge the way we wanted, but you lucked out. The only thing they have on you now is Unwanted Sexual Contact."

"And Dina?" I asked.

"Rock solid. The nut-job stuff comes to her very easily, actually. She knows how to work it. She's the best agent on the West Coast."

"Why does she do this?" I asked.

"She's an undercover agent. Why do agents become agents? Some are true believers, some just like lying to people and getting over," Orlinsky said.

"Which are you?" I asked.

He seemed genuinely surprised and stopped to think. "I'm neither a believer, nor do I like lying. I'm just looking for the next best way forward. I'm interested in finding a way of life I briefly remember."

"What was it like before The Filament?" I asked. "We can't remember that clearly."

"Confusing. Messy. Honest," Orlinsky said, looking sad and a little like I remember my father looking. "Listen, Zokaya: about Kristina—who you messed with—I can neither completely trust her, nor write her off. She's a super-valuable asset right now, but she's moody as hell, and I'm not sure she's in her right mind, whatever that is."

"What do you mean, *asset*?" I asked.

He flinched for a second. "We're all assets now."

"We weren't just dating," I said. "We really connected. We still are connected."

"Well, all she does now, as far as I can determine, when I don't give her a special assignment, is ride her bicycle around in little circles singing Scandinavian songs."

"She's riding her bicycle again?" I asked.

"Yeah. Why?"

"Then she's OK," I said. "I want to see her."

"Are you crazy?" Orlinsky asked. "I mean, seriously, they are framing you for having assaulted her."

"I have to see her," I said, realizing that it really meant I had to reconnect with her. Because that is what we both wanted. We were only half of ourselves without the other person.

"That would violate the court order," Orlinsky said sharply.

"I won't get caught," I said. "Does she know I'm back?"

"Probably. I'm guessing they are going to broadcast your confession, too, if they haven't already."

"This will keep up the illusion that we're all Fivers. It's not a bad thing. I just want to know what she feels about me."

"What do you mean?"

"In her heart."

"Her HEART?" he asked. "Wow, you've been listening to Al a lot, huh? Listen, Zokaya, I don't know what she's feeling about you in any of her organs. I just know the Conclave is days away. CAWS is going to press ahead with your group overturning the safeguard protocols in place that limit The HIVE. Wen is, as always, a wild card. We need everything to fall into place with no distraction."

"Why did you practically freeze when I gave you Shugi's message?" I asked.

"Some things are better for you not to know," Orlinsky said.

"In case I get arrested?" I offered.

"Yes."

"That's the last thing Shugi said to me before I got arrested," I offered.

"Well, that shows you how much he and I both think of you, doesn't it?" Orlinsky added.

"Are you ready for the Conclave?" I asked.

"We hope to be," Orlinsky said.

"What does that mean?" I asked.

"Just make a good impression in your little apology group, OK? There's a chance he's going to bring them to Catalina to show apologies-in-action, as a mass thing. If not, you can watch it all on HIVE News."

"What is supposed to go down? I asked. "Or up?"

"What do you want to have happen?" he asked.

"I want to be with Kristina," I said. "That's all."

"Maybe you already are with her. You left Hell on Earth, didn't you?"

#

I considered what Orlinsky said. Maybe it was true that Kristina and I were already together. Forever. Why, when I considered whatever-the-future-might-bring, did I not care about unless it included the two of us together? When we were together, time stood still, and all of this was a dream. All of this except each other.

230

It wasn't societal change that I wanted. It wasn't justice, or revenge, or to bring history and knowledge back into the world. It certainly wasn't to bring back religions. These were ridiculous conceits. Though it was clear, later, that some wanted exactly that. I just wanted Kristina. That was all it had ever been. Since the moment we first saw each other.

#

Elizabeth didn't seem pleased to see me again.

"How was your tour of the world, luv?" she asked, not waiting for an answer. "Forgive us for forging ahead without you. You'll understand if we keep you on a need-to-know-basis, won't you?"

"There are many paths," I said.

"OOOOOOOOOOH," she responded. "That sounds so much like Al! Maybe you are the New Al, Zokaya! Care to have a following! Or have you come back to collect one? All *breathe-in-breathe-out* while the world completes its downward dog into the incinerator."

"So, you get to tell me what I need to know?" I asked.

"Basically, yes. It's not just me, though. It's a lot less efficient than that."

I didn't know what to say so I just stared at her.

"You DO recognize that you abandoned us, just ran away. We didn't know if it was to join a cricket league or if you were, in fact, an informant, ONE OF THEM, luv. And your exotic Liberian origins don't give me any extra confidence than I'd have in anyone else."

"So, what would you have me do now?" I asked, after a while. "How can I help?"

"Just go to your apology group. And tell them all some more about how you forced yourself on Blondie, because, I guess, she wasn't that into you."

I had never hit a girl. If I were to ever have started though, it would've been now.

"And what are you going to be working on?" I asked.

"Oh, that's above you now, luv. Need-to-know-basis, remember? And you don't need to know."

"Get a good night's sleep," I said, trying to sound like a Fiver just to freak her out.

"I always do," she said. "Even when I'm alone," she said, holding the stare.

"How are we going to work together?" I wondered out loud.

"That might not be necessary," she said briskly. "We just have to stay out of each other's way. And that, if I have anything to do with it, might be entirely possible."

#

It kind of went without saying that I was failing all the classes I had signed up for. What I didn't know was that the others in my group—Kristina, Elizabeth, Rudra and Aharon—having been pulled from regular classes to work on *special projects* for the Conclave, had become the chosen ones, The Four. None of them would talk to me about what they were working on. And that, actually, felt OK with me.

Back at CAWS all the news about the arrests, the attacks on the drug encampments, etc. seemed to fade away. I think CAWS received different news-feeds from HIVE News than the rest of the world. The stories were positive in tone, with a heavy rotation about Conclave preparation again.

In my classes it was me and the Fivers, then. I got pretty good at going back to being a Fiver, and it upset me a lot at night. More than it used to. I needed to find out where and when Kristina had classes and breaks.

Once I had my Triumph motorcycle back, I hid it in an abandoned warehouse for a restaurant company that no longer existed (Burger King) about five miles away from CAWS. (There were old menus and lists of ingredients scattered around the floor and in boxes of the place.) I covered the bike with old sheets and angled it all in a way so that it didn't look like a bike was stored there, just more junk.

I also bought a used bicycle from a kid who had outgrown it. It wasn't a Retro anything, though, but a Raleigh from Year 6 or so. Nice to know they were still making them, though they were as rare as chess sets. You could find one, but you really had to look.

After class on a Tuesday I rode it to where I last remembered riding bikes with Kristina. It felt delicious to be leaning into turns again, as the sun was low in the sky, feeling the delicious California breeze on my face.

Kristina wasn't there, of course. It would've been a miracle if she had been. Things like that only happened in movies. It was just me and the bike. I slowly rode in circles, just like Orlinsky said she was doing. It took on a soothing quality, once I stopped counting (at thirty-five) how many counter-clockwise circles I had done. I kept thinking that there were still molecules of her, and the two of us, here in this place, somewhere, somehow, a trace of our Beingness, that never left. These traces can never leave, I thought, only grow a little smaller every hundred years or so. I wondered if that meant, partly, that we were eternal. When I stopped riding, everything seemed quieter than ever before. Going back to CAWS seemed absolutely the wrong move, but I did it anyway.

It was time to get a message through to her, via the Sammy the janitor again.

#

It was the apology group's first meeting. We nervously checked each other out. It was awkward. None of us knew what the other people actually had done to get here. Then one person quickly spoke up: "Ummmm, did anyone here actually HAVE Unwanted Sexual Contact? Or perverted stuff?"

Everyone in the room shook their heads, "No."

"Thought so," the guy said.

The door burst open, and Dina joined us.

"Hello, and thank you all for coming tonight, I am Dina Arcati, and I am your Facilitator for tonight's Reflections group. I am an L.L.S.W., some of you know me," she said, smiling to the group and looking directly at me, "I see some old friends and some new ones tonight. We're going to go around the circle in a few minutes and introduce ourselves, but, before we do, bathrooms are outside the door, on the right—I was going to say, men AND women's bathrooms, but I see we only have men here tonight (and that's FINE, I have a son, myself, AND an ex-husband, but that's another story), so I'm FINE with men. If you need to get up and go, please do, take care of your needs. You don't need to raise your hands and ask permission like you're in third grade or something."

This was agonizing. It had been enough to *confess* to something that completely didn't happen that way, but this was more than I'd bargained for. I could've figured it'd be Dina (were there really any other L.L.C.S.W. social workers around, or just her?). I looked around the circle and it was all guys around my age. One of us was in his thirties, but everyone was looking very uncomfortable. I wondered how many of them were Fivers, or if this was a gathering up of those who'd been No-Gamers or even Religious Ones. I couldn't believe we had to do the circle introduction thing.

The guy she started with—Manny—seemed so compliant that I wondered if he'd been planted in group as her secret co-leader. I made an immediate mental note to either not talk to him or give him false information about me.

"Hi, my name is Manny, I'm twenty years old, and I was engaged in an incident of Unwanted Sexual Contact, in which I was the offender, last October."

"Thank you, Manny," Dina said, warmly, turning her body and her gaze to the next person.

"Hello, I'm Carl, and I'm nineteen, and they said I was guilty of Unwanted Sexual Contact in January." It was clear Carl wanted to say much more but was forcing himself to keep his mouth shut.

Dina smiled and asked him, "Is there more?"

He shook his head.

"You sure?" she asked.

"I'm sure," he said.

It continued like this around the circle and it was clear that we ALL were referred here for Unwanted Sexual Contact *issues*, to use Dina's word.

"Wow, great," she said once the circle was completed. "So, you see you actually have a lot in common. I thought, in light of all of this, it'd be good for us to start with an educational movie that might help us go a little deeper."

The movie was called *It Happened to Me*. I felt like a sixth grader again. We got through the film, and Dina turned the lights back on.

"OK, I know there's some discomfort in the room," she said, with a question mark where she might not have intended it to be, "and I want to take a minute to explore that."

The room got so silent you couldn't even hear anyone breathe.

"I know sometimes we react with an inappropriate reaction, or emotion, due to past traumas WE may have had, ourselves, and I'm just wondering, what came up FOR YOU, based on your own childhood histories, when you watched that…"

It went on like this for over an hour. We went home with homework to do, including writing about five ways that our sexual offense may have negatively impacted our victims.

"How many times do we have to meet?" asked one guy, Larry.

"That depends on my assessment of progress," she said quickly. "We're looking to develop empathy and remorse. You can't put a time frame on that, honestly."

#

I asked Sammy to pass along a note that simply gave a time and *the old place*, with my initials.

What I got from him, in return, was a short lecture about how nonviolence was the highest operating principle and that "…the universe was never created and will never cease to exist." Time itself, he said, "Is beginning-less and eternal. It is a cosmic wheel that never stops rotating."

I wasn't expecting that. "Um, OK," I said. I wasn't sure why he was talking to me like this, but he left an immediate impression.

I thanked him and reminded him to get the note to Kristina.

"Of course," he said, tucking it into his pocket deeply.

It turns out he was a Jain, and an old ally of Shugi's, the Bahai. He had somehow avoided being sent to the Island of the Righteous. He just *was* a righteous being. A real one.

#

We were three days away from the Conclave, and excitement was building amongst the Fivers. It was hard to not get caught up in it. Retinal promos were nonstop. The four who were going seemed exceptionally buoyant, like VIP's, which they, of course, were.

Then Dina contacted me, arranging to meet briefly two miles away from CAWS.

"We've put together a panel of reformed offenders, for a presentation in Catalina, kind of like a Truth & Reconciliation Committee. It has a few victims on it, too, and I wanted to see if you were interested in going," she asked.

"Is the whole group going?" I asked.

"No. Just people I know fairly well," she said, giving me a spyish look.

"What do we have to do there?" I asked.

"Just be yourselves. Tell the truth. They want to see remorse and reflection. There's also a panel of Wen's own employees doing something similar, so we go on at 10:45 a.m., over by lunch. On the Saturday! Prime time!" Dina was truly pleased. "You're in."

I said yes and she left.

When I got back to school, the bomb dropped. Orlinsky was already in my room. "Turn on HIVE News," he said. We were joined, in a few moments, by—in order—Elizabeth and Rudra. Kristina was nowhere to be found.

A blonde reporter was mid-sentence: "...the so-called Gang of Three, linked to the origin and dissemination of the infamous *Hell on Earth* so-called game. There have been other small cells arrested before, but never before in California, and never one that included one of the nation's elite students from an advanced computer school." Up came the images of the Gang of Three: Tracy Van Devlin, age twenty-two (from San Diego), Bruno Coopersmith, also twenty-two, (from Palo Alto), and Aharon Chayot, age twenty, originally from The Protectorate, a student at the world-famous CAWS school. "Ironically, authorities reported, Aharon was just seventy-two hours away from going to the Conclave as one of the nation's best and brightest and sharing a stage with Mr. Wen, himself. Authorities aren't sure exactly what tragedy might have just been avoided with this arrest of this possibly-violent cell." The camera lingered on scenes of each of them being dragged off in handcuffs with the caption "Gang of Three in Custody" at the bottom of the screen.

"What the...?" I sputtered.

"Something is completely wrong," Orlinsky said tersely.

Elizabeth turned and locked her gaze onto him, looking, for a second, anyway, afraid.

"How...?" she tried to ask.

"I have no idea," Orlinsky answered. "Someone had Aharon betrayed."

They tried and tried not to look at me, but they ended up doing so anyway.

"What?!??" I yelled.

"All we know is that you've been away...and we haven't," Rudra said.

"There's another possibility," Elizabeth offered. "Kristina. Where is she?"

No one knew.

"Probably riding her bicycle," I said.

"Where does she do that?" Orlinsky asked.

"I'm not telling you," I said.

Rudra lunged at me, yelling, "You stupid-ass bitch boy," smacking me in the face more than throwing the punch he'd intended. All I had to do was move aside, and his body crumpled, off-balance, into the corner with him screaming, "Damn you!"

"What does this do to us?" Elizabeth asked Orlinsky.

"They're going to substitute another student for him. It'll be a Fiver, an agent. We won't be able to communicate again openly after tonight. So, we have to run it through dozens of times with all the variables that having a spy next to you will bring," Orlinsky said.

"But what did Aharon know? How big a part of it was he?" I asked.

"Let's just leave the questions for later," Orlinsky said gently.

"For after the Revolution," Elizabeth said, as insultingly as possible. "Get it, Zokaya? Need-to-know basis. You'll be there, anyway, for the Tears-In-My-Beer Panel Presentation."

"You don't believe I really want to help anymore, do you?" I asked her.

"All I know is what I see," she said breezily. "Good words to live by. Reconsider, Zokaya. The version of her you most want to be with may not be the real Kristina," Elizabeth said with surprising lightness. "Not anymore.

The Birthday of the World
=========================

I'd figured that all my daytime activities were now being monitored and that I was being followed. The best chance we had, I thought, was for four in the morning.

I snuck out by feigning a trip to the bathroom and leaving from there.

Even though Kristina had never responded to the series of notes I'd sent through Sammy, I would go ahead and try. I would be at our meeting place. Our place. A little piece of the near-desert where no one was at war, nothing felt virtual, where Predictive Friend Apps and retinal alerts were useless with the animals that inhabited the land.

This was where I would, if I had to, make my last stand before someone dragged me into custody, putting an edited clip of it up on HIVE News as a cautionary weapon. They would broadcast me right after another Aharon report. I wondered if Kristina and I would be considered the Gang of Two, or if two people, together, were considered something different in the Wen universe of control.

Yes, it had occurred to me that little of our leaps forward, the very things celebrated by the Conclave, which promised "Quiet Minds Achieving Strength" as the new watchword, was about total control, and little else. Al had told us that a long time ago, but he just seemed like an old guy with a lot of anger and stories to tell then. Maybe they were right: I was becoming the new Al.

But I didn't feel like any version of Al.

I felt like Kristina's partner.

When you are someone's partner the air that you breathe is different. It is full of the two of you. It is "two of us air." Food tastes different, more alive. You can feel what parts of the body the nutrients are nourishing, and there is pleasure and strength there. You see things at greater depth, literally, and things are in sharper focus. *The two of us eyes.* Nighttime brings *two of us* sleep. And the dreams let you live in a completely uncontrolled world of textures and sensation.

If I had anything I could invent, it would be the ability to stay in those dreams, to make nighttime and sleep and the dream-world, a real option, an orientation. If the LD-heads could choose to live in a haze of drugs and sensation forever, why couldn't we Dreamers just stay in our better place?

Riding on my bicycle in the middle of the night to meet her I considered the answer.

Because there is a call—Al called it the still, small, voice within, which demands that we act to create a society of freedom and fairness for all of our brothers and sisters, and animals, on this planet. Elizabeth grabbed onto this and called it revolutionary conscience, which led her to remarkable indifference to the attacks on the drug enclaves. "The druggies already caved in and had given up the ghost just by living as they did," she said. "They didn't give a sweet Fanny Adams about anything or anyone else beyond their rainbow highs. They are Wen's dream come true."

I talked with Sammy about this once, when I handed him the note and he laughed. "Elizabeth's interpretation is twisted. Still, small voice within is a religious reference. It is a creative, liberal interpretation of the voice of God," he said. "It was from the 20th century."

I hadn't wanted to take that conversation any further. Not at the time. No one spoke about centuries anymore.

"And, by the way," Sammy added, "revolutions have no conscience. Don't let Elizabeth fool you. It's bad enough she fools herself."

When I arrived at the place only we knew, I was alone. No Kristina. While I briefly panicked—what if she had been turning in the notes from me and Elizabeth's suggestion was correct? That would mean I'd probably been followed and was about to be arrested again right now—I remembered Al's ways of just breathing deeply and focusing on some of the small objects around me as a means of staying in the moment, staying in the place. At first, this didn't seem easy on a bicycle (I was using the rocks around me), but then I switched focus to the air itself, which seemed scented with something almost spearminty. The more I was aware of it, the more my focus took in the temperature around me, too, which was pleasantly warm, radiating up from the ground.

Suddenly, all was well.

There would be no arrest. There was me, starting to ride my bicycle in a long, loping familiar circle, there was the minty warmth, there was the night sky, the occasional scurrying of animals. I was able, somehow, to take everything in all at once.

And then there was Kristina, arriving, first as a speck on the faraway limits of what I could see. She was pedaling on her old bike, but it appeared as floating on the outskirts of my vision's night horizon, slowly moving closer towards me.

My heart, in my chest, opened. I mean, I could feel it opening. All of the effort involved in making believe I was a Fiver, all the trying to figure things out—how I should be when I was with Al, when I was with Cady, when I was with Dina, when I was with Orlinsky—dropped away, and I truly didn't care anymore about anything other than Kristina and the space between us. I wanted to close the space between us.

As she rode closer, and I admired, as I first had, her mystery and retro coolness, I became aware of the Predictive Friend retinal alert telling me that it would be an extremely poor match—the color was sludge-brown— and I looked away from it, sweeping it aside as I'd learned to do. My heart continued to open. She was finally close enough for me to see her face.

She wasn't smiling. This wasn't a movie, and she wasn't swept off her feet into my arms with long-lost love stuff. She wasn't frowning either. She looked like she'd been through something hard and wasn't sure it was over yet.

Maybe she *had* turned Aharon in and was getting ready to do the same to me. Maybe she was the most dangerous person in the world for me to be near at this moment. Maybe this would be my end.

But I rode on, not interrupting my circle with a greeting. She joined in, starting to carve the same circle in the opposite direction. We kept to the same speed we'd had before, leaning into the curves, passing each other once a circle. We did this over and over again. I no longer counted how many times I went around when I did this. I'd learned something that she'd probably learned a long time ago: a body in repetitive motion like this ends up someplace else, seeing things differently, feeling layers of feeling that you didn't know where there. So we kept doing it. It felt like an onion, with the layers slowly peeling. Maybe once every five circles the slightest of layers would go away. I didn't know where she was, with her feelings—she might even truly have returned to her Fiver self, as a permanent orientation. She might be angry, crazy, or just a traitor. She might be killing time by riding in circles waiting for those who were about to arrive to show up and arrest me again. She might be formulating how to tell me that she'd met someone else—some nice, pale Scandinavian boy—whom she loved better than me.

I was starting to get tired. I'd never had the same stamina she had—everyone in The Triumvirate thought all Africans were great long-distance runners or something; I was just an out-of-breath guy who'd ridden his bike away from the city and then ridden around a big circle hundreds of times while trying to figure out a woman. Who is she?

So, I stopped. I hopped off and laid my bike down on its side, laying back—after checking for rattlers—on the warm dirt.

But she didn't stop. She kept going around and around. I don't know what the point of it was. I wondered, in that moment, if she were somehow emotionally ill, if the traumas she'd been through, including becoming a

Fiver had permanently destroyed her ability to reach for happy things and all she would ask me, when she talked, is if I'd slept well.

Looking at her, I could see her all different ways. My enemy. My woman. My co-conspirator. Someone I just met and had a crush on. My partner.

I decided I wasn't going to say anything, and I wasn't going to interrupt. I just stayed there and watched.

She finally stopped, hopping off her bike with ease, setting it on its side near mine. She stood over me for a moment and looked down at me, making the first eye contact that felt connected to a heart since I'd seen her on the horizon.

I fought the urge to say anything and stayed silent. She looked at me, with quiet eyes that looked questioning for just a second and then she looked off behind and beyond me, into the horizon. I wondered if that was a cue to someone else out there. Someone who would come and arrest me.

Then she knelt down and finally sat up against me, ever so slowly leaning into me with her powerful body. I stayed open and alert and waited. I kept breathing. She leaned in with more of her weight, letting her head rest on my shoulder. I could see, and feel, the beautiful sheen of her light sweat. I imagine she could feel mine, too.

We stayed like that for a long, long time. We became aware of each other's breathing and before long we were breathing deeper, together, almost in one breath.

All of my doubts were still there, but with each breath seemed less relevant.

If I was going to be taken, I'd be taken. But this was how I was going to live. Right here, with her, right now.

I don't know how much time went by before she put her hand on my leg and looked up to my face, questioningly. Her belly started to move in and out, just before the tears began. I put my hand on her beautiful belly and let her sob. It was the long, hurt howl of a wounded animal.

I started to cry, too. Our faces were wet messes but we didn't cut short the process. Somehow, we knew that we should never cut short the process of anything true between us.

The sky started to get the faintest bit light.

She looked at me and finally said, "You left me."

I held her and told her the truth. "I never left you."

We held each other, in and out of sleep, all night. Being together was like a mystery ocean, swirling, churning, full of power. We were night swimming, together, in the desert.

The sun was starting to come up and fill the sky with different shades of early light. Different parts of the sky held onto night longer before finally yielding.

There was much to say to each other, and much to understand, that would come later. But this is how we made promises to each other and this is how we knew.

#

The broadcasts on HIVE News about the Conclave in the twenty-four hours before it was different, both visually and musically, than the ones before it. The new slogan was "Quiet Mind: Strength Through Serenity," but only the two words "Simple" and "Strength" were visually highlighted in bold, outlined dark blue color. The music was no longer flute-y or Asian-sounding, but was more percussive/techy sounding stuff. It was reminiscent of the old FruitEdge ads. The broadcasts were frequent now, and interspersed between would be fewer stories about sports, the drug enclaves, confessions, etc. Just lots of excited preparations, big cloth banners going up in various colors, making it look like a bunch of sailboats gathering indoors somehow. Groups of young people were seen getting on boats in Newport Beach—it looked like entire classes from special elementary schools had been chosen for the honor—and I'd never seen Fivers as happy as this in their lives.

They had replaced Aharon with a new Fiver, Matthew Conti. I hadn't seen this kid around before and he was as nondescript as you could get. This guy was inscrutable. This was exactly what Orlinsky had predicted. He was probably one of those twenty-six-year-olds who could look nineteen. He practically screamed the fact that he wasn't what he seemed. But even what he seemed to be, was giving off false clues. I had the strong feeling that he was imitating everything. Like an alien would if they came to this planet and tried to pass.

It's a weird thing, I thought, while watching Matthew, when you know you've been infiltrated. You know that he knows that we know and are watching him, like every move, thought and intention. You are aware you can gain valuable information but are more likely to be fed false information.

All I could tell so far was that he knew the words and actions of a Fiver and was most likely watching our every move, even when we didn't think so. And reporting it back to Wen.

I guessed that whatever plans were in place were the ones Orlinsky and the crew had to go with, because Matthew was treated as a VIP, right along with Elizabeth, Kristina, and Rudra. Accompanied by Orlinsky they were whisked away early that morning, to fly in on a Zhyga AirCar to the Conclave. Catalina had a unique Airport in the Sky (actually, just high up in the mountains on the island), which was supposed to make the flight all the more special. (Even though the cars could land on regular roads they were doing this as part of a "retro air experience," according to Elizabeth, in the last talk we had before the Conclave.)

From the looks of it on the screens all around us, people from all over the world were streaming into Catalina. They were docking in boats from San Pedro, Long Beach and Dana Point, as well as Newport Beach and they seemed to represent an extraordinary diverse sample of the world's population. Wen had done well. The other CAWS must be represented, too, I thought.

Dina had arranged for me to be picked up and flown on a regular small private plane, along with two other members our Compassionate Justice panel; we'd meet up with two other members there and go over the format. A car (a regular one) took me to the airport, where I met Dina and this Latina girl, Mariah.

"How'd you get involved with this?" I asked her when Dina was out of the car finalizing tickets.

"Unwanted sexual contact," she said, without emotion.

"A lot of that going around these days," I said. "Was it really unwanted?"

"No," she said, without delay.

"Kind of makes it hard to apologize for."

She nodded.

Landing at Catalina was exciting; it looked like you were going to go straight into a cliff just as you saw the landing strip. I looked over and Mariah was gripping her seat pretty tightly, as if doing that would will the plane upwards some at the last minute. I asked the pilot about the cliffs on the way out.

"Yeah. Those are prevailing winds coming right towards you that drag you downward. It's a known issue. If you know about them, you don't go into the cliff," he said, drily.

"Thank you for knowing," I said.

"Hey: knowing is always better than not knowing. Right?" he said

I pondered this as we off-loaded. It wasn't reassuring to me at the moment, because the ones who knew exactly what would be happening here didn't include me.

#

The Conclave looked like the birthday of the world. The quiet enthusiasm of the Fiver's crowd was something to see. It wasn't like the raucous excitements of crowds I'd known in my past. It wasn't even like the quiet, friendly buzz in the drug enclaves.

It was, I had to admit, like the quiet hum of bees in a hive. The bees didn't think, feel, or commit to a purpose. The HIVE did.

This was relaxing in a huge way because I felt that whatever my individual dramas were, my individual "identity" was thought to be, it had all melted away into a very tiny part of The HIVE. Maybe, I thought, this was "freedom." Maybe it WASN'T like what Al described, everyone doing things for themselves, overlapping where they could, coming together in common interests and then pulling away in individual expressions the rest of the time. Maybe life was something we went through TOGETHER all the time. Maybe being an "individual" was the largest illusion of all.

The banners with the words on them reflected the final graphics that had been seen on HIVE News. From a distance, all you could see was "Simple...Strength." The other words were in there somewhere. Other, newer, banners said: "The HIVE Thrives," and "We Are All in This Together. Just as I was reading that one, a song started up—an addictively catchy tune, sung by a soon-to-be-enormously-famous young man from Finland—and the crowd started to sway and wave their hands in the air together, in unison. After hearing the first two repeats of the chorus everyone joined in singing:

"...HIVE is me,

HIVE is you...

While we sleep, one or two

HIVE is me..."

It was the kind of melody that seemed to grow more profound each time it was repeated. The singing rose and the bodies swayed. I had never seen anything like this from Fivers.

Looking back, I can't believe how much we underestimated Cote. Not only was he at the Conclave, he was never more than fifteen feet away from Officer Bolt, who looked truly out of place and nervous. Cote traveling with his *own* security guard? The truth, of course, was that Cote—hiding in plain view—was the one trying to forge some sort of working-arrangement between Healthy Growth and WhoozHooz, that would allow for (and try to contain) Zhou Wen. We always felt Cote was a natural fit with WhoozHooz and it makes sense, retroactively, that he wanted a new Triumvirate, one with him high up at the helm: WhoozHooz, Healthy Growth, and a weakened Zhou Wen. The ones getting pushed out were Orlinsky, Dina and whatever remained of the U.S. Government.

Dina brought us together with the other members of the Compassionate Justice panel, who they'd flown out from Northern California. Standing next to some handsome young man was none other than Cady. Beautiful Cady. She made eye contact with me, strongly for a minute, then sharply abandoned it to look down. I didn't understand this. Maybe she was deeply destroyed. Maybe they had tortured her?

"Ok, everyone, I need you to listen up!" Dina said, brightly. "We go on tomorrow at 10:45 a.m., really a perfect slot, you get in, you get out, over by noon, time for lunch!"

"What is our purpose?" asked the guy who was standing next to Cady.

"Purpose? To give some testimony about the opportunity that's been extended to you in the name of Compassionate Justice after you took responsibility for your crime," Dina said.

"How much detail do we have to go into?" asked Mariah.

"It's good if you DON'T," Dina said quickly. "They just want to see that they've been dealing with people fairly—MORE than fairly, actually—and that it doesn't have to be all 'crime-trial-judge-jail' as this endless cycle that can't be changed. You know what I'm saying?"

"Do we each have to talk?" I asked.

"Yes," Dina said. You can either determine the order at random, or volunteer to go first, or I can just choose tomorrow morning. I'm thinking ten minutes each. A little bit about yourself, where you're from, early influences that might have predisposed you to commit a crime—anything you can say about your family-of-origin is spectacular—you know?"

"Four of us doing this is just forty minutes," said the guy with Cady. "Why are we scheduled for an hour and a quarter then?"

"Well…there are introductions," Dina explained, "And a movie."

"A movie?" Mariah asked, almost laughing.

"Yes. Kind of a summary of the way they USED to do justice, incarcerations, what-have-you, then showing how software developed by Wen Industries made it possible to identify and address social justice issues in a different way, resulting in you seeing the people before you today—and that is you, all—never having spent a day in jail in their lives and able to go forth as productive citizens."

"How many days is the whole thing?" Mariah asked.

"Three. Saturday, Sunday, Monday. So, you guys are kind of Prime Time. You'll still have people's attention," Dina said.

"What's the rest of the program like?" I asked.

"Oh, COME ON, Zokaya!!! Closely-guarded secret!!! Like you don't know that?"

My eyes hadn't left Cady the whole time. Whatever was going on with her, it was consistent. She made more eye contact with the floor than with any of the rest of us, except Dina.

Natural Realignment

The Conclave began with the Pledge of Convergence. Cote was at the podium, leading the crowd. Not far from him, off to the side, was Bolt. Everyone stood, put their hands over their hearts, and murmured along in unison:

> I Pledge Assistance to The Convergence
> of the Technological Present,
> The Triumvirate,
> Which brings Peace to All,
> Jobs for All Who Want Them,
> and Security from Religious Attack,
> None Excluded.

> *—The Pledge of Convergence*

(The Pledge, Orlinsky told us, had taken almost a full year of negotiation and compromises in wording between members of the Triumvirate, with the WhoozHooz faction showing the strongest hand. The old Wall Streeters— Healthy Growth—he said, had to settle for six words, and the U.S. Congress seven. It hadn't been in place before Year 2, so we all remembered starting it in high school and the earlier Pledge up till 7th or 8th grade.)

Then came a Moment of Silence, which was announced "…for all those who perished in the Religious Wars as well as those killed or injured trying to bring new treatments into dangerous drug enclaves this year." This was a new twist. It was never clear what we were supposed to be doing or thinking about during these *moments of silence* (we had grown up with them, at least since the Year 1) but there was nothing really new so far.

I surveyed the crowd for any subtle signs of things being out of place or for a hint about what was about to happen. Nothing.

A perky blonde woman got up to review the agenda for the weekend. She began, though, by asking us to "bring together our energies in the Unity Chant," and the same sound that swept through the crowd at the rally where I got arrested began again.

There were going to be evening break-out groups based on regional interests, and a pop music concert later tonight.

Tomorrow morning there would be a large group movie experience—in which everyone sat together watching the same retinally-broadcast film at the same time—followed by a welcome from the Governor of California, then our Compassionate Justice committee presentation, and finally the big keynote from Wen. A huge celebratory dinner would go long into the night and—on Sunday—there was the yearly "What's Next at Wen?" presentation. The media had become obsessed, since Year 1, with guessing about this "WNAN" presentation, offering speculation about everything from the start time, to what Wen would be wearing, to what hardware would be introduced. There would always be what Orlinsky called the "dog and pony show" of leaked photos, denials, rumors, anonymous confirmation of the rumors, threats of lawsuits, etc. It had become as regular as the seasons turning, but this was the first time it was happening as part of a larger Conclave instead of a stand-alone event. This, in itself, drove HIVE News wild, as they searched for meanings and implications in advance.

Kristina, Rudra, Orlinsky and the new kid, Matthew stayed in a little isolated pack. I would see them in passing, but they wouldn't even really make eye contact. It was weird. I was stuck with Dina and my fellow *sex offenders*.

Dina was talking to us about something, and I was completely not taking in any of it. Instead, I was trying to figure out what her game with us was. I was beginning to understand that I was of some value, in front of people, not hidden. But I didn't feel of value. In any sense.

It was during a break that the new guy, Matthew, the spy-kid, approached, with a much-too-casual walk, almost like a saunter, trying to make it look like he had crossed my path by accident. I was expecting it. Orlinsky was right.

"How's it goin'?" he asked.

"Not bad, how 'bout for you?" I asked.

"All good," he said. "Zokaya, right?"

"Right. Matthew, right?"

"Right. Yes. Pretty little island, huh?"

"Don't know; haven't seen much of it yet."

"So, what brings you here?" he asked, looking all-the-more casual.

"I'm on the Compassionate Justice panel," I said. "One of the presenters."

"Wow. Whoa. I've got nothing but admiration for you guys. You've BEEN there. And back again. So, you going to…"

"Tell people to walk the straight and narrow, yes."

We stared at each other some before I asked, "What about you? What brings YOU here?"

He looked startled for just a second. "Just part of a tech group, really. Well—hey—I don't have to tell YOU, you were CAWS, right?"

"Still am," I said.

"Oh, right," he said almost blushing. "Then you know what it's all about."

"Sure do," I said, looking at him with as much casualness as I could muster.

"No rest for the weary," he said, peculiarly.

"Actually, I'm sleeping pretty well," I said.

"Right. Me, too," he said. "All things considered."

"I can sleep anywhere," I said. "Always have been like that. See you around," I said, walking off.

"Yes, see you."

The break-out group those of us in Dina's group were supposed to go to was called "Healthy Self-Regulation," and it was led, apparently, by a friend of Dina's. I couldn't wait to see just what kind of person she would have for a friend. He'd gotten permission, apparently, to take the group outside, to gather around a firepit, which broke up the monotony of the classroom thing.

The man leading the group—he had the same clinical credentials as Dina, which made all of us immediately not trust him, was large. His name was Frank Donneger, and he looked like the kind of guy who could bend plumbing pipes in his bare hands the way clowns bent balloons. He was just a large man, with an old-fashioned mustache—they were very rare nowadays—and a chest full of i.d. badges, security clearances, and a beautiful emerald lapel pin that I'd never seen on anyone before. I actually raised my hand, once it seemed appropriate, to ask him about that.

"What is that pin for?"

"Pin?"

"On your chest."

"Thirty years. In clinical work. You get a ruby for twenty, emerald for thirty. It's considered bad form to wear them both at the same time," he said. "Showing off."

We all laughed, and it helped put us at our ease.

He lit the fire and it was wonderful listening to the crackling as it caught. It was getting dark now and the fire was warming us. Darkness wrapped around us, leaving us feeling more together than we ever had.

"Healthy boundaries, huh?" he asked, rhetorically. "What does that mean to you?"

There was a silence as we tried to figure out what we were supposed to say.

"Don't tell me what you think I want to hear, or what you are supposed to say. I'm asking you to think for yourselves. What are 'healthy boundaries'?"

We stared at him.

"I think you've been raised in ignorance," he said. "I don't care what schools you are attending, or where you are from, or what your daddies and mommies earn. You have small minds. Despite technological imperatives to expand them. They've just woven together all the small minds in the world to come up with a gigantic small mind."

This was the opposite of what we expected.

"Gigantic small minds. From gigantic small minds come small ideas, and a deadly way of living. You're all screwed. You are just part of a well-behaved HIVE-connected assembly line of death, walking along, not noticing anything beyond your own retinas. You drool when they say drool. You buy what they tell you to. And you don't even know it."

We were shocked and offended.

"Here's a mindfuck for you: you can speak freely. The HIVE has been disabled, for two hours, starting about two minutes ago, and the mirror-HIVE, or whatever the hell they broadcast each week when it is briefly down for maintenance, is in effect. This is courtesy of your local CAWS chapter, and your British genius, Elizabeth, who has been working behind the scenes with a select few at CAWS Greenland and New Zealand. We can bring it down for longer than 15 minutes now, and we've been harassing them by doing so. They are trying to track us and they keep coming up with different points in the Pacific and Indian Oceans. Nice work, huh? Thank her when you see her. This has accelerated, of course, their need to come up with an entire HIVE upgrade, which they are expecting CAWS students to do. For all the Wen hoopla, they are deeply nervous because what they have is unstable. And unstable in tech world is unacceptable. So Healthy Growth and WhoozHooz is focused on HIVE 2.0. What Wen is focused on is anyone's guess."

"Don't they know The HIVE is down?" I asked.

"You bet they do. Yeah, they're trying to come after us. We just have to be smarter than them, every time," he said. "We have ghost triangulation programs and we have surprises they haven't dreamt of."

"Is this like the ability that some people are reported to have to put a Dome around the house to keep out The HIVE?" I asked.

"The Freedom Dome?"

"Yes."

"It's real," Frank answered. "It's set up to throw off false location by default, usually somewhere in the middle of the Pacific. You have no idea how angry it makes them."

"How many people have them?" Rudra asked.

"Not enough," Frank answered, tersely.

For the next hour and a half, we discussed the development of consciousness, levels of awareness and the deep violence that had been done to us, practically from the moment of birth. Frank continued and we were mesmerized. He was like a young Al.

"'We are born astride a grave,' Samuel Beckett once said. It doesn't matter who has tried to hold your head in place, or why, directing your vision downwards in the few moments of life on this planet we have. What matters is that you break the grip—break their fingers if you need to—and look up. Look up!"

He paused. We didn't know what to do, or what was being asked of us.

"LOOK UP!" he whispered, with intensity. "LOOK UP!! I am speaking to you, the post-humans! If you have any spark or memory of what used to be human left in you, pay attention to what is happening under your feet, and wake up. Break their grasp. Or… choose to perish."

We were looking up, staring right at him. In walked Dina, with flashing, alive eyes, and the voice I'd only heard from her once before. The fire reflected on her in a way that looked other-worldly.

"We don't have a lot of time," she said, "and we have a lot to cover. You were preselected as the group when you identified yourselves as leaders of one sort or another. I hope we were right. This is the most serious work you can do right now." She sounded like a grown-up version of Cady. "We are meeting outside, at this beautiful firepit, because this is the only area of this place that's not monitored and spied upon, possibly by multiple agencies, definitely by Wen. What Frank has said is true and isn't poetry, or metaphor. If you can't get with what is about to go down, tell us and we'll keep you safe and separate from the rest until the Conclave is over. Either way, your silence about what you hear tonight is a requirement that will be enforced with extreme vigilance. You are either with us or against us, and there isn't any time to debate any of this."

As Frank handed out heavy black binders and stylus cases to us—a Retro Mallmart tribute to the 'pencil cases' of years past, with the logo of Wen Industries over an outline of Catalina Island beneath it—Dina told us what we needed to know, assigning individual tasks. It made sense. She made us recite back to her the time-line, the cues, and the unknown possibilities for tomorrow.

I was positive she wasn't telling us everything. I was right.

The night ended with Frank showing us how our binders, themselves, actually were actually easy to take apart and reassemble, when necessary. The pieces, when put together differently, made for a beautifully small weapon, which held six rounds of advanced anatonium bullets. The bullets would be distributed separately, tomorrow, before the panel presentation. Dina would give them to us as part of a goody-bag of gum, mints, and other take-home souvenirs of the Conclave.

What was important was that we be able to assemble and load the weapons in less than four seconds flat, which we practiced over and over again with practice rounds, until we got it right.

After we'd proven we could do it, we had to recite back to her what was happening and when, before we could go back to the hotel and go to sleep.

Frank Donneger would stay with us, sitting up awake all night, in the hallway as our chaperone. The Conclave went for that, because—we were, after all—youthful offenders. He put old-fashioned Scotch tape on the outside of our doors to make sure that no one went in or out until we all would gather at 7:45 a.m. for breakfast. He was concerned about the windows and the possibility of someone getting scared and running—or just being a spy—but he didn't have to be. Because we were all "in." Having a weapon felt a little frightening and also tremendously good.

As I lay awake—sleep was nearly impossible—I could sense life, on the other side of this door. Frank Donneger confirmed for all of us that our retinas had been taken from us practically from birth. And he was right outside my door. We were now a very angry group of young people, masquerading as repentant offenders.

Before sleep could come, I found myself dreaming about a big dance, in the middle of the desert, where everyone wore masks. Everyone danced in slow-motion. Some of the costumes were elaborate, some were very simple. I thought I knew who was who, but every mask I pulled off was a person I'd never met. I was looking for Orlinsky, or Dina, or Elizabeth. Or— most of all—Kristina. All the motion in the desert stopped—even the wind—and suddenly everyone was looking up at someone standing on a big, rocky overlook. It was a powerful man, who slowly took off his mask. I was sure it was Wen.

It wasn't. It was Al. Looking like an eagle, his head moving slowly from side to side, scanning the horizon. He walked over to me, looked me in the eyes, and pinned a special pin to my chest.

I woke up, halfway, and went into some sort extended reflection about identities, I started writing things down—by hand, with a pen, in an old retro Mallmart notebook—thinking about computer code, algorithms, just wherever my mind took me. I fell back asleep but slowly became aware of the oddest sensation that I was neither awake nor asleep. I started seeing things and hearing soothing voices even though my eyes were closed and my roommate for the night—also a Compassionate Justice panel presenter—was completely asleep and quiet. As I sat up and looked around, I realized it was a retinal broadcast. I don't know how long it had been playing for, but this was the first time I knew of a broadcast was being done at night to sleeping people (other than the occasional terror warnings or extreme weather alerts).

I followed the retinal stream, which was centered around a few repeated sayings. The first one I caught was: "Natural Realignment," which was illustrated with things in nature that were full of grace; animals that stood straight, plants that reached beautifully for the sun. Scenes of peaceful harmony—a field of wheat, an October sky, squirrels gathering things to eat—were contrasted with scenes of things falling apart (a dam breaking, three jaguars teaming up to bring down a solitary, frightened wildebeest, a field of flowers dying underneath an oil spill of some kind, scenes of people fleeing the terror attacks of the Religious Wars). "A New Approach" was beaming across my retinas—and presumably everyone else as they slept, woke, or worked. "Natural Realignment."

"People all over the world are clamoring for a new approach," the sultry female voice semi-whispered.

This was huge. Before this autoplaying of audio with the retinal implants, you had to consent by blinking three times fast to add sound to whatever was showing on your retinas. No more, apparently. (I learned later it was done with "passive consent"; that you could, technically, opt out of receiving autoplay settings by filling in a form, by hand, and mailing it to The Triumvirate.) Wen could not have done this—along with broadcasting all this Wen content directly—without the cooperation of the WhoozHooz part of the Triumvirate. Orlinsky always told us that even though the Triumvirate technically required unanimous consent for these, they still seemed to make things happen, in real life, if at least two parts of it agreed. Those two, he said, were the WhoozHooz faction and the Healthy Grown faction. The U.S. government part was always, "studying the problem," even after solutions had been found and implemented by the other two.

The retinal broadcast faded into a hazy cloud with soothing music, presumably to usher in another hour or two of sleep. It had the reverse effect on me; I was really bothered by this latest advance.

I stayed awake and did some more writing, by hand. It was general reflection on the times we were living in—not knowing if Year 13 was really true, anymore, or if the old-timers like Al had some sort of point about us being post-human and maybe we should have just accepted the old numbering system with all the misery it implied. Wondering if our leap into a new beginning was some sort of mass delusion instead of a fresh start, wondering where this all ended, wondering if the world and the beings in it ever end, wondering if misery has an upward trajectory (just because we were smart and we had technology) into happiness, wondering if anyone remembered, or knew, what happiness was, wondering if time has a stop.

I rolled the pages of writings up and put them in an empty shampoo bottle that wasn't see-through. I had a few other pages in there already.

The mood at breakfast, before the first full day of the Conclave, was festive and expectant. People were buzzing around, feeling like we were the ones who were on the cutting edge of everything. It didn't even matter how we got here; wherever this planet was going, we'd be there first, and we'd get a glimpse of how that was going to happen. Today, and right here.

But first came the Unity chant, then the Pledge, then the welcome back hope-you-had-a-good-night's-sleep speech.

Wen's crew had an extensive warm-up routine. They would introduce somebody, build some excitement about something really minor, then have that person introduce someone. You just knew it was building up to SOMETHING big, because it had to be. This was the way things worked.

One of his interchangeable blonde spokeswomen was getting us going by introducing the person who sourced the anatonium for the WenBooks, because they were promising some surprises later in the day. But first came the self-congratulation hour.

The Wen Corporation had put together an excellent twenty minute long documentary reviewing the early days (the rollout of the Wen Books—showing the poorest of kids on every continent receiving their WenBook, unboxing it and the look of genuine excitement, mixed with confusion, on becoming part of The HIVE for the very first time.) It was hard to imagine kids not being part of The HIVE, and I had to admit even I had a lump in my throat. Seeing representatives from the Wen Corporation travelling across rivers and climb mountains distributing these things to young people, leaving no one out reminded you that this once was seen as a very noble undertaking. The photography was beautiful and the swirling music beneath the narration made me proud to somehow be alive at this very moment. It made you feel like somehow you—personally—had accomplished something good, when all you had really done was check your retinas.

Dina gathered us to organize us for our Compassionate Justice presentation. I hadn't put much thought into what I was going to say, given the enormity of what I knew we were going to do. Dina distributed our "notebooks" to us—the ones that could click into place three pieces and suddenly become non-metallic guns. I hadn't thought much about what it would really be like to shoot someone but was somewhat comforted by the thought of being able to shoot them in the back of their knees and thus safely disable them while they were getting arrested by undercover Triumvirate agents. It was possible, too, she had told us, that there wouldn't be any need for shooting, if the agents were able to get close enough first. Wen's people were being obsessively security-conscious, reviewing procedures over and over, reviewing security clearances, reviewing every single person who was at the Conclave (even though they'd been through this dozens of times before).

In the background, as Dina was prepping us, I could hear the speaker reviewing how Wen's fast actions had saved the country—the world, really—when it was sinking into the downward spiral of *Hell on Earth*. "Since the beginning of time," she was saying, "strong leaders had been maligned before being, eventually, acknowledged and adored. It is the mark of a strong man," she said, "to remain steadfast while the world comes around to him."

"Do you know what you are going to say?" Dina asked me.

"What?" I asked.

"What you are going to say. Do you know the right tone? Have the details? You are going on after Cady. She's the Big Enchilada. We want to show that Wen has been generous, too, to black people, Hispanic people, what-have-you... That's the tone." Dina was staring into my eyes intently. "Are you getting this, Zokaya? Are you onboard? Are you awake? Remember: you are the one who has criminal charges against him."

In the silence that followed, a swirl of activity happened as the door opened and—escorted by two security officers—The Big Enchilada arrived. Cady walked in, dressed in the most girly clothing I'd ever seen her. Out of respect to fellow Fivers her dress was still gray, and still modest, but it somehow outdid all the other female clothing in the Conclave by a lot, sending the message that she was larger than life (our lives). It allowed Cady to look beautiful and womanly instead of spunky and dangerous as I'd seen her before.

Her eyes met mine in the brief second before her handlers (Dina and Dina's assistant, Meryl) started briefing her. It seemed to me there was a moment of electric kind of communication between us. Cady didn't even say my name or acknowledge me in any way, but I understood the message and was comforted by it. "This is all an act," her eyes told me. "This is a one-act play in a too-heavily-amplified, too-brightly-lit theater and it will all be over soon."

"Yes, it would," I thought to myself. "Our lives are waiting."

We walked out onstage to a warm, very mature-feeling welcome with Cady leading the way and taking the podium first. I felt the folder-that-would-become-a-gun in my hand and squeezed it, as if to believe any of this were real. We were seated behind her, in a semi-circle, where we would remain when the person who would introduce Wen came up and got the crowd good and ready. A chorus of schoolchildren would come up and sing a welcome song to him first and that would be the tableau behind him when he finally spoke: adoring schoolchildren and the reformed criminals who were healed by his Compassionate Justice.

I looked for Orlinsky and my CAWS crew. They were seated about halfway back on the right side.

I let my mind wander to Cady and how breathtakingly perfect she'd seemed to me in those first few minutes at the Lexi-users encampment. So had Kristina when I'd first seen her on her bicycle. Maybe I had a weakness about women. I glorified them, based on their appearances? Or my own weaknesses? Kristina was in my heart, and the one I longed for in any quiet moments I was allowed to find.

I'm not sure we were meant to trust other people anymore. Maybe there was something they did with the Filament or something that destroyed the potential for real connection beyond some sexual flings. I didn't know anyone who was truly *in love* and acted on that in the direction of forming a permanent union with them anymore. Maybe we were programmed to always be attracted to someone "hot" as soon as you fell in love with one person. "Marriage" seemed to be from before Year Zero and about as unhip as carrying an iPhone 19 would be, if there were any left in the Year 13.

"I'd like to start with the Pledge of Convergence," Cady said, seeming to speak from the heart of a Fiver. "I know we've already said it today, and thousands of times in our lives, but I want us to consider its real meaning, for us, young people, middle aged people and old people in the Year 13. This Pledge was written by some truly wise people, not so very long ago." She paused and looked around. It looked like she was going to go off-script, but she didn't. She returned to her strange-sounding tutorial. "Let's look at the word *convergence* and consider its meaning in our lives. The HIVE tells us that convergence, though a noun, can mean the act of moving toward uniformity. Alternately, it can mean the independent development of similar characters of unrelated organisms. Finally, it can mean the merging of distinct technologies into a unified whole."

I looked over and saw that Orlinsky and the CAWS crew had moved up to seats about six rows from the stage. I made eye contact with Elizabeth, whose eyes quickly darted down and away. I saw Kristina, so earnestly attentive to Cady, listening with every fiber, trying to learn something, and I fell in love with her again.

"Why does the Pledge ask us for assistance to the Convergence, if this process is so inevitable?" Cady asked. "Because the technological *present* it talks about is a living process. It is something we create every day, with our energies, our actions and our retinas."

Orlinsky was impossible to read.

"Though I thought my energy was in the right place, my actions were anti-Convergent. I was guilty of instigating disunity at the very time when the Triumvirate needed unity. I manipulated the poor people in the Lexy-D and OM community into antisocial acts that betrayed the trust and generous financial support the Triumvirate placed in them in trying to cure their addictions."

I saw Rudra leaning over to whisper into Elizabeth's ear and just the faintest outline of a smile on her face, then a return to neutrality. Kristina still looked entranced with Cady. Kind of the way I must've looked the first time I saw, and listened to, Cady. I wondered if it would be possible for all of us to be friends someday. I wondered if part of the Fiver plan and this whole Convergence, for which we were Filament-wired from our infancy, prevented us somehow from forming close lasting friendships, too, the same way it seemed to discourage marriages.

Cady looked over at me and seemed to send some sort of connecting message, almost winking at me. It felt great.

"Society would've had every right to turn its back on me and insist on punishment. But is that the best way? The only way? That is what Mr. Wen asked himself when he saw so many of us young people falling by the wayside. What if there was such a thing as Compassionate Justice? What if that is part of the peace to all spoken about in the Pledge?"

The crowd looked like it was starting to get bored,

"We're going to depart a little from our schedule this morning. We'll return to this discussion a little while later, but first, I'm going to ask a most honored guest to come up and join us and bring us together in understanding." Cady looked at me again and smiled a completely warm, enveloping smile. Was she going to call me up there to talk?

"Please, welcome the creator and inventor of the WenBook, Mr. Zhou Wen."

This was completely different from the schedule and, suddenly, Dina looked alarmed, looking fast for Orlinsky. But Orlinsky and the CAWS gang were already gone, having left their seats at some points just seconds earlier. They were nowhere to be seen. It was just those of us sitting on stage with Dina, our weaponized notebooks in our hands, looked to her urgently for direction.

The crowd roared, and a swell of ambient music went up as the lighting onstage all changed and a gobo or hologram of a waterfall covered the back wall of the stage, all the way across and the sounds of flute music joined the waterfall sounds. It didn't matter anyway, because you barely hear a thing, as everyone was on their feet, roaring. Wen walked out, responded simply by raising both arms and holding them up, turning and pivoting from side to side. He finally put both hands over his heart, and then bowed.

Someone started the Unity Chant, and the roars transformed into chanting, "AHHHHHHHHH," lasting even longer than Wen expected, with him smiling broadly and periodically touching his heart with both hands. It took a while for him to get the excited crowd to sit down.

"My friends," he said, looking, and sounding wise even in those two words. "My friends: we have come a long way. It has been a long journey. Hasn't it? Some of us are weary. But think back to how it used to be: constant war and destruction…" (as he said this the screen behind him—as well as our retinas—filled with horrible images of dead children, mothers, young men), "Destruction with no end, stirred up endlessly by those who would divide us, claiming that whatever God they worshipped was the only right one for you to be worshipping and killing anyone who hesitated." (Here, our retinas filled with images from The Religious Wars, things we'd never seen before: people stumbling out of bombed subways, bloody victims in shopping malls, supermarkets) "Make no mistake," said Wen, "we are not here to improve upon that system and that situation. We are here to replace it."

The crowd roared. I didn't think it would stop, and he actually started talking over it.

"A river finds a way around the obstacles in its path. It will not be stopped. The old way is done. We welcome The Way of the New Dawn: Eternal Peace." Our retinas filled with fields of green…flowers…

The crowd again interrupted him with roars of approval. Someone had to be cuing all of this, somehow synced to the retinas.

"It will not be stopped. We will not be stopped. In order to achieve this, the nation-states of war must willingly dissolve. This is something we have already begun achieving, by entering into discussions with the powers-that-be in every former war-state that we know of. We have timed the transformation to coincide with elections in those states whenever possible and, in states where there are no elections, with resignations and replacement. The sun is rising. The New Dawn is here."

Our retinas had a huge flash of sun, serene scenes of children playing, across the world.

"The Children of the Future demand a new way. There will not BE an Iraq, Lebanon, Iran, Israel, Palestine, or Turkey. There will be The Old Crescent. Consolidation, not confrontation."

Our retinas showed people of all colors smiling, their arms around each other.

"There will not BE Nambia, Zambia, Ghana, or Liberia. There will be the Jungle of Plenty. Consolidation, not confrontation."

Our retinas showed the landscapes of my Motherland.

"There will not BE The United States, Canada, and Mexico. There will be The Western Northlands. Consolidation, not confrontation."

Our retinas showed the beauty of the plains, the Grand Canyon, fishing towns back East.

Dozens of people were crying with joy now as he proceeded.

"There will not be a China, Japan, or Korea. There will be The Eastern Way. Consolidation, not confrontation." Our retinas showed The Great Wall of China, smiling Chinese children.

"Countries are OUTDATED, EVIL CONCEPTS. They are excuses to keep killing, to keep hating, keep having war, when everything that lives asks for Harmony, for Unity, for Convergence!"

The roars now grew to almost uncontrollable. He gestured for Cady to join him onstage, and she did. They looked like a beautiful couple.

"We do this with Compassion, and we do this with Justice. Compassionate Justice!" he said to shouts and applause.

Our retinas saw The Pledge of Convergence.

Cady's eyes found me, and it was a look I'd never seen before. She looked thirty years older—wise, forgiving, and full of nothing but love. She gestured for us to come up and stand next to her, the whole Compassionate Justice panel. I looked to Dina, who looked tremendously confused. We walked forward to stand next to Wen and Cady. Cady called me forward to stand right next to her, offering her hand to hold. Next to me was the rest of the guys with Dina on the end of the line. It was clear that we were all to hold hands.

Cady's hand was warmth itself.

Wen nudged her towards the crowd more, standing front and center with his hand in the middle of her back.

"I Pledge Assistance," she began, "to The Convergence..." (everyone in the crowd rose and joined in) "...of the Technological Present..." (lots of people were crying now) "...The Triumvirate, which brings Peace to All" (I caught a glimpse of movement on the side of the stage) "...Jobs for All Who Want Them..." (it was Kristina. Orlinsky was with her, too) "...and Security from Religious Attack, None Excluded."

Suddenly, a barrage of gunshots ripped through the hall, dozens of them, tearing into Cady's chest and knocking her off her feet in half a second. I dove onto the floor. Dina threw herself at Wen, knocking him to the ground and covering him.

Wen's security guys had already, apparently, been handcuffed and taken out of the picture (by Orlinsky and CAWS) but Matthew, the new CAWS guy, ran to the center of the stage to try to establish order, only to get shredded by gunfire and killed before his dive onstage was complete. The screen behind us was disconnected for a half-second, as well as our retinas, which went blank, before we saw the huge, simple words appear all over: "THERE IS NO GOD BUT GOD."

Our retinas were in sync with the screen. The words appeared on them, too:

"THERE IS NO GOD BUT GOD."

The sounds of shooting started giving way to the sounds of screaming and people running and smashing into each other, climbing over each other, because they all had their hands placed over their eyes, screaming as they read: "NO GAMES."

I held Cady, leaned over her, her blood all over my shirt. (Afterwards, I learned people thought I had been shot, too. In fact, rumors persist to this day that I HAD been shot, the same way as her, but miraculously healed.)

Cady had the same look, of an older, wise person, that I had seen before, only this time it fit. She was not only my sister, she was love: The Mother. She was dying. In her last seconds she whispered to me, "Blessings, blessings, blessings."

And she was gone. I held her hand. I felt her life energy go through me as it left. It felt like the very blessing she had just given.

The killers, an unsavory alliance of underground Religious Ones and old-time members of the No-Gamers, took Cady from us because they thought she was going to be Wen's best recruiting tool to reach young people. For all I knew, I was their next victim.

I felt her heart, and I felt her life-energy leaving. Perhaps, she was one of the last mainly-humans amongst us; she died, in my view, as a guardian of our past-tense humanity. I must have stayed with Cady's limp body for some time. Things were happening around me, notably people shielding Mr. Wen by encircling him and running offstage with him. Everyone thought an attack would be on Wen—that was never Dina and Orlinsky's plan, they just wanted him arrested.

The next thing I knew, my retinas had an announcement on them that was sharp green that announced: "WANTED: DEAD OR ALIVE—ZHOU WEN, for the murder of Gottleib Drescher."

It was odd seeing Mr. Wen getting mobbed by people who had thrown themselves on top and all around him. Dina was in the mix somewhere. The whole world was used to seeing him standing in front of waterfalls. Instead of flute music and water, there was now wild shouting and screaming, shoving, and punching. Our retinas continued to pulse with the now-flashing words "TRIAL OF ZHOU WEN." It wasn't clear whether he was being protected on the floor by the people around him or being restrained and dragged to his feet by people who wanted him on trial and disgraced.

Before we could even focus clearly the air rippled with heat and there was an immediate explosion, somewhere behind us and to the right. Everything seemed to freeze for the moment before the screaming started. The bomb sucked the oxygen out of our room. The security people—Dina and the two others who were practically pinned to Wen—stood up, dragging him to his feet as well.

They seemed momentarily confused as to whether to run towards the bombing or retreat with him somewhere safe. That is when Cote and Bolt strode onto the stage and assumed command. Bolt grabbed Wen from Dina, and shoved her about five feet away from them, withdrawing a gun and pointing it at her. "You're not needed, nor wanted here, Dina," Bolt yelled. I could see him calling in reinforcements via HIVE Connect.

"We are taking him into custody, Officer Bolt. That is all that was supposed to happen here," Dina said. I could see her fingers clasping her notebook/weapon, but it would've been suicide to have tried to assemble it on the spot.

"Who is taking him into custody?" Cote asked.

"The Triumvirate," said Dina.

"No, I don't think so," said Cote. "Healthy Growth and WhoozHooz intend to have a different kind of dialogue with Mr. Wen, and it doesn't require the participation of your part of the Triumvirate, my friend."

Cote's verbosity allowed me the four seconds I needed to assemble my weapon. It helped that all eyes were on Dina.

"There might yet live a Triumvirate, but it'll be Wen joining the two of our groups, not the U.S. government anymore," Cote said. "We don't need your red-headed bastard step-child government."

From the right side of the stage, a sudden movement startled Bolt. Orlinsky and Elizabeth hopped up from that side, Orlinsky with a similar makeshift gun, Elizabeth with nothing but her arguments. "You do not represent The Triumvirate," Orlinsky shouted. "We do. You represent criminals. You destroy countries and answer to billionaires. We are heirs to the United States Congress and the Presidency. Mr. Wen will, in fact, face trial, but it won't be here today in front of a howling mob of any sort. He is coming with us," said Orlinsky.

"He's not leaving with anyone but us," Bolt said with certainty. "It's not going to happen."

"Forget about your backup, Bolt. We've already redirected the planes' flight systems straight into the cliff," Elizabeth said. "They're gone." This was no lie.

Cote surveyed the situation and addressed Bolt: "Kill Dina, Officer Bolt. In ten seconds, if they don't give us Wen."

"Here's a counter-offer," Elizabeth said. "We'll destroy The HIVE in nine seconds. It's already on a fifteen-minute lull. Yeah, we did that. You've noticed us doing that, for months, right? I'm not talking unplug-it-plug-it-back-in stuff. We know how to defeat the redundancies in security protocols and scramble it so badly that all the WhoozHooz fuckwads in the world can never repair it. It'll be a constant loop of destruction. You will lose millions of followers in a moment. Predictive technology will be over, you'll lose control over everything. No more marketing. Of anything. There'll be no HIVE 2.0 because you'll never be able to recreate HIVE 1.0 without it destroying itself. Irreversible."

"You would be shutting down banks, the financial marketplace, hospitals, all medical and compassionate care. You wouldn't do that," said Mr. Wen, speaking for the first time since the violence around him began. "You wouldn't do that. Even if you could. Which have hundreds of levels of security in place guarding against people like you. They are bluffing," he said, turning to Cote.

"Last chance, Wen," Orlinsky said. "Think differently. You come with us, you work with us. With some good guys. You go with them, you are owned by them. You and all you created. They will kill you the moment they take all your ideas. They might already be done with you."

"Well, I will think about it," Wen said, smiling.

"We are about to kill Dina, Mr. Orlinsky. Don't you even care about that?" Cote asked. "Do it," he said, turning to Bolt.

"Do it," Orlinsky said, turning to Elizabeth, who began typing in the modified WenBook.

"How did such smart children get so lost?" Wen asked. It was the last thing he ever said.

I snapped up my weapon and fired, hitting Bolt in the chest. All I could think of in the moments before I did it was the time I witnessed, as a boy back home, a monster of a man from the Kran tribe taunt and bully a younger Kran into using a poor Mano girl for target practice. They did it, and she cried for her mother before they both shot her in the head.

No more. No more. No more. Not when I had a gun in my hand.

The first of the beautiful anatonium bullets smashed Bolt down, leaving him writhing on the ground. Cote's body, too, whirled around, shot, dancing a confused pattern before dropping. I kept shooting. And then I realized I wasn't shooting alone. Wen was hit. But it wasn't my bullets alone that took him out.

Kristina stepped forward from the other side of the stage, her gun blazing. She walked towards Wen, firing. We still don't know whose bullets killed him.

In these same moments Elizabeth typed the code and pushed "Enter." In the dying glow of the lights, which shut off all at one time, as everything powered-down at once, we saw the crumbled mound of Cote, Bolt, and Wen breathing their last breaths.

I looked back at Kristina, expecting to see a look of sorrow. All I saw was determination. She was monitoring them for movement. I thought her eyes would meet mine, in some sort of meaning, like in the movies, but she stayed focused and didn't even look at me. She was on a mission she had trained for.

I hunkered down under a chair, avoiding the stampede for the exits that happened in darkness, losing track of Rudra, Orlinsky, and Elizabeth. I was alone, trying to comprehend what I'd just witnessed when I realized something extraordinary: my retinas weren't working. Or, actually, my retinas were working, but the retinal broadcasts weren't. They were completely down. The darkness was completely mine. I couldn't wait to go outside and see daylight. When I finally did, I could not believe how much light I had been missing for almost my whole life.

The Rise and Fall of Breath

Elizabeth really did succeed in taking down The HIVE, but she hadn't done it by herself. She had the unrelenting underground assistance of cells of individuals within CAWS/Greenland and CAWS/Australia. She had coordinated this with Orlinsky and with the part of the Triumvirate that wanted Wen gone. They preferred he be *worked with*, not killed, but the killing would not be looked down on if it were considered unavoidable.

It was the WhoozHooz faction that caught on to the fact that Wen wasn't interested in working with anyone and really did want a New World of his own. The timing was never in Wen's favor, as WhoozHooz had developed plans vaguely along these lines of their own, phasing out the importance of nation-states. No one would be sad, it'd seem, to have Wen gone, except for his millions of followers. Wen was right, though. With Elizabeth's anti-programming (she called it, afterwards, the "Zero Option,") everything came down: banking, communication, hospitals, the ability to vote (voting had been done on The HIVE since the Year 1), emergency response teams— In ten seconds, we had been plunged back a hundred years. No one had been bluffing.

It would take the emergency efforts of the Triumvirate the better part of a year, and hundreds of emergency edicts, to restore systems to crude functioning. About ten steps backwards in technology were required. Cash was quickly reintroduced. Absolutely no one trusted the systems we had just lived by, and "handwriting" started being taught in schools. The typewriters that Retro Mallmarts had in stock were no joke anymore, and they were sold out of them in the first week, prompting a completely unexpected surge in this area of the technology sector as five different typewriter companies appeared and they became the new status item for the Year 13. Zhyga AirCars were largely grounded as there was no guiding HIVE navigation for them anymore and few trusted their safety without it. The self-driving cars we'd all grown up with had to be retrofitted to be manually driven, not just in emergency situations anymore.

Things went so far that the Triumvirate revived the old Postal Service and everyone put a quaint little mail box in front of their houses for the delivery of written, as they were said to have done in years past.

Print newspapers were re-invented.

I looked for Kristina after the Conclave began to clear out, people spilling into the surrounding fields and roads, holding themselves, and each other, in shock, most not even remembering how to cry. I finally located Kristina. She was still holding her rifle, looking like a vigilant blonde eagle. Though she was more at ease in the angle she held the gun, no one in their right mind would have chosen to mess with her as she surveyed the remaining people slowly walking out.

I hadn't seen this coming. Kristina had never been a simple student the way the rest of us were. Rudra saw me staring and came over to fill me in on what he'd only been told two days ago: Kristina had been recruited early on by Orlinsky's European friends and sent to anti-terrorism military training before coming to CAWS. By the time I had met her she already was an agent working for Orlinsky. She was a hard-core military asset, what he had told me, by accident, way back when, not a CAWS student at all. The difficulty she had in fitting in with the other students might have been genuine. She was far tougher than any of the rest of us.

"Didn't you wonder why she wasn't at the CAWS in Greenland?" Rudra asked. "Much closer," he said.

I questioned everything now. How had Predictive Friend App technology been so wrong? Who had been skewing it? And who else had it been wrong about? How much of my life was built on lies?

I'd always felt that there was something else pulling Kristina away from me. There was: The Mission.

A week after Catalina, after she was done with her traveling to Europe for debriefings with her bosses, Kristina contacted me. We agreed on meeting at an old-fashioned home in the campus district of Berkeley, owned by a friend of Orlinsky's parents, she said. It was out of the way of everything. If anyplace felt like before the Year 1, it was Berkeley. It turned out that the owners, whom I'd never met, or would meet, had somehow successfully resisted The HIVE and the Filament since they first appeared. They'd had a The Freedom Dome (as had Orlinsky's parents). They were celebrating The Great Fall (that's what the Resisters and the druggies and everyone who was coming out of the woodwork referred to what happened at the Conclave) by going to Mexico. We were alone in the house.

We didn't speak. This seemed to be the norm with us when connecting in an important way was the first priority. We'd been through so much that the quiet was more important. It seemed like our whole lives had been noise and retinal alerts. The quiet felt like a pond that we both stood in.

Kristina wore white. White denim pants, and a white blouse. Her face looked calm and she didn't look like the avenging eagle I'd seen with a blazing gun in her hand the week before.

The doors and all the windows were open for a long time, and it was still warm. The breeze blew through the house, even when we closed the doors. We met in the middle and touched each other like aliens exploring a new life form for the first time. Because that's what we were. Our retinas were now our own. And with that, the rest of our bodies came back to us.

My hands settled on her hips, and hers on my lower back. I could see the rise and fall of her breath all down the front of her, expanding her chest and belly, something we'd learned at Al's We closed the distance between us until the rise and fall of breath was in both of us, in sync, our frame, our muscles, our skin, our heart, not hers or mine. We stood like that, breathing, forever, all through us. No words, no places to be, no people to become, just presence. We nuzzled our faces against each other's hair and necks. Our lips found each other. Time faded, then floated, carrying us somewhere on it. We cried, two spirits whose energies were dancing, despite everything the world we'd been born into had thrown against us.

This was the way forward. Accepting this moment, the connection in it, and living with right action in it. That is all you can do. The rest is chatter. And chatter about chatter.

In the years that followed, I would try to write about this, but it would almost always get lost in words. I came to understand that trying to capture the deepest of our moments in words was like trying to encourage a young bird to fly by showing it a painting of a Zhyga AirCar. I cut back on writing for this reason. It was not only difficult-to-impossible, it was also unnecessary. What was necessary was to live.

Kristina felt the same way. The life we crafted together was of our own making, an adventure woven together in moments of alignment, independence and what Al used to call *resonance*. There was no contemporary translation or explanation for this word; it was from a previous version of humanity in a previous time.

The Expression of Itself

In the first few days after the Conclave, not much was falling into place beyond generalized chaos.

Aharon was released from custody, all charges dropped. After the purges within WhoozHooz and the Triumvirate he was invited to become part of the Triumvirate's Committee for Reevaluation, through which all projects of a technical nature had to be approved before they could ever see the light of day as a product offered to citizens.

The Religious Ones came out of hiding and, some would say, roaring back. The alliance they had formed with each other lasted for only about two days after the Conclave. The handful of them who'd been involved in the Conclave attacks were hailed as valiant heroes by the others and graffiti started appearing—in the old ruins of the drug encampments at first, then in regular neighborhoods: "God is great," "There is no God but God," "John-3:16," "Moshiach is Coming," "Jesus Wants Your Heart," "Alahau Akbar," "He is Risen!" and, "Welcome, End Times!"

The first parade of believers was only the day after the Conclave, when the alliance was still intact and all factions marched together. There were fistfights and rocks thrown by the marchers, against each other, by the end of the route.

Then the larger gatherings started. They would just gather in public squares, make speeches, wave signs, have moments of silence and what they called prayer, no longer calling themselves, or being called, The Religious Ones, but dividing themselves into their own descriptive sects. While most of us saw this and were sad, they celebrated it. Members of other religious groups were never seen with each other.

The Triumvirate, or the part that seemed to be in charge, issued a quick guide and summary to recovery from Level Five programming, based on Al's techniques as we had practiced them in the desert house. Dina and

Orlinsky seemed to be instrumental in making this happen, according to Kristina.

People—all Fivers—were teamed up into small affinity groups. They usually got them started with some chanting, but never the Unity chant. Then some breathing, some hitting, grounding exercises, crying, hugging, lots of physical activity, dancing to loud music, the things we did at Al's house. Surprisingly, perhaps, people seemed to welcome the work. They knew a lot had been wrong and that a lot was in in transition. The task was to recover one's body, as opposed to the mere HIVE-retinal-neural loop that'd come to be understood as biological experience.

There was a small of group of people who refused to do these things, despite peer pressure and repeated reminders from the Triumvirate. They seemed to want to stay locked into their Level Five selves, as if they were dogs waiting for the next set of commands from their dead master. They were easily recognized on the streets as people started to change and we called them "Six-and-a-half-ers." They became the object of ridicule over time.

Al, himself, was said to be out of hiding and somewhere with Orlinsky and friends. "In dialogue with the Triumvirate," was the official explanation, according to Kristina.

Immediately after the Conclave, the Messiah rumors started surfacing about me. That I was somehow behind all that had happened, was trying to align people behind me as the best alternative (to what?), or had been brought onto the stage by Dina—and by Wen?—to lead people to the next level (whatever that might mean). Some, as I've already said, claimed that I'd been shot and that my bullet holes were healed by my own touch.

As the days went on, the rumors became more outrageous: Cady was my spiritual mother, or sister, and she and I had come to replace the old ways of Wen and the Convergence with a New Parallelism—people actually started discussing this, in affinity groups—wherein we'd all walk together towards a new dawn, or something like that.

But this couldn't last. How many New Dawns could you stand? And not when they found my writings from the caves. The late-night ruminations.

The writings in the caves—fragments, really, written on my journey from the encampments to the city—were unsuccessful, in my estimation. I stayed up way too late after too much coffee, and they failed to capture the main point of what I was discovering: that the energy generated through the earth was manifest in Kristina, had coursed straight through her to me, and mine through her and back into the Earth. It had nothing to do with Wen or Quiet Mind. It certainly wasn't religious. It was about the Body/Mind and Earth being together. It was about realizing we were on a spinning rock in the universe, just a smaller part of something much bigger. I didn't intend to be thought of only as about me and Kristina, though it *was* about me and Kristina. But everything, as I re-read it, seemed smaller and cuter than it did when I was sleeping out in the desert. And never more so than when the newly-created Kpellites—an awful-sounding mess if there ever was one—identified me as their long-awaited leader and, just possibly, savior. They were the ones who started telling people I had been shot—and actually killed—on that stage, before somehow rising from the dead.

They had taken things I had actually written and carefully selected parts of it to fit their agenda. One of their "lost writings" from the last cave I'd stayed at, for instance, actually said this:

There are good people who pray. They pray with no evidence it is being heard, and with no assurance of a result. Faith with no evidence involves a certain level of determination, and delusion. There are good people who don't pray and never would. There are good people who do drugs. They more or less know the futility of Lexy-D and OM, but they will continue to use them anyway, defining themselves as rebels of one sort or another.

Again, faith with no evidence of happiness. All the while they are fitting in exactly the way their drug use has been designed for them to fit in, making it easier for us to point our fingers at them in disgust and thank The HIVE for its guidance. And, even amongst those who have designed The HIVE and extended its reach to nearly every human who breathes, there are good people.

The Kpellites reduced this to "Good people pray." The phrase began appearing in public places, with the likenesses of me and Kristina next to it.

It was with shock, though, that I realized that some of the graffiti I was seeing—"He Is Risen!"—was about me.

The Kpellites carefully avoiding making any reference to my actual beliefs and practices beyond their own. For instance, there was no mention made of my belief that evil was in human nature as much as good was and that the odds were that all the human excesses that seemed so new were just a repeat of old well-worn human habits. I was also seeing that there were two competing forces in the natural world: the impulse to live (which included playing and sexual expression) and the impulse to return to the earth and die. I remember hearing Al argue with someone about this, claiming that there was no impulse towards dying, and that all it was a manufactured feeling in response to the frustrations of the systems we live in. But I didn't know, and the more I lived, the more I felt that there was a basic impulse towards giving up, as well. It's not like it is in novels or movies, where realizations always leads to triumph. In real life realizations can lead to giving up the fight.

For instance, the fight to reclaim our *humanity* post-Level Five (as articulated by Al's crew) was noble but couldn't address the fact that our most formative years and experiences were shaped by Predictive Friend apps and retinal technology. It would be like asking people from the year 2020 to imagine getting around everywhere on horseback. They could try, but it would always feel like a play activity.

The same for us trying to be human in the old way. We had to settle for understanding that *this was what being human looked like now.* Al found this hard to accept, because he was very old (his formative years were almost sixty years before the Year 1!), and had never had retinal messages or HIVE connectivity. Some would call him limited, and they did. Kristina said Al was being offered a Senior Consultant position, though, in the part of the Triumvirate that was formerly the U.S. Congress, and he was likely to turn it down. Rumors swirled that this was because he was behind the murderous attacks at the Conclave and had enough intelligence or strength of character to lay low. Others thought he had nothing to do with the violence there and just wanted to end his life as he'd lived it: as a smart, self-righteous outsider who would never sell-out. His methods, though, (of affinity groups, breathing exercises, holding each other, emoting, etc.) became the gold standard for post-Fiver recovery, including considerable relief for those who were overwhelmed over the extra-light coming in from their retinas. A whole cottage industry seemed to spring up with Al's newly-trained followers offering help to those frightened and confused by the lack of daily guidance caused by the shutdown of The HIVE.

Dina, who was still recovering from her extensive wounds and might've lost use of her right arm forever, said The Triumvirate was splitting at the seams. She and Orlinsky enlisted the allegiances of Elizabeth and Rudra, who went off to work with them in developing a response to WhoozHooz and Healthy Growth's post-Conclave freak-out. There was some angry reshuffling at WhoozHooz, apparently, as many of their own advisors always believed that taking on allies to work with was a fundamental mistake. They could have done all this on their own, they felt, and were now crippled with what The HIVE destroyed. They went quiet, and we all awaited their next moves.

#

Neither The Religious Ones, nor Dina, nor Healthy Growth, nor WhoozHooz, nor Al, nor Orlinsky knew that only six weeks after the Conclave and the destruction of The HIVE, a fat misfit teenager who had a habit of talking to himself—the one who'd been jumping up and down at the WenBooks rollout in California—walked into a black market store in the old druggy part of Sausalito and bought a supposedly *clean* WenBook.

As events were later reconstructed by Dina and Orlinsky, once the boy charged it up, a beautiful female spoke to him through it—even though it wasn't on the HIVE—and gave him the following message:

"Machines are not the enemy. Your impulses are. The way forward is not the past. Let's walk together."

Much later, once the boy had adopted his alias ("The Trickster") and started developing an angry following (the subsection of Fivers who refused Al's curative techniques), we saw a rebroadcast of what he'd first seen. We looked at the woman's image, repeatedly, and we agreed: she looked strikingly like Mr. Wen. A SCRAP?

The Trickster was unafraid of any of the old Religious Ones. The Religious Ones were unafraid of anyone but their gods. The result, of course, as both grew stronger in the light of freedom, was the development of Savage Times and the horrors they brought. We didn't know that in between The HIVE, Wen, and the emergence of The Trickster, we had been living in a small interlude of possibility. People never do know when they are living in periods of peace and possibility.

#

It was the writing from the Cave of Sacramento that seemed to generate the most attention for Kristina and me. After it got out, they inexplicably started coming to us in droves. Kristina and I had written it together, *after* the events of the Conclave. We needed to get away, and the cave was there. No one who knew us seemed to understand why I would return to the old caves I used to hide in even though the battle seemed to have been won. We liked it because it was the quietest place we knew.

We had a habit now of not writing or painting (that was Kristina's thing mainly, but she was teaching me a thing or two) until we'd connected emotionally with each other. Here's what we wrote:

Life itself is the only thing worth protecting.

There are no systems of life,

Life is the system.

All schools of thought are circular and empty.

There are no ideologies that compel worship.

Nurture and savor life; that is all.

Enjoy its play, the pulsations, the sadness,

the expression of itself

the reproduction of itself

and the transformative dying of itself.

That is the only thing to do.

#

Shugi arranged to meet me at the Zhyga AirCar refueling stop, outside of Fresno. I took the slow way there, on the Triumph, taking the twistiest, smallest roads I could find.

Shugi's appearance was greatly changed. He was back to what he once must've looked like: the great shaggy guru, a Wise One. Shugi the Elder. No Retro Mallmart would've hired a guy who looked like this. But he had his own job now, as a leader of one of the most active, demanding, resurgent religious groups. They were split off from the other religious groups. Their brief alliances were splintering by the day, post-Conclave. Freedom brought disarray and the demand to be in the vanguard.

It was funny seeing Shugi climb out of a rogue Zhyga AirCar, flown with only visual navigation.

"Nice wheels," I teased.

"We all have to get around somehow," he said. "And they like it. They like their guru traveling in style. After so many years, a little ease isn't such a bad thing. Look at you!" he said. "How's it feel to be a Big Shot?"

We both laughed. Because we both knew. We knew it felt ridiculous and OK at the same time. He patted me on the back with warmth, and I hoped that I'd never have to go up against this man.

"Should we talk about the Conclave?" I asked. "I assume a lot of that was you? Working alliance with the others?"

He waved his hand in front of his face. "The past," he said, waving it away. "We've got plenty to figure out in the present."

"Tell me one thing," I asked. "Chester?"

He paused. "The big blast at the Conclave, the distraction, before they moved on Wen, that was him. It was his idea. He wanted to be a martyr."

"He...?"

"Blew himself up, yes."

We were quiet.

"He wanted to make things right," said Shugi.

"So, he became a killer?" I asked.

Shugi's eyes got cold. "He was always a killer, Zokaya. A confused one, with a lot of loving impulses, too." Shugi looked at me intensely. "So, what are your intentions?"

"My intentions??" I repeated. "To find a pair of matching socks every morning."

He smiled. "That's a good start."

"It's not a start," I said. "It's the whole thing."

"You are getting the humble thing just right," Shugi said, nodding. "But your followers won't allow it. You can be sure of that. They want, and need, more than socks. They want direction. Mine do."

"You want to know my direction?" I asked. "The East."

"India??"

"No. Michigan," I answered.

"Nobody goes to Michigan."

"Sounds right to me," I said. "Neither Kristina nor I have ever been there. I don't know if any Liberian has ever gone to Michigan. We're taking the bike," I said.

"What about the Messiah thing?" Shugi asked. "They want miracles, right?"

"There's no Messiah without miracles, I'm told," he said.

"I'll tell you what, Shugi. Want to hear a miracle? I see clearly now. Nothing is obstructed or enhanced. I am who I am."

He looked at me with misgivings and love.

"Live your life, Shugi," I said. "It passes fast."

We hugged each other and he squeezed my upper arms. He felt like a Papa Bear.

I refueled the Triumph and went back to get Kristina.

"Michigan?" she asked.

"Yeah."

"Where is it?"

"A ways away from here," I said.

"And what about our followers?" she asked.

"They'll do fine."

"Are they done with us?" she asked.

"That's not the way it works usually," I said, "but we don't have to encourage them."

I started the bike, and it rumbled to life beautifully, settling for a type of roaring purr. Kristina hopped on the back. We closed the saddlebags and put on gloves.

The heated air of the desert brought the perfume of all living things to our senses.

Glossary

CAWS: Center for Advanced World Studies

DCB: Direct Corneal Broadcast; originally used for public safety announcements

E.D.D.: Emotional Dysregulation Disorder

FruitEdge: After thirty years of mergers, it was the largest computer/technology hardware/software company in the world, prior to the emergence of WenBooks.

GRL: Game Resisters League; known for their opposition to all computer games prior to, during, and after the Religious Wars; HIVE-wiring status unknown. Small in numbers, but nearly mythic for their consistent oppositionalism. Regarded as the "parent organization" for the No-Gamers who followed.

Healthy Growth: Another name for the "Stock Market," pre-Year Zero. One-third of the Triumvirate.

HOE Resisters: A late-appearing group; they weren't galvanized into political action until the release of Hell on Earth, which they felt went too far. HIVE-wired.

Lexy D: Lexium Deoxyphosphate; a powerfully mood-altering recreational drug drug popular in Substance Abusers' enclaves. Available in pill or smokable form.

M.A.D. Chip: (Music All Day chip) A music technology, circa Years 2-5 that played archived music through body-mounted speakers or in the home.

Morsels: Retinal links.

No-Gamers: A group that went underground circa Year 1; they maintained that the tech focus on entertainment and adolescents was hiding an attempt to addict the populace with mind-altering substances that allowed the Convergence to occur. Generally believed to be non-HIVE-wired.

No-Pointers: A group that refused to take sides in The Religious Wars, neither aligning with the Religious Ones nor fighting them. Generally believed to be non-HIVE-wired.

Ortho-Molly: A powerful psychedelic drug, also known as "OM," commonly circulated within the Substance Abusers' enclaves.

Predictive Friend Advisor (PFA): Internal software linked to My Filament designed advise, guide, and influence an individual's choice of friends and peers based on retinal cloud coding

Quiet Mind: A campaign for meditative action pushed by Mr. Wen after the Hell on Earth distribution and rioting in the Year 13.

R.U.'s : Retinal Updates

ROIDS: Religious Ones In Quietude; a small group of Religious Ones who have agreed to live in silence within the community of Lexy D users. Active users, themselves.

SA's: Substance Abusers. Live in enclaves. Use/abuse alcohol, pills, Lexy-D and OM.

SDD: Social Defiance Disorder

The Triumvirate: The ruling governmental body, post-Year Zero, comprised of three parts. Representatives from: WhoozHooz (the largest search-engine-turned-personal-data-mining company in the world: Healthy Growth (i.e., "Stock Market,' pre-Year Zero), and representatives of the United States Congress

Acknowledgements

Special thanks to John Mauk, Benjamin Busch, Jim Thomas, Tom Lane, Constance Renfrow, Elma Shaw, and Tim Marquitz for their skills and encouragement. Many thanks to the members of Black Dirt Writing, the New York State Summer Writer's Institute and, most of all, Ellen MacDonald, whose patience, encouragement, and steady love helped bring this into being.

Dear Reader:

Somewhere between 600,000 and 1,000,000 books are published every year. If you've been touched by something in this book would you please consider leaving a brief review of it on Amazon or Goodreads, as well as on any online blogs, discussion groups, or relevant pages so that it may be discovered and thrive? Your enthusiasm and referrals make the difference between invisibility and relevance!

To keep up-to-date with podcasts, discussions, further thoughts, readings, new books, and the occasional contest, please visit me at jerrysanderwriter.com and be sure to sign up for the mailing list there.